USA TODAY Bestselling Author

DEBRA
WEBB

THE
LIES
WE
TELL

mira

ISBN-13: 978-0-7783-0831-7

Recycling programs
for this product may
not exist in your area.

The Lies We Tell

This book is dedicated to my older daughter, Erica Webb Green. Erica, thank you so much for being such a great help with this series. From research to proofreading, you have been invaluable. One day you will write and publish amazing stories of your own and the world will love them! You are an inspiration to us all! Love you!

THE
LIES
WE
TELL

RIP

Carlos Sanchez
September 3, 1948–October 24, 2019

Mr. Carlos Sanchez will be prepared for burial by DuPont Funeral Home. Friends and family may contact the funeral home for information regarding arrangements.

One

Herman Carter looked old. So very old.

The past five months in jail awaiting trial had taken a toll on the seventy-one-year-old man. He'd lost weight, and his gray hair lacked its usual sheen. But it was his eyes that told the real story. Dull, listless, resigned.

Rowan DuPont felt no sympathy.

Renewed indignation tightened her lips. This man—a man she had known and trusted her entire life—had deceived her. He had taken advantage of her father…and betrayed so many people. For no other reason than greed. He could toss out his excuses about his wife's illness, but the truth was he had hurt people, using Rowan's family and the funeral home that had belonged to her family for 150 years.

He deserved a far heavier punishment than she imagined the court system would eventually dole out. *Eventually* being the key word. The trial wasn't scheduled to begin for another three months. The wheels of justice indeed moved slowly.

"Did you get my letters?" His voice sounded rusty, as if he rarely found a reason to use it.

"One every week," Rowan said, her voice stiff, no matter that she had repeatedly attempted to relax. No matter that she did not want to be here, this meeting was necessary. Furthermore, it was essential that she proceed with caution where her personal feelings were concerned. She needed him cooperative. Revealing her utter disdain would not aid toward that end.

Herman had written to her every week since his arrest. Until yesterday, she had not opened a single one of his letters. She had felt no desire to read anything he had to say. He could not be trusted in any capacity. Yet, unfortunately, he was the one person still living who was well versed in her family's history. He and her father had been best friends their whole lives. With her father dead going on a year now, Herman was the only person who might be able to help her.

For five months she had attempted to dissect her mother's journals. She had searched the funeral home, as well as the living quarters, from top to bottom. One by one she had questioned neighbors, business associates and anyone else who had known her parents. She had learned nothing useful toward her goal of uncovering the facts surrounding the deaths of her sister and her mother.

Perhaps the truth had died with her father.

Rowan still struggled with the loss of her father. The idea that he might have lied to her made adjusting to this new reality all the more difficult. A part of her refused to believe he had lied, despite the rumors and innuendos she had encountered. The trouble was, she had to know for certain. Herman Carter, the man who had stolen body parts from the dead to sell on the black market, was the sole person on this planet who might be able to help her find the answers she sought. However hard she had searched to find the facts some other way, ultimately, she had realized *this* was her only choice. He was her final hope.

The thought of living with the uncertainty was something she was not prepared to do. Too much hinged on knowing the whole truth.

"Is that why you're here after all this time?" Herman asked, a spark of hope lighting his dark eyes. "Did my words persuade you to forgive me?"

Rowan clenched her jaw long enough to restrain the urge to laugh in the man's face. *Forgive him?* Not in this lifetime. All those weeks and months she had ignored his attempts at communicating. She had fully expected to continue on that course. Then, the day before yesterday she had hit a wall, run out of viable options for finding answers. With no other alternative, she reluctantly began to open the letters and read each one, twice. They told her nothing useful. Rather, his words had repeatedly expressed how deeply sorry he was and how desperately he wanted her forgiveness.

Forgiveness was the one thing she could not give him. Beneath the table that separated them, her right knee started to bounce. She braced against the outward display of her emotions and said what needed to be said. "No."

The optimistic gleam that had appeared in his eyes died an abrupt death. "Then why are you here?"

"I'm here for information." Rowan squared her

shoulders and stared straight into his defeated gaze. "You owe me the truth, Herman. The whole truth."

He shook his head, turned up his shackled hands. "I've told you and the police everything I did. I don't know what else I can do."

If only the issue were so simple. "I don't need the truth about what you did, Herman. We know what you did."

His shoulders drooped. "I don't understand what you're saying, Ro. I did bad things—but never at Du-Pont. Never. It was Woody who crossed that line, not me. I wouldn't have done that to Edward. And it only happened once. Even if Woody hadn't ended up dead, I guarantee you he wouldn't have done that again."

Really? She was supposed to be grateful he did his stealing from the dead at another funeral home? Unbelievable.

Focus, Ro.

Sticking with her agenda was imperative. The chief of police had allowed her this extended visit with Herman for that specific purpose. She wasn't allowed to discuss the ongoing criminal case with Herman—not that she had any desire to do so. The chief—her longtime friend, William "Billy" Brannigan—had allowed her to use this interview room rather than the usual visitation area with the metal bars and Plexiglas. Today could very well be her one chance to speak with Herman in this sort of setting. The elderly man was likely going away for the rest of his life.

Aim for the emotions. "My father considered you family, Herman. You meant a great deal to him." She moistened her lips. "To both of us."

"Edward meant a great deal to me. You mean the world to me, Ro."

His words were true. Rowan heard the sincerity in his tone, saw it in his face.

"I've found quite a few disturbing notes in my mother's journals. I'm convinced my parents were keeping a number of troubling secrets. I want to know what those secrets were."

"We all have secrets, Ro. Even you." He gave her a knowing nod. "It's part of being human."

Anger whipped through her before she could stop it. "None of my secrets involve murder. I'm certain you can understand how uncovering those sorts of secrets is of particular importance under the circumstances."

Circumstances. More frustration and anger swirled inside her. The circumstances involved a serial killer. One of the most prolific serial killers in recorded history. One who, less than a year ago, had been her dear friend. *Dr. Julian Addington.* The monster who murdered her father and dozens upon dozens of others.

A monster whom, until recently, she had believed she had brought into her father's life. Now she wasn't so sure.

She wasn't very sure of anything, frankly.

"You've asked me repeatedly to forgive you," she reminded him. "If you want my forgiveness, then you need to help me." She had no intention of forgiving him even then, but she wasn't above dangling that particular carrot.

"I swear I'll help you any way I can," he promised. His earnest words urged her to trust him, to believe in him as she once had.

There was a time when she had considered Herman

a second father, or a trusted and loving uncle. How could she not have recognized he was not the man she believed him to be? How had she missed the signs?

The same way you did with Julian.

A lump swelled in her throat. How was she supposed to get past the idea that she had been so damn blind? Both her education and her work experience were in the field of psychiatry. For years it had been her job to read people—to see what the homicide detectives on her team did not. She had been quite good at her job. Not once had she failed to solve the case...*until Julian.*

Julian, and then Herman, had proved her a fraud.

Herman owed her for that betrayal and by God she intended to collect.

"All right. I'll put together a timeline of dates and events. Billy will pass along my questions and then we'll meet again to discuss anything you recall about those dates and events. If you let me down—"

"I won't." Herman leaned forward. "Tell Billy to give you the key to my house," he insisted. "Estelle was a stickler for keeping up the family photos. She documented every family event and special moment we shared with your family like a regular historian. You might find something useful there. Doesn't hurt to look."

To Rowan's knowledge there had been no evidence found in the Carter home and the house had subsequently been released by the department. Hopefully Billy wouldn't have a problem allowing her inside. Speaking of which, she glanced at the clock on the wall—Billy would be waiting for her by now. He'd promised her half an hour.

"I just need one favor from you."

Rowan drew back at his words, putting some distance between them. How dare he ask her for anything after all that he had done?

He held up his hands, the shackles rattling with the move. "It's not for me, exactly. I'd like you to see that flowers are put on Estelle's grave every year on her birthday. It's coming up next month and I've worried that I won't be able to arrange the delivery. Your father always did that for your mother and I surely would like to do it for my sweet Estelle."

She wanted to say no but that would be wrong. It wasn't Estelle's fault her husband had hurt others. His actions were part of the reason Estelle was dead and he was living with that painful fact. No, that wasn't entirely true. The cancer had been killing her, and she'd simply ended things early after learning what her husband had done. It was bad enough to face the pain of the disease each day. Who wanted to deal with the investigation into the criminal affairs of the man she had loved and trusted? Giving up the battle had been easier.

"Fine. I'll ensure that Estelle has flowers every year on her birthday." Rowan would have done it, anyway.

Herman nodded. "Thank you. That's all I ask."

Rowan slid her chair back from the table and stood. A few feet away, outside the door, two guards waited to return the old man watching her to his cell. She was beyond ready for that to happen. She needed out of this room. Away from another of the men in her life who had betrayed her. Except she needed his help. Her personal feelings had to take a back seat for now.

She pushed in the chair she'd vacated. "I'll be in touch again soon."

When she turned her back to him, he spoke again.

"Your daddy was a good man, Ro. Whatever else you believe, believe that."

Rowan forced one foot in front of the other until she reached the door. She walked out of the room. The guards went inside to reclaim custody of their prisoner. Rowan kept moving down the corridor without looking back. She didn't stop until she found Billy.

"How'd it go?" he asked.

She shrugged. "Well enough, I suppose."

Billy pushed away from the wall where he'd been waiting. "You can tell me all about it over lunch."

Rowan had no appetite, but she'd learned over the past several months not to mention details such as those to Billy. He worried about her, fussed over her. As much as she appreciated their friendship, that aspect was often frustrating. Outside work, she had lived a solitary life in Nashville. Her evenings had most always been spent hovered over a case file until she fell asleep. The occasional night out with friends always involved *work* friends and even those occasions were rare.

"Lunch sounds good."

He glanced at her. "You're getting better at hiding how you really feel."

So, he was onto her. "Lunch has never been high on my priority list."

It was true. She often forgot to stop for lunch. Even as a child, she and her twin sister would play and never think to stop and eat. Their mother had fussed when they finally made their way home. Not that Norah Du-Pont was much of a cook. Generally, Rowan and Raven had prepared their own meals. But that detail didn't prevent Norah from saying a mouthful if she happened to be home and noticed the time of day when her daughters finally showed up. Norah had been a little scattered and she'd spent a lot of time traveling. Their father had always been the primary parent. Which was likely why both she and Raven had been well versed in the preparation of a body for burial before they were old enough to date.

Billy opened the passenger-side door of his truck. "Burt called. He's sending business your way."

Burt Johnston was the county coroner. Since the exposure of the black-market body-part brokering, a good number of folks in the community who passed away were transported to a Tullahoma funeral home for their services. Rowan was grateful for any business Burt pointed in her direction. Gardner's, the only other funeral home in Winchester, had almost gone out of business under the weight of the lawsuits. No matter that her family had avoided any lawsuits, DuPont's hadn't slipped by unscathed. Clientele had dropped off considerably.

Fortunately for Rowan, her overhead costs were minimal, allowing her to ride out the storm. Gardner's apparently wasn't so lucky.

"Anyone we know?" she asked.

Winchester was a small town. Most everyone knew everyone else. The small-town atmosphere was part of the reason Rowan had been determined to move on to a larger city when she left for college. But she'd learned the hard way that she couldn't hide who she was simply by expanding the number of faces surrounding her. Strangely, she had decided she liked the idea of knowing the folks around her. Less likely to be so blatantly betrayed.

Then again, there was Herman. Knowing him

inordinately well hadn't prevented her blindness to his betrayal.

No, Rowan decided. What she liked about being back in Winchester was that she had grown up here. She had been labeled and pigeonholed at a very young age as the undertaker's daughter. Though she was the undertaker now, folks still saw her as the undertaker's daughter and she understood exactly what was expected of her and where she stood in the community. Whatever she did or didn't do, little would change in terms of how folks viewed her. Strangely, there was something comforting about the status quo.

"Never heard of him," Billy said in answer to her question about the new intake. "One Carlos Sanchez, seventy-one. A neighbor discovered him, deceased, in his apartment over in Bell View."

Bell View? Rowan didn't know Carlos Sanchez but she did know Bell View. Run-down, roach-infested apartments and run-down houses, operated by the closest thing to a slumlord that resided in Winchester.

"Cause of death?" Couldn't be murder, or the coroner wouldn't be releasing the body so quickly. He would, instead, be sending the man to Nashville for an autopsy.

"Heart attack."

"Any family?"

"Nope. His friend showed Burt and my officer a letter of instruction Sanchez had told him about. The letter expressly instructed that his body was to be taken care of by DuPont Funeral Home and stated that the insurance policy to cover the costs had been taken out with an insurance company downtown. The policy number is in the letter."

"I guess the man knew what he wanted."

Lots of people made advance arrangements. They just didn't generally live in Bell View.

Rowan had learned from experience that the one thing you could count on was that life never failed to toss out the occasional surprise.

She wondered what other surprises she would discover about Mr. Carlos Sanchez.

Two

Carlos Sanchez lay on his back on the mortuary table, his head resting on the head block. The overhead lights cast a harsh glow over his nude—save for the covering over his genitals—form. The man had lived a hard life. His body told the story. There was no hiding anything at this point. The craggy lines on his face and discoloration of his weathered skin spoke of decades of smoking and alcoholism, perhaps the abuse of other drugs. The numerous scars and the missing plug of cartilage in the helix portion of the right outer ear indicated he'd participated in more than his fair share of physical altercations.

Despite his advanced age, his body was lean and wiry. Muscle tone appeared firmer than average. None of the usual sagging along the arms and legs or in the abdomen area. Rowan would wager that he'd worked out regularly until very recently. Among the vast array of inked numbers and symbols on his body was a tattoo of a heart on the left side of his chest. A rose vine covered with thorns curled around the once deep red tattoo and extended up and across his shoulder, around his throat and disappeared. Interesting.

As a member of the Special Crimes Unit in Metro Nashville's homicide division for several years, she had seen a bit of everything when it came to tattoos and piercings. For some, certain symbols were considered a style statement or a testament of loyalty or faith. It never ceased to amaze her what some folks would do to their bodies toward that end. When it came to criminals, the markings and piercings were often related to their motivations. Other times it was entirely environmental.

She doubted she would ever know what had motivated the man lying before her. Unless someone came forward to claim him, he would be buried with little or no pomp and circumstance in a local cemetery.

After preparing the disinfectant and germicidal solutions, Rowan pulled on her gloves, then slipped on an apron. She generally wore jeans and T-shirts to work for comfort and because they were easily laundered. The first step was to cleanse the body and massage the extremities. Massaging the arms and legs was essential for helping to relieve the rigor mortis to some degree. This step not only helped her make the body more presentable for viewing, but it also facilitated the flow of fluids during the embalming process. She had checked his vitals already. No matter that the coroner had pronounced him dead, it was standard protocol that Rowan confirm that conclusion. The presence of rigor mortis and lividity were obvious signs of death, yet she still checked for clouded corneas and then for a pulse in the carotid artery. The former was present, the latter was not.

No question, Mr. Sanchez was assuredly deceased.

As she rolled the body to its right side, her gaze automatically tracked the vine tattoo drifting from his neck to a spot in the center of his back where a wreath of thorns encircled a name.

Norah.

Rowan's heart skipped as she reread the name. Norah was her mother's name. The hair on the back of her neck stood on end but she shook off the eerie sensation. Lots of women were named Norah. She cleansed the back of his body, then lowered him onto the table once more. As quickly as possible she completed the remainder of the cleaning-and-massaging process. Touching his body suddenly unnerved her. The sensation rarely occurred during this process since she had learned as a child to distance herself emotionally from the work. As inhumane as it sounded, during this particular step it was important not to see the body as a person any longer. Removing bodily fluids and replacing those with chemicals was an admittedly gruesome, no-turning-back step. It was important to remain objective and to focus on the task.

Despite her training, she found doing so difficult this afternoon. Because of the name tattooed on the man's back, she supposed. Any little reminder of her mother often unsettled her.

"Finding your mother hanging from the second-story stair railing when you're twelve years old can do that," she muttered.

Norah DuPont had committed suicide only a few months after Rowan's twin sister, Raven, drowned in the lake. Rowan was left feeling as if her mother had preferred to follow Raven into death than to try to get on with life with her surviving daughter. Not exactly an enduring memory. Rowan had never been particularly close to her mother, anyway. Raven had held that cherished spot.

As a psychiatrist, Rowan had learned that it was typical for one child to be closer to a particular parent than the other. Rowan had been closer to her father. At least she'd always thought so. After his death, she'd began to wonder if she knew either of her parents as well as she had once thought.

That was the thing about secrets. Secrets never stayed secret forever. Someone eventually discovered them and then it was often too late for the bearer of that secret to set the record straight. There were so many things Rowan wished she could ask her father.

Pushing aside the troubling thoughts, Rowan sealed Mr. Sanchez's eyes and mouth, ensuring his jaw was locked into position with wire. She set his face in a neutral-looking expression since he didn't strike her as the sort of man who smiled often. She studied those thin lips for a moment, then inspected his rugged face. He looked more like the kind of man who growled orders or snapped harsh words. Since there was no family to ask, it was safe to conclude that no one was going to complain about the expression he wore in death.

With the superficial steps out of the way, Rowan hesitated before moving on to the next part of her work. For about two seconds she argued with herself, but the daughter—the woman—in her won. She slipped off her gloves and rounded up her cell phone. One by one she snapped photos of the tattoos. Satisfied she had documented what could potentially turn out to be evidence if this man somehow knew her mother, she pulled on her gloves once more. She made the necessary incisions and inserted the tubes, then turned on the pump that would drain the blood vessels and usher preserving chemicals into those same veins and arteries. In the past it had been necessary to use more topical cosmetics for adding color to the complexion, but nowadays dyes and additives were combined with the embalming fluid to help restore the body's natural coloration. In fact, accessory chemicals could now be customized for each body. A person could look as healthy and attractive in death as the family desired. Of course, the topical enhancements were still needed for most clients, depending on the body's condition and the wishes of the family. Like everything else, all it took was a well-trained mortician and money.

The process of embalming required upward of forty-five minutes. While the pump did its job, Rowan noted the chemicals and amounts she had used for Sanchez on the whiteboard. When services were completed, she would ensure that all the notes were added to his file. Charlotte Kinsley, Rowan's personal and mortuary assistant, had contacted the insurance company to initiate the payment process. At this time there were no known surviving family members. Still, Rowan had asked Charlotte to select moderately priced items with which to fulfill Mr. Sanchez's services. Eventually next of kin might be located. Rowan felt confident he or she would appreciate any remaining moneys.

With the embalming complete, Rowan removed the tubes and closed the incisions she had made. She prepared Mr. Sanchez for storage in the refrigeration unit and moved him there. Another hour of cleanup in the mortuary room followed. By a few minutes past five, she retreated to the second-floor living quarters. She had no visitations tonight, which was rare. There was generally at least one every day of the week. As much as she appreciated a reasonably steady stream of business, she was grateful for tonight's reprieve.

Upstairs, Freud, her German shepherd, wagged his tail. "Hey, boy, you need to go out?"

His ears perked up and he headed for the stairs. Rowan sighed and tromped back down the stairs she'd only just climbed. The house was a well-maintained historic home that had served as a funeral home its entire existence. The mortuary services were handled in the basement. The funeral services and delivery access were on the first floor. The second and third floors served as the family living quarters. More often than not Rowan used the back staircase—the one located by the delivery entrance at the rear of the house. Part of the reason, she imagined, was because her mother had used the grand second-story landing that overlooked the lobby and front entrance to hang herself.

What kind of mother hung herself in the open only minutes before her daughter would arrive home from school?

Rowan had stopped dwelling on that question years ago. She'd spent far too many years obsessing about her inability to be enough for her mother. With a couple of clicks on the keypad, she disarmed the security system and sent Freud racing across the backyard. The security system had been installed back in May, when

Julian Addington decided to invade her life here in Winchester.

The bastard.

How could she have known him all those years—as his patient and then, later, as his friend and colleague—and not recognized what he was? A monster. One of the most prolific serial killers to date. He'd turned her life upside down. How could she possibly have considered continuing her work with the Nashville police department's Special Crimes Unit when she hadn't been able to spot the killer right under her nose?

The answer was she couldn't. Subsequently, she had resigned. Resigned and come home with her tail tucked between her legs.

Rowan wrapped her arms around herself. She should have pulled on a sweater. The October weather had turned a little chillier than usual. Or maybe it was the memories. From the moment Julian had murdered her father, all sorts of secrets had started to surface. Her mother, Norah, had apparently had an affair with Julian. Julian's seventeen-year-old daughter had come to Winchester more than a quarter century ago looking for the woman who had stolen her father's attention. The theory was that the daughter, Alisha, had murdered Raven and then, according to Julian, Rowan's father had killed Alisha in a fit of rage and revenge.

Rowan wasn't prepared to believe her father had done such a thing. But every time she dug a little deeper into her mother's journals, she found something else that suggested her father was capable of all manner of hurtful deeds.

Still, she had found no proof he was a murderer.

A frown tugged across Rowan's brow. Her mother

had called herself a writer. She'd worked on project after project and taken frequent research trips, but nothing ever came of the work that somehow consumed her existence. Oddly, none of the projects was ever finished. Most appeared to revolve around mysteries and murder.

The memory of Mr. Sanchez's damaged ear flashed in her mind. The image was somehow familiar. The scar on his left hip whizzed into focus in her mind's eye next.

"Freud, come!"

When she had persuaded Freud to follow her back inside, Rowan locked up, set the alarm and then climbed the stairs, two at a time. Rather than start dinner or go up to her room on the third floor for a shower, she went straight to her parents' bedroom. She sat down at her mother's desk, turned on the lamp and started thumbing through the journals. Her mother had described all sorts of murderers. The details were always lush and well-defined. Norah had been a talented writer in that she captured the essence of time and place extraordinarily well. Her characters were clearly drawn. It was in the execution and follow-through of the plot where she collapsed.

A victim had clamped down on his ear once, tearing loose a small plug, serving as a constant reminder that he could never be careless again. Leaving any sort of evidence was far too risky.

Rowan reread the passage. She skimmed a few paragraphs before and after to see if there was any mention of which ear. There was not. It was a foolish notion, but the idea wouldn't let go. She went back to the beginning of this particular project and started to skim the pages. She pulled one knee up to her chest, got comfortable and read.

His Latino heritage was evident in every square inch of his hard body. His dark hair was long and shaggy, his equally dark eyes piercing.

The fact that the man in refrigeration downstairs was Latino was not lost on Rowan. "Don't be ridiculous, Ro."
She was not a child, and this was no episode of some creepy horror show. This was life, coincidence. Rowan continued skimming.

Dragging her fingers across the scar on his left hip, where he'd taken a dagger, made her tremble.

"Now, that is creepy." Sanchez had a scar on his left hip, in the area of the iliac crest. Coupled with the name *Norah* tattooed on his back...
Rowan shook her head. "Impossible."
Still, she kept reading.

My name on his skin would forever proclaim that I belonged to him. He was a killer and yet I did not fear him... I craved him.

Rowan sat back. Reminded herself to breathe. This could not possibly be what it appeared to be.
She laughed, couldn't help herself. She'd spent the past five months learning that nothing in her life was

what it appeared to be. Why would this be any different?

She had to be certain.

There was one person she could trust without fail. *Billy.*

Rowan went in search of her cell phone. She found it in the kitchen, where she'd cut up an apple earlier. She put through the call to Billy's cell. She knew what needed to be done, but she was no longer in law enforcement, though Billy had asked her to assist him with cases. This step, however, required more than an advisor.

Billy answered with his usual greeting. She couldn't help smiling. He made her feel like she belonged. He'd always had that effect on her. "Hey, there's something I need to talk to you about. Would you be available to come over, now or later—whatever works for you? I could call in some takeout."

The two of them shared enough meals to be an old married couple. But neither of them had time for marriage. They were too focused on work.

"Actually, I just pulled into your driveway."

Rowan walked to the front window and looked out. Billy's truck sat in front of the main entrance to the funeral home. As she watched, the driver's-side door opened and he climbed out.

"Come on in. Use your key—you know the code."

"Will do."

Billy was the one person in the world she trusted completely.

When she'd tucked her cell into the pocket of her jeans, Freud jumped to his feet and barked. "Take it easy, boy, it's just Billy."

Freud glanced at her, then curled back into his bed. Rowan opened the door and watched as Billy strode along the hall between the second-story landing and the living quarters.

"Hey." He smiled and reached up to remove his hat as he crossed the threshold.

Billy Brannigan was a cowboy through and through, from the boots to the hat, but, more important, he was a true gentleman. And he was charming and polite, exactly like the heroes in the romance novels women swooned over. It really was a miracle that he'd made it all the way to forty without getting married. There wasn't a single woman in Franklin County who wouldn't love to land the handsome chief of police.

But the man swore that he just hadn't met the right woman yet.

Not that Rowan had any room to talk. She was swiftly approaching forty and she hadn't been married, either.

All work and no play. They were certainly a pair.

"Hey yourself. I know why I was calling you, but why were you coming to see me?"

"You first," he urged, hat in hand, face way too serious.

She knew that face. Rowan crossed her arms over her chest and shook her head. "Just tell me what's happened, Billy."

"Herman had to be taken over to the hospital. His blood pressure shot up sky-high and wouldn't come back down. They'll be keeping him for observation for a couple of days."

Rowan's heart started to pound before he finished speaking.

"They've got his numbers stabilized now," Billy

added quickly, obviously noting the worry in her eyes. "But I knew you'd want to be made aware of the situation."

"Maybe it was my visit." Guilt heaped onto her shoulders. "I wasn't very nice to him."

Billy shrugged. "I don't think this was related to your visit. The doc on call said his medical record showed a history of high blood pressure. They're going to adjust his medication and he'll most likely be fine."

"He's under guard, I presume." Foolish question but the need to hear the words was too great to ignore.

Billy nodded. "He is, and no one can visit without prior authorization."

Her eyebrows shot up. "Has anyone requested authorization?" From the moment Herman had been arrested, his family had turned their backs on him. Not that she could blame them or that she intended to feel any sympathy for him even after hearing that he was ill. She didn't. Would not. He did not deserve her—or anyone else's—sympathy.

"Not yet." Billy frowned. "What did you need to talk to me about?"

"It may be nothing." Suddenly the idea felt entirely foolish. "But I'm thinking you should run Sanchez's prints."

"You mind sharing your reason?"

"I think he might be a killer."

Three

Rowan turned off the hair dryer and set it aside. She studied her reflection as she ran the brush through her hair. Growing up, everyone had insisted that she was the spitting image of her mother. The comments had made her happy at first, but then later, after her mother died, she grew to hate those well-meaning observations. Yes, she had the blond hair and blue eyes, the pale skin. But so had Raven, her twin sister. The difference had been in the softer edges—the line of Rowan's jaw, her nose. Those details were duplicates of her mother's. Raven's features had been sharper, ever so slightly more angular.

The differences were hardly noticeable to most people. Even Herman hadn't been able to tell them apart if they didn't want him to. But their mother and father had always known who was who.

Rowan tossed the brush onto the counter and reached for the moisturizer to complete her nightly ritual. She had hoped to hear something back from

Billy after he checked out Sanchez. So far he hadn't called. It was possible the deceased man's prints hadn't been in any of the databases. If that were the case, Billy would have called by now and told her as much. Then again, he was the chief of police. He might have gone out on a call. Winchester was a fairly small town, but it wasn't crime-free.

Taking a deep breath, she slid on her glasses, turned away from the bathroom mirror and headed to her room. With the cooler nights, she'd added lounge pants to her favorite bedtime T-shirts. This old house had a fairly new heating-and-cooling system, but it was simply impossible to properly heat and cool a house as old as this one. A room was either too warm or too cool, particularly on the upper floors. Thankfully, the inconsistency wasn't an issue on the first floor. Keeping the temperature low was vital when it came to slowing the decomp rate. The viewing and visitation times could become an issue if the temperature was too high, particularly with a large crowd of family and friends.

She grabbed her discarded clothes and tossed them down the laundry chute. It was early still. She typically didn't get to bed before midnight. Sleep eluded her for a while after that. Then the usual dreams woke her. It was the same old routine that had haunted her since she was twelve years old and had watched her sister's coffin being lowered into the ground.

Rowan dreamed of Raven more often than not. Thankfully the dreams were generally brief and vague. Raven in the water—the same dark water where she'd drowned. In the dream, she would call to Rowan, urging her to come into the water with her. A few months ago Rowan had begun to dream of her mother, which

was something she had never done, not even immediately after her death. But those dreams had ceased
in recent weeks. She no longer awakened from the
disturbing arguments between her mother and a man
whose voice Rowan could not identify. She was grateful those unpleasant memories, or whatever they were,
had stopped interrupting her sleep. Dealing with far too
regular reminders of her sister's death was bad enough.

She recognized that the dreams of her sister were
related to survivor's guilt. Why had Raven died and
she lived? The fact that Rowan had been so upset with
her sister for going to a party that Rowan hadn't been
invited to made matters worse. Pile their mother's sub-
sequent suicide on top of that and Rowan had barely
survived beyond the age of twenty. Two attempts to
take her own life had sent her down a different path—
one that ultimately had cost her father's life.

Hugging her arms around herself, she wandered
down to the kitchen. Finding a possible connection to
Sanchez in her mother's ramblings had dragged recent
history back to the forefront of her existence. Until she
had the answers she sought, this would be the way of
things, she supposed. Moving beyond the past would
be impossible until she solved the mystery still sim-
mering there.

She placed the kettle on the stove and set it to heat.
Maybe a cup of tea would help warm her up.

While she waited, she stared out the window across
the backyard. No matter that this was a funeral home
and there had always been at least one dead person in
the house, Rowan had felt safe and happy here as a child.
But that was before. Now this was the place that some-

how hid all the secrets related to her mother's and sister's lives and deaths, leading up to her father's murder.

Rowan had no idea when she came home after her father's murder that her childhood in Winchester was tied to Julian Addington. They'd met in the hospital when she was a freshman in college, after her second suicide attempt. Julian had taken her case, become her mentor and friend. She'd had no idea that he'd been watching her all those years—most of her life. Apparently, Julian and her mother had carried on an affair. The details surrounding their relationship remained somewhat murky. Rowan felt confident it was true but there were questions. Questions with profound implications.

Did her father know about the affair? Did Julian's daughter, Alisha, come to Winchester twenty-seven years ago with the intention of killing Raven and Rowan? Had she only succeeded in murdering Raven? And who had really killed Alisha?

Rowan hadn't known about the affair or Alisha until five months ago, when she stumbled upon the girl's remains not a dozen yards from where Raven's body had been found nearly three decades ago.

Finding those remains had lured Julian out of hiding. He'd been close, watching Rowan. All of which only further convinced the FBI that Rowan was somehow involved with him as more than a friend. She felt relatively certain those suspicions had lost most of their impact after she shot Julian. Of course, he had escaped, anyway. Unfortunately, she had no idea as to the extent of her injury related to the shooting. The good news was that he had not contacted her in all the months since that day. If the world was lucky, he was dead.

Considering that the massive manhunt had turned up no sign of him, it was a reasonable possibility.

His former wife, Anna Prentice Addington, remained in Winchester. She'd taken up temporary residence in the historic bed-and-breakfast. Her cohort, former LAPD detective Cash Barton, was never far away. The two firmly believed that if Julian was still alive, he would eventually come after Rowan again. Until then, they intended to stay close. Anna insisted she was not leaving until she knew what really happened to her daughter.

Rowan desperately wanted that answer, as well. Julian insisted her father had killed Alisha, but Rowan could not believe such a wild accusation. Her father wasn't that kind of man.

But then her father had had secrets, too.

Not nearly so many as her mother.

Rowan shut off the stove. She slid her feet into her shoes and headed for the front door. As if he'd sensed the change in her mood, Freud lifted his head and watched her cross the living room. When she unlocked the door that separated the living space from the corridor that led to the main staircase, he jumped up and followed.

At the top of the stairs, Rowan hesitated. No matter how many times she used these stairs she couldn't pass the second-floor landing without thinking of her mother's death.

There were many things Rowan didn't know about her mother, but one thing she was absolutely certain of was how very selfish the woman had been.

She hurried down the stairs, Freud trotting at her side. Without pausing, she turned and made her way along the first-floor corridor and through the staff-only doors. She opened the door to the refrigeration unit and flipped on the light. She walked straight to the only gurney in the unit and drew back the white sheet. Why would this man leave instructions for his body to be prepared by her funeral home? Had he, too, been watching her? Like Julian? For Julian, perhaps?

"What do you want from me?" she demanded of the dead man.

Her mother had written about this man as if she had known him intimately. How many affairs had Norah DuPont carried on? The fact that Rowan could not answer the question was just another indication of how little she really knew about the woman.

Rowan stared at the cold, lifeless body. Had this man been a friend of Julian Addington's, as well? The age was right. When she was a kid, sixty-five or seventy had seemed ancient—elderly. Wheelchairs and nursing homes had come to mind. But that was no longer true. Not only was Rowan older, but people were also healthier now. Took better care of themselves. The average seventy-year-old today was like the fifty-year-olds of the past. It was nothing to see a man or woman well beyond sixty running in marathons.

Maybe Julian and Mr. Sanchez had belonged to the same murder club. Her gaze traced the thorny vine that crawled up his chest, disappeared across his shoulder and down his back until it reached that thorny crown that surrounded Norah's name. It seemed more and more feasible that Norah had been a member of that same club.

The front bell rang. Rowan jumped. She pressed a hand to her chest and took a breath, then quickly covered Mr. Sanchez. Exiting the refrigeration unit, she ensured the door was closed securely and listened for the bell again. If there was an incoming body, she generally received a call, particularly after hours. Not to mention that anyone who made deliveries was well aware that coming to the rear entrance was standard protocol. She didn't accept deliveries through the main entrance.

"Damn it." She'd left her cell upstairs. It was possible someone had called and asked for instructions.

Leaving the lights out, she walked into the lobby and over to the row of windows next to the front entrance. She peeked between the slats of the blinds. Billy's truck sat in the drive. If she pressed her forehead to the glass she could see part of him where he waited at the door.

Her pulse sped up. Hopefully he had news.

She hurried to the door, deactivated the alarm and unlocked the dead bolt. She pulled the door open and stepped back to allow him inside. "Did you find something?"

He nodded. "I did."

She closed the door behind him and locked it. "Do we need coffee or a drink?" When he didn't bother removing his hat, she understood he wasn't here to stay. He was on his way someplace else.

"We don't have time for either. We should get over to Bell View."

Adrenaline fired in her veins. "Has something happened?"

"When I ran his prints—even before I had any results—the feds called me."

Surprise flared in her chest. "The feds?"

He lifted one broad shoulder and let it fall. "Your favorite fed."

Josh Dressler.

"What did he have to say?" She didn't dare breathe as she waited for Billy's response.

"He'll be here in the morning with the necessary paperwork to take Sanchez off your hands."

"Really." Her arms folded instinctively over her chest, and her gaze narrowed. "Why would he do that?"

About a dozen scenarios streamed through her head, none of them particularly appealing. Her instincts had been right. Sanchez was a killer. From the sound of things, he'd left his mark with broad strokes.

"I'll explain on the way." Billy looked her up and down. "You okay to go, or do you need to change?" He gestured to her fuzzy slippers and thin lounge pants.

She needed jeans and sneakers and her contacts. "Give me three minutes."

Fifteen minutes later they parked at the curb on Knight Street in the Bell View neighborhood. No matter that it was dark—streetlights had the place lit up like a runway. More and more exterior lighting had been added over the years in an effort to cut back on the crime carried on in the area after dark.

The neighborhood consisted of a couple of blocks of government-subsidized housing and a large apartment building that should have been torn down fifty years ago. Instead, a fresh coat of paint was slapped on every decade or so and the rotten steps and railings were replaced only when a safety inspection failed. The clientele had declined over the past half century, and then about a decade back, the stats had done a turnaround.

Based on what she'd seen since her return, overcrowding was now a major issue in Bell View.

Sanchez hadn't lived in the subsidized housing or the dilapidated apartment building. He had rented one of the shacks that had once been part of a motel. The office sat in the center of the property. Small, squat buildings that had started life as motel rooms with kitchenettes stood in a horseshoe pattern around the office.

"Have you been inside?" she asked as she climbed out of the truck.

Billy came around to her door. "Since the death didn't involve foul play there was no reason to go back in once the body was removed. After that call from Dressler and the download of Sanchez's rap sheet, I called the manager. He's an old friend of Chief Holcomb. He gave me the key to Sanchez's place."

Until four years ago, when Billy took over, Luther Holcomb had been the chief of police for as long as Rowan could remember. Holcomb was one of those lawmen who did things old-school and sometimes his tactics weren't exactly legal.

Is what you're about to do legal?

Rowan ignored the question and followed Billy to the third cement-block box on the left. What Billy was about to do was crossing the line, there was no arguing the reality. He was a good man and he would never cross that line unless it was for her. The last five months or so he had taken chances and crossed far too many lines—all for her.

"Wait."

He turned to meet her gaze before opening the door he'd just unlocked.

"As much as I want to go in there and see what we can find potentially related to my mother, I can't let you keep doing this for me, Billy. You—"

He turned back to the door, opened it and walked inside.

Rowan blew out a breath and followed him. The overhead light came on at about the same instant the smell of stale cigarettes and cooking grease invaded her lungs. The space looked to be about twelve feet by fifteen. Old linoleum floors were hardly visible, with the bed and dozens of gray plastic storage containers taking up the square footage. Two shirts hung on a rod attached to a shelf on one wall. Beyond the smell and the overflow of stuff, the place appeared reasonably clean.

"Where was the body?"

Since there was only one room, besides what looked like a tiny bathroom in the far corner, the body had to have been on the bed or on the floor.

Billy jerked his head toward the other side of the room. "On the floor next to the bed."

Rowan glanced around again. "Does it matter where we start?"

He pulled gloves from his jacket pocket. "Up to you." He passed one pair to her and tugged on the other.

Cold slid through her veins. "Okay."

Gloves on, they started with the bed. Checked under the mattress and box spring, inside the pillowcases. Under the covers. Then they moved on to the small bedside table. Nothing in the drawers. A few dishes and a couple of pans in the cabinets. Some canned goods and a half loaf of bread. The refrigerator was filled with beer, the cheap stuff. A carton of cigarettes sat in the freezer compartment.

With nothing left except the storage containers, Rowan turned to her friend. "You understand that if we find evidence my presence could jeopardize whatever investigation follows."

It wasn't a question. He knew this the same as she did.

His jaw hardened and he tightened his lips for a moment before he responded. "Dr. Rowan DuPont, I hereby deputize you until further notice. Happy now?" He reached for a container.

There had been a few moments in her life like this one, but right now Rowan couldn't help wondering how she possibly deserved a friend like Billy. "Absolutely."

She flashed him an exaggerated smile as she reached for a container. She placed it on the floor and crouched down next to it. This whole endeavor could be a waste of time, but Billy was willing to help her satisfy her curiosity, even if it meant skirting the boundaries of the law. One of these days she hoped to have the opportunity to back him up the way he'd backed her up so many times.

The container lids locked into place on each end. Rowan popped the release on one side and then the other. The instant she removed the lid, the odor of chemicals crashed into her senses. Inside stood two stacks of what appeared to be books. Seven—no, eight. All appeared to be antiquated and were bound in leather. She picked up the top one on the left stack and opened it.

There were no pages, just more of the leathery material she recognized as skin that had been preserved via some sort of tanning process. She picked up the folds of skin and opened it up. The face staring up at her sent her tumbling back onto her butt.

When she found her voice, she said, "We're going to need a forensic team."

Four

The faces were from mostly male victims, but two were female. There were twenty-six in all.

Degloved. The skin had been completely removed from the underlying connective tissue and muscle. Generally, avulsion injuries such as these involved ripping or tearing the skin away from the tissue, but that had not happened in these instances.

With gloved hands, Rowan gently examined the final mask of skin. The edges were clean and fairly smooth, like the others. Whoever had removed the faces had first made a meticulous incision around the entire boundary of the hairline, in front of the ears and then down and beneath the chin, tracing the mandible. Finally, the skin had been removed with painstaking slowness to ensure there were no sudden tears, or thin or uneven spots. The work had been executed with surgical precision. There was, of course, no way to determine if the removal was completed postmortem, or if the victims had still been breathing.

As if that was not grotesque enough, more skin had been removed, presumably from the bodies of the victims, and tanned like leather for use as a binding. Each face was ensconced inside its own book. Each book was unique in texture and varied ever so slightly in color, maybe due to age or maybe related to ethnicity.

Rowan shook off the disturbing sensation that had rushed up her spine and camped at the base of her skull. "Judging by these—" she placed the last of the more than two dozen books into another large evidence bag "—Mr. Sanchez collected quite a few victims."

Billy placed the lid back on the container before him—thankfully, it was the last one. "The rest are photos and touristy souvenirs along with dozens of spiral notepads. Most of the ramblings in the notepads are like stories. He waxes on about wherever he is— the landscape, the sky, the way the air smells. Then he talks about the people he meets. Describes them in detail, but no names."

Rowan shifted her attention to her friend. "Sounds like my mother's journals."

With every single discovery in this cramped house of horrors, Rowan grew more convinced that there was some sort of connection between her mother and this man—this probable serial killer. She shook her head. What was she thinking? Of course, he was a serial killer. The evidence sat right in front of her.

"I was thinking the same thing." Billy's gaze touched hers. "Based on what you've told me."

Growing up, the strangest thing about her family was the fact that her father was an undertaker. Her sister died but other kids lost siblings, too. Her mother's suicide was not entirely unheard-of. But this—she glanced around the sleazy room—was the sort of strangeness that put one in the eye of media storms. Rowan had done her time under media scrutiny. After her father's murder and Julian's abrupt exiting of the closet as a heinous serial killer, Rowan had been hounded by the authorities, as well as the media. *This* did not bode well for her future sanity.

The bottom line was that her mother had apparently been involved with both Julian and Sanchez. The other known details at this time were that Sanchez had at least twenty-six victims to his credit and that his name was most likely not Carlos Sanchez.

"Dressler is going to have a field day with this," she muttered.

Billy checked his cell. "The evidence techs are twenty minutes out." He glanced around. "Anything else you want to look at before they get here?"

"The notepads."

He pointed out the two containers with the spiral notepads. Rowan set to work. Growing up, her mother had often been so preoccupied with writing that she had little time for her children or her husband. Rowan and her sister, along with their father, had indulged her whims. Life had been simpler that way. Rowan had wondered later when she decided to write her own book, *The Language of Death*, if she had inherited from her mother that need to pour her soul onto pages. The release of the book had garnered far more attention than Rowan had expected, even landing her an interview on a popular national morning TV talk show. But Rowan had written about truth and her life growing up in a funeral home. Her mother's work had been fiction.

Or had it?

Rowan flipped quickly through notepad after notepad. She skimmed the headings, scanning for anything familiar. Dates, places, notations about jobs he picked up, but nothing that triggered a memory of anything she'd read in her mother's journals.

"They're here."

Billy's deep voice startled her after the long minutes of silence. Rowan closed the lid on the container and stood. "I didn't see anything that connected with my mother's writing, but I can't rule out the theory without a closer, more thorough inspection."

He nodded. "We tried. Nothing else we can do tonight."

They had tried. What else could either of them do at this point? Rowan had an obligation to share her concerns with Agent Dressler. She would not put Billy in the position of having to do so. This was her problem, so she would deal with it. Billy had already done more than he should to help her and to protect her.

The evidence techs took over the scene. Detective Clarence Lincoln arrived to supervise the search and collection.

"Hey, Ro." He flashed her a smile. "You and Billy have to learn not to allow work to interfere with your social life."

Rowan laughed. "What social life? I was just finishing up the preparation of a body before I came here." She hitched her head in Billy's direction. "Maybe he has a social life, but I do not."

"You two kill me." Clarence glanced around the room. "No pun intended."

She managed a chuckle but opted not to question his statement. There were a few people around town who wanted to play matchmaker with Billy and her, and Clarence was one of them. The three of them had gone to school together. As much as she had lusted after Billy from afar as a kid, they had become good friends. Great friends, in fact, but nothing else. Clarence was wasting his breath.

Billy Brannigan was the most eligible bachelor in the county, and Rowan doubted he had any interest in the woman who spent most of her time with the dead. There had been moments when she'd felt a tingle of something primal between them, but there was no way in the world she would risk their friendship for a moment of physical satisfaction. Besides, she was the object of a deranged killer's obsession. She had no intention of dragging Billy any deeper into that unpleasant situation than he already was. Billy was the closest thing to family she had left. She did not want Julian using him to get to her.

Needing air that hadn't been closed up with a killer for God only knew how long, she stepped outside and inhaled the cool night air. The ruckus had roused residents, drawing them outside their doors onto stoops. They stood or sat on the steps, watching and waiting for whatever might happen next. Smoke curled in the air from the end of a cigarette. A cell phone or two flashed photos. Did any of them know they had been living next door to a killer? Had he bragged about his exploits?

Only one way to find out. Rowan stepped down to the sidewalk and started toward the nearest neighbor. The cell in her pocket vibrated against her hip. She tugged it out. The name of her security company flashed on the screen. Rowan paused and accepted the call.

"Rowan DuPont."

"Dr. DuPont, the alarm has been triggered at the funeral home. Are you safe?"

"I'm not at home." Rowan looked back toward the squat building with all the cops going in and out. "I can be there in ten minutes."

"We'll send the police now. Approach the property with caution, Dr. DuPont."

Rowan reminded the dispatcher to warn the officers about Freud. Most everyone knew there was a big old German shepherd at the funeral home, but she wanted to be certain. Beyond that, she wasn't sure she said goodbye or even thanked the dispatcher. She shoved the phone back into her pocket and went in search of Billy.

The funeral home's back door stood open, the wood near the lock splintered where a crowbar or similar tool had been used to force it open. The two officers who arrived first had gone inside, turning on each light as they searched an area. One of the officers, Ray Trenton, had served on Rowan's protection detail a few months back. Freud recognized Trenton and allowed him and his partner into the living quarters. Billy insisted Rowan stay outside with a third officer until he had checked things out himself.

Another of his overprotective moves.

Frustrated, Rowan stood in the center of the front parking lot and waited, arms crossed over her chest. There were folks who wrongly believed that funeral homes kept cash or the valuables of their clients lying around. Others would go after the chemicals for enhancing the effects of drugs. Soak marijuana in embalming fluid, allow it to dry and the effect of the drug was elevated. Dangerously so.

"Idiots," Rowan muttered.

A couple of times when she was a teenager there had been a break-in at the funeral home. Once, Gerald Scott had decided he wanted his wife back home with him. It was the only time her father had ever lost a body, if only for a few hours. The other time was when Tony Syler and a friend had sneaked down to the mortuary room during his aunt's visitation. They hadn't stolen anything, just snapped pics of each other on the embalming table.

No one had ever stolen any of the chemicals.

"Damn it." She exhaled a big breath of frustration.

Anticipation welled inside her as Billy strode out the front entrance. His long legs ate up the distance between them, her worry rising with each step.

"How much was taken?" she asked. How many kids would be harmed by those chemicals? *Damn it, damn it.* This was the last thing she'd expected. She'd have to get new locks on the mortuary room and the storage closet where she kept the chemicals. Anything to avoid this issue in the future.

He shook his head. "No chemicals were taken, Ro." Billy glanced back at the funeral home. "Whoever broke in, they had only one goal."

She frowned, afraid to breathe. If not the chemicals…

"They took Sanchez."

"They took a cadaver?" Why in the world would anyone steal a freshly embalmed corpse? Unless it was a family member. But neighbors insisted Sanchez had no family. Of course, these were the same neighbors who apparently didn't know he was a killer.

"Afraid so." Billy hitched his head toward the entrance. "You can come in now. Have a look around to make sure nothing else is missing." He shrugged. "I should probably call Dressler and tell him what happened."

"Better you than me." Rowan did not envy him that task.

While Billy passed along new instructions to the officer who had been waiting with her, Rowan headed inside. Freud greeted her in the lobby. Rowan scratched him on the head.

Trenton gave her a nod. "He was raising the devil when we arrived. As soon as we opened the door on the second floor, he rushed down the stairs and to the refrigeration unit. He's got good ears."

"He's a good dog." Rowan gave Freud another scrub behind the ears.

The fact that Trenton had been able to open the door to the living quarters told Rowan she'd failed to lock up on the second floor. A dead bolt wouldn't have stopped the intruder, she reminded herself as she thought of the back door. Most likely, if he'd gone up the stairs, Freud's deep, threatening barks had sent him back down.

But this break-in hadn't been about her or what she might have in her private rooms or anywhere else in the funeral home. This had been about the man—the killer—lying on that gurney in refrigeration.

Rowan moved toward the refrigeration unit. Trenton's partner stood by the open door. She didn't try to go inside, no need. She glanced beyond the door, noted the gurney still in place, the sheet she'd had draped over Sanchez's body abandoned on the floor. It was possible one intruder had dragged him out, but she couldn't see one man—even a particularly strong one—carrying him out. Sanchez was a good 170 pounds. Not to mention the rigor would have made moving him unwieldy.

"You think we're looking at two perps?"

Rowan turned to face Billy, who had obviously read her mind. He did that a lot. No surprise. They'd known each other a long time. Thought alike in many ways.

"I don't think one could have managed alone, especially without the gurney."

"Evidence techs will be here as soon as they finish up at Sanchez's place. Meanwhile, we should talk about Dressler."

Great. Rowan resisted the urge to roll her eyes. "I need coffee. Is the kitchen off-limits?"

Billy shook his head. "No reason to believe he entered the living quarters. Coffee sounds good to me, too."

He followed her upstairs and she set the coffee maker up to brew. She'd no more than pressed the button when the scent of coffee filled the air. She'd never been a nighttime coffee drinker but there were times when it was necessary. Having cops roaming the funeral home in the middle of the night was definitely one of those times.

"Dressler is justifiably upset," Billy said as he settled at the table. "I think it was important to him that he had the body." Billy shrugged. "Maybe to prove the guy's dead."

"It won't be difficult to lift DNA from the drain in the mortuary room. I've cleaned up already but I'm sure he can find something. Maybe on that gurney, as well."

"You still photograph the corpses?"

She nodded. "Always. If the body I embalmed was the man Dressler is looking for, there is no question about him being dead. He is as dead as the proverbial doornail."

"You photographed the tattoo?"

Rowan poured two cups of coffee and moved to the table. "I photographed them all."

"Dressler's going to want your theory about the name."

She sipped her coffee and made an agreeable sound. "Don't worry, I'll be cooperative."

Billy stared at his cup as if wrestling with the decision of whether to infuse his veins with caffeine or not at this point. "I'm not exactly a fan of his, but I'd like to be there when he talks to you."

"I wouldn't want it any other way." There was no love lost between Billy and Dressler. Rowan wasn't sure of the reason. One of these days she would ask him. Maybe today, after she met with the haughty agent.

"Do you mind if I have a look at the journals with the references to the man you believe to be Sanchez?"

"Why not?" She stood. "Follow me, Chief."

They abandoned their coffee and she led the way to her parents' bedroom. Not that she needed to—Billy knew this house as well as she did. The journal she'd pulled from the others was on her mother's writing desk. Rowan opened it to the pages she had marked with paper clips and passed it to Billy.

When he'd viewed the final marked page, he passed the journal back to her. "Sure as hell sounds like the guy."

Rowan nodded. "I have no doubt. The only questions

in my mind are how did they know each other and what was his real name?"

"I'm sure Dressler will share what he feels he can." Billy's tone contradicted his words.

"What came back on his prints?"

"The prints were connected to about a dozen homicide cases, but the owner of those prints was not identified."

"Then he is a serial killer." No surprise there.

"If he's not the killer, then he was some sort of accomplice since his prints showed up at all those scenes. Different cities, different MOs."

"Any of them missing their faces?"

Billy shook his head. "Not even one."

Disgust churned in Rowan's belly. "It's worse than we imagined."

"I believe so."

Which meant Rowan's mother could have been involved in dozens of murders. How the hell had her father not noticed there was something horribly wrong with his wife?

Unless he suffered from the same ailment.

No. Her father was not a killer.

Was he?

Five

Rowan clutched her coffee mug in both hands. The cold had leached deep into her bones. She stood in the refrigeration unit staring at the gurney where Sanchez, or whatever his name was, had been lying before his body was stolen.

Who would go to the trouble to break into a funeral home and steal a body?

She and Billy had tossed scenarios back and forth until the wee hours of the morning. The possibilities were endless. A cult follower who admired the killer's work. The family member of a victim who knew who he really was. Another serial killer who wanted to consume his remains in some sort of bizarre ritual or who wanted to fuel a sense of power by mutilating his decomposing corpse.

Sanchez had no family or any friends as far as anyone knew.

"I have to talk to that neighbor."

Freud whimpered as if he disagreed with her conclusion.

Rowan turned to find him waiting at the open door. She blinked. Shivered. The pullover sweater and jeans were no defense against the frigid air pumping from the fans of the refrigeration unit.

"Don't worry, boy," she said as she joined him in the corridor and closed the door. "I haven't lost my mind yet."

It only looked that way from time to time.

Her cell vibrated in her back pocket. She reached for it and checked the screen. The text message spilled across the screen.

Thomas Harvey ready for pickup.

She messaged a thumbs-up to the sender. "Time to go to work, Freud."

Rowan took her mug to the lounge. Around three this morning, when she still couldn't sleep, she had decided to start leaving Freud with free rein in the funeral home whenever she was away. After moving back into the funeral home earlier this year, she had concluded that leaving Freud in the living quarters if she had to go out for any reason was the best strategy. With the cleaning team and other staff members in and out, it had worked out better since Freud could be a little intimidating. But everyone on the DuPont team knew him now so there was really no need to do so. Perhaps if an intruder heard his ferocious bark beyond whatever door or window he'd chosen to illegally enter, he or she would think twice about breaking in. On the other hand, Rowan wasn't sure Freud could have stopped whoever made off with Sanchez's body. Worse, he might even have been hurt.

"Maybe you should stay upstairs, boy."

He cocked his head and stared at her with those pleading dark eyes.

"All right. We'll try it this way and see how it goes."

A quick trip upstairs for her bag, and to lock up, and she was ready to go. At the west side exit, she set the alarm, leaving the motion sensors inactive since Freud would be running around. Then she climbed into her father's hearse and headed for the hospital. For the first couple of months back she had avoided using the hearse. It had felt strange sitting in the driver's seat— her father's seat. She'd left pickups to Woody, her former assistant, and to Herman. When they were both gone, the task had shifted to Charlotte, her only full-time assistant.

Driving the hearse was actually easy—just like driving a station wagon. The front seat and dashboard were no different than any other vehicle. Certainly, the mechanisms that made the vehicle operational were the same. The primary modifications were the curtained rear windows and the casket rollers and pins for stabilizing the load being transported in the cargo area, which included a flatbed where a back seat would have been.

Winchester was a fairly small town, particularly when compared to a place like Nashville. Most of the time a drive to practically any destination in the county required less than twenty minutes. No heavy traffic, no exit bottlenecks and rarely any road construction. She would never have believed that the slower pace and perpetual quiet would suit her, but it did.

Her life might even be considered dull and quite normal if not for the Julian Addington nightmare hanging over her head, along with those long-buried DuPont secrets that kept scratching their way to the surface.

The pumpkins, hay bales and cornstalks adorning most storefronts reminded her that Halloween was only a few days away. Black cats, spiders and ghosts populated more front yards than not. The end of the year was scarcely more than two months away.

It didn't seem possible that it had been so very long since her life in Nashville fell completely apart.

Surprisingly, for the first time, she noticed she didn't experience that hollow feeling she once had when she thought of that painful time all those months ago. Her new life was growing on her.

As she pulled into the hospital's rear parking area, big black spiders appeared to be crawling over the brick walls. Spiders were more reasonable than skeletons, she decided. One of the houses on High Street had skeletons crawling up toward windows and onto the roof. Some folks went all out for the holiday. Before she could stop the errant thought, she wondered how Herman was doing. He was a patient in one of those rooms, and though she wanted to pretend she didn't care, it was impossible not to. He'd been a part of her family for as long as she could remember, and no matter what he had done, she couldn't erase him so easily.

Pushing Herman out of her thoughts, Rowan considered that she and Billy had discussed the possibility that the stolen body was a Halloween prank. Sanchez might very well be somewhere close by. In her opinion, that scenario was one of the less likely possibilities they had considered.

Perhaps it was someone else in the area who was connected to one or both of her parents and their many secrets. Or maybe to Julian. It still felt strange when she considered that for her entire adult life, she had believed she and Julian first met during her freshman year of college. It was hard to fathom that he had known her since she was a child, had kept tabs on her to some degree all those years.

The concept that she should have her DNA compared to his nudged her again. Hard as she tried not to toy with the prospect, she couldn't help wondering if he had done all of these things because she was his biological daughter. She had accepted the strong probability that he and her mother had carried on an affair. If she and Raven had been his biological children, it was possible his daughter, Alisha, discovered this additional travesty and set out to destroy her illicit siblings.

Didn't matter what DNA told her, Rowan was a Du-Pont. No test was going to change who she was. To that end, why bother? The results would only give the FBI something else to use against her and would be a slap in the face of the memory of the man who had raised her.

She backed up the hearse to the loading area and climbed out. A press of the call button notified the morgue attendant she had arrived. A couple of minutes later, Thomas Harvey was loaded and Rowan was headed back to the funeral home. She'd already called the family for a meeting and then she'd left a message for Charlotte to see if she could give her a hand with the unloading.

When her cell vibrated in the seat next to her, she worried that Charlotte was unavailable. Rowan hadn't had any luck with finding another assistant willing to work part-time to take some of the load off Charlotte. Folks were looking for full-time jobs with benefits, neither of which she could offer at this time.

Billy's name and smiling face flashed on the screen. Rowan wasn't sure whether to feel relieved or concerned. If Special Agent Dressler had arrived already, he would just have to wait.

She grabbed her phone and accepted the call as she braked to a stop at the intersection of Hospital Road and College Street. "Hey, Billy."

"Where are you?"

"I just picked up Thomas Harvey at the morgue and I'm headed back to the funeral home." There was an uneasiness in his voice and no small amount of frustration. "What's going on?"

"Herman is missing."

Rowan glanced in her rearview mirror at the hospital building behind her. "Missing? When did this happen?"

"As best we can tell, between one and four this morning. The nurse took his vitals just before one. When she went back at four, he was gone."

"I'm assuming he was secured and had at least one guard." Rowan shook her head. How could this have happened?

"The guard went to the bathroom just once. He thought Herman was asleep. When he came back, he stuck his head in the room and all looked to be as it should. Herman had tucked pillows under the sheets to give the appearance that he was still in the bed. And, yes, he was secured to the bed rails with a handcuff. No clue how he unlocked the damn thing. I'm at the hospital now watching the security video feed to see if anyone besides staff went into his room. Just be watchful, okay? We don't know his agenda. He may have revenge on his mind."

"Or joining his wife," she pointed out. "If I hear from him, I'll let you know."

After tossing her phone back onto the seat, Rowan barreled out onto College Street. If Herman killed himself or disappeared, she would have no hope of learning the truth. She couldn't trust anything Julian told her.

She had to find Herman…and stop him from doing whatever the hell he had planned.

Charlotte was waiting at the funeral home when Rowan arrived. They unloaded Mr. Harvey and Charlotte had agreed to begin the preparations so Rowan could talk to the family, who were waiting in her office already. Once the arrangements were sorted out and Rowan ensured Charlotte had everything under control, she grabbed the keys to her small SUV and rushed out the door. Last month she'd traded her car for an all-wheel-drive crossover SUV. Winchester didn't get that much snow in the winter, but it did endure its share of icy roads. Besides, she liked the way the vehicle handled and the ability to use the cargo and back seat areas almost like the bed of a pickup truck. The best of both worlds.

Even more important, it was perfect for all those back roads in the area. Rowan had driven to each place in the county her mother had mentioned. She had strolled along the riverbanks and followed paths into the woods. Though the scenery had been interesting, particularly as fall descended, she'd found nothing useful in her journeys. Each location appeared to have been a rendezvous location and the one thing they'd all had in common was remoteness. Rowan had concluded that if her mother had met men like Julian or Carlos Sanchez at those locations, she'd had a serious death wish. As independent as Rowan was, she had taken her weapon and Freud on her excursions.

Then again, Julian might have presented himself as a good and caring person to Norah, as well. He'd done exactly that with Rowan for two damn decades. She hadn't known he was a killer until just before he murdered her father.

What a fool she had been, and her father had paid the price.

Or so it seemed. Rowan made the turn toward the cemetery where Herman's wife was interred. Not long after her father's death she had learned that Edward DuPont had kept a few secrets of his own. For instance, the fact that he had known Julian before Rowan introduced the two of them. Or the idea that the two men had met for drinks at a local bar back in January. Julian insisted that Edward had finally admitted killing Alisha, Julian's daughter.

Rowan did not and would not believe him.

Still, how could she not have known her father was keeping secrets? Why hadn't he told her that he knew Julian on some level?

Frustrated all over again, Rowan parked and emerged from her SUV. This was the primary reason she couldn't allow Herman to disappear or to take his life. It had taken her all these months to realize she needed him. Maybe it wasn't about recognizing the need, but putting aside her pride and acknowledging it. She had been determined to rid her life of all those who had betrayed her.

"How's that working out for you?" she muttered.

It wasn't. At all. Though she could not trust Julian, he knew things she wanted to know. The problem was filtering the truth from all the lies he spewed. Herman could help her with the process...if he only would.

The sleek marble marker now standing at the head of Estelle's grave carried her name and dates of birth and death. Herman's name and date of birth were there, as well. The date of death had been left blank, as was the custom when one partner passed and the other was left behind. Rowan scanned the cemetery. No sign of Herman. Bare branches shifted in the breeze, the cold air making her shiver. Leaves tumbled across the graves, some smacking against headstones. Fall cleanup was right around the corner. As a child she'd loved raking the leaves from around the grave markers. She had made up stories about the folks she didn't know named on the headstones. At age eleven, she'd mentioned to her sister the stories she came up with for the dead people she didn't know in the cemetery. Raven had thought she was mental, as she'd put it, with a roll of her eyes that perfectly matched Rowan's. Norah had smiled and said Rowan was a storyteller like her.

At the time, Rowan had felt a sense of pride. Now she felt nothing but resentment and a burning need to find the truth.

She scanned the acres of headstones once more. "Where the hell are you, Herman?"

The cemetery was deserted. If Herman had stopped here, he was long gone now.

Sliding back behind the steering wheel, she decided

to try his house next. His personal residence was likely the first place the police went looking for him, but it was worth a drive along the block. Would give her a few more minutes of hope before she had to admit defeat and acknowledge the fact that there was a very good chance Herman had cut and run.

Two police cruisers sat in the driveway of Herman's home. Billy's truck was there, too. Rowan kept driving. No need to get caught up in that aspect of the search. If Billy found him, he would let her know. Billy had never let her down. Not once. He understood how desperately she needed answers.

Her cell vibrated against the console. She picked it up and said hello without checking the screen. One of these days she needed to take the time to set up the connection between her new vehicle and her phone. Then again, she wasn't sure she wanted it to automatically connect every time she got into the car. There were times when she had no desire to be interrupted by the phone. Not that she allowed a call to go unanswered, anyway. The funeral home line was forwarded to her cell whenever she was out, and that made ignoring calls a risk she couldn't afford to take.

"Ro, it's Charlotte."

Her assistant's worried tone drew Rowan's full attention to the call. "Hey, Charlotte. Is everything okay?"

"There's someone here to see you."

Rowan had been wrong. The emotion she heard in Charlotte's voice wasn't worry. It was fear. "Great." Rowan infused as much pleasantness as she could muster into her tone. "I'm almost there."

Another three minutes and she would be back at

the funeral home. Not nearly fast enough if there was trouble. Should she hang up and call Billy?

"I'll let *him* know you'll be here shortly."

Him. Surely Julian wouldn't appear out of the blue like this? Would he have the nerve to show up at the funeral home when Rowan wasn't there? How could he be sure Charlotte was calling Rowan? She could be calling anyone. It didn't sound as if her phone was set on the speaker option.

No. Julian was far too smart to make such an elementary mistake.

As if the other woman had read her mind, Charlotte said, "I offered him sweet tea, but he said he wasn't thirsty."

Sweet tea. *Herman*.

"Tell him I'm turning onto First Avenue now."

"Okay."

"And, Charlotte…"

"Yes?"

"For now, let's keep his visit to ourselves."

"I promised him I would. We're waiting in your office."

"I'm pulling up to the funeral home now."

Rowan ended the call, shoved the gearshift into Park, shut off the engine and hurried from the SUV. Charlotte was nervous and Rowan didn't blame her. She hated putting the younger woman in this position, but it was necessary.

Since the front door was still locked and Rowan had to use her key to get in, she wondered if Herman had come to the back door. If he'd rung the bell at the loading entrance Charlotte would likely have believed it was Rowan. Otherwise she wouldn't have opened the door without checking first.

Inside, Rowan locked the door behind her and headed along the hall toward her office. Her pulse rate rose with each step as she rounded the corner and hesitated a few feet away from the open door.

"Are you sure you wouldn't like some coffee or tea?" Charlotte's voice trembled ever so slightly.

"I just need to talk to Ro."

Herman's voice sounded weary. No sympathy, Rowan reminded herself.

She strode the final few steps into her office and produced a smile for Charlotte. "Sorry to keep you waiting."

She nodded to the visitor waiting in one of the two chairs in front of her desk—the chairs family sat in to go over the options for their deceased loved one. "Herman." Turning back to her assistant, she suggested, "Charlotte, why don't you get back to Mr. Harvey? Herman and I have some catching up to do."

"No." Herman shook his head adamantly. "She'll call Billy or Colt."

Colt Tanner was the county sheriff. Like Billy, he would not be happy about Herman's escape. The older man appeared extremely agitated. Not surprising. He was no spring chicken and he'd just escaped law-enforcement custody. He was a criminal awaiting trial and now he was a fugitive.

"She won't call anyone. Will you, Charlotte?"

Charlotte shook her head just as adamantly as Herman had. "All I want is to get back to work. This is none of my business and I don't intend to make it my business, Mr. Carter."

Herman visibly relaxed.

"You go ahead. I've got this," Rowan assured her.

Charlotte nodded and stood, vacating the chair behind Rowan's desk. She still wore the apron and gloves she donned when preparing a body. "Let me know if you need anything."

"If you call anyone and they show up," Herman warned, "I will make you sorry." Herman withdrew a small handgun from the pocket of his trousers.

Charlotte let out a squeak of fear. Rowan wasn't particularly scared; she was just disappointed. "Go on, Charlotte. We'll be fine."

Charlotte stared at Rowan for a moment as if she feared leaving the room. Rowan gave her a nod to go on. No need for both of them to be stuck in here with an armed man running out of time and options.

When Charlotte had gone, Rowan addressed the man before her with dead calm. "The gun is a bad idea, Herman. You should put it away."

He placed the weapon in his lap. "This is not about hurting you, Ro. I just need you to listen to what I have to say."

"You couldn't call me? I would have come by the hospital."

He shook his head. "I don't have much time."

So, he intended to run. How was it that this kind, seemingly caring man, whom she had known her whole life, had come to this?

She sat down in the chair behind her desk. "What is it you expect me to do or to say?"

"Nothing. I just need you to listen."

"All right. I'm listening."

"There are things you need to know." He leaned

his head to one side in a sort of shrug. "But he won't allow me to give you the answers. You have to find them for yourself."

"Who won't allow you?" A blast of outrage roared through her as much at the idea of who he meant as at the reality that he, too, had just admitted to some connection to Julian Addington, the bastard who'd started all of this.

Herman's chin lowered but his dark gaze never left hers. "You know who. He wanted me to give you a message. He gave me the chance to do what I need to do, but passing on a message to you was the price."

Rowan stilled, and even her ability to breathe seemed to stall. Julian had sent someone to get Herman out of the hospital.

"You're all that's left of her, Ro, and they will *all* want you."

Rowan stared at the man who had spoken—a man she had thought she knew inside and out. "What does that mean, Herman? Who is *they*?"

He shook his head. "As much as I want to, I can't help you, Ro. I can't even help myself."

The pounding of footfalls echoed from the lobby. She jerked at the sudden sound, her gaze drawn to the door and the corridor just beyond it. Billy's voice followed the pounding. Charlotte had called him.

Damn it.

"Don't forget what I told you, Ro."

Her attention snapped back to the man seated a few feet away. "Which part?"

"Billy has the key to my house. There's a lot of history in that house, Ro. All you have to do is look for it."

"Are you saying—"

He lifted the handgun.

Her heart stuttered.

The muzzle poked into his temple. "Goodbye, Ro."

"Herman, no! You—"

He pulled the trigger and the blast of the bullet leaving the barrel and plunging into his brain didn't quite drown out the sound of her scream. Blood and brain matter splattered across one side of her desk. She blinked. Herman slumped forward. The gun thudded to the floor.

She couldn't move. Helplessness, outrage and hurt roared inside her. Something warm trickled down her cheek. She swiped at it, expected tears, but it was blood.

Billy and two of his officers burst into her office.

One officer took possession of the weapon while the other checked Herman's pulse. It wouldn't do much good, since most of his frontal and right temporal lobes were missing.

"Are you hurt?"

Billy crouched beside her, but she couldn't look at him. She could only stare at the man who had let her down yet again.

How would she ever find the truth now?

Six

Charlotte walked out of viewing room one. Billy had decided to conduct his interviews there since the funeral home office was a crime scene. Rowan's chest tightened. Her assistant looked shattered. Had every right to. Herman had practically held Charlotte at gunpoint until Rowan arrived. Although she was thirty-one and a strong woman, she hadn't been exposed to the murders and criminal acts Rowan had seen every day while working with the homicide division. This wasn't the sort of thing a young mother of two elementary school–aged kids who lived in Winchester typically dealt with.

"Will we be okay for Mr. Harvey's viewing tonight?" she asked, her voice wobbling.

Rowan almost smiled. She was so very grateful for this woman. She'd just experienced a serious trauma and she was worried about how they would take care of business.

Who knew how long it would take the evidence techs to finish up in the office. "We'll be fine. We can close off the corridor beyond the restrooms and lounge if necessary."

Charlotte nodded. "I'll take care of the memorial pamphlets before I leave, then I'll be back at five to help prepare."

"Thanks, Charlotte, I don't know what I'd do without you."

Her assistant managed a smile before heading to the back. Thank God they'd moved the computer and printer Charlotte used to the supply room. Rowan had wanted her to have her own space—a perk for finally agreeing to learn the embalming process. They'd taken a portion of the supply room and set up a very nice office, complete with a new large-screen computer and state-of-the-art printer. No more running across town to the print shop.

Rowan wanted to shake Herman's dead body for blowing his brains out in her office. Of all people, he had known what a mess he would leave behind. Damn it. *Damn him!* Why would he do this? She still needed him, damn it! Emotion burned her eyes and she wanted to scream at herself for feeling anything for the man.

Billy appeared at the door of the viewing room. "You ready?"

Rowan took a deep breath and moved toward him. Her arms tightened around her waist in hopes of keeping the trembles in check. She'd started shaking when Herman's body was taken away and she hadn't been able to stop since. More than anything, it annoyed the hell out of her.

When Billy didn't immediately step aside for her to walk into the room, she met his concerned gaze. "I'm worried about you, Ro."

She dredged up a modicum of bravado. "Herman's the one who's dead."

He nodded. "He had a reason for taking the risk he took coming here and he had help. Until we know how and why that happened, your safety is my top priority."

Of course it was. Billy was the big brother she never had. Her safety was always his top priority. This should make her feel relieved but somehow it only frustrated her more. "Let's get this over with."

He stepped back, gestured for her to pass.

Rowan sat down in the chair he'd pulled away from the back row. He'd arranged another chair so that the two were facing. Billy lowered his tall frame into the chair opposite her. Sitting next to or across from Billy was as familiar to her as breathing. She'd known him her whole life, and they'd been friends most of that time. As an adolescent she'd done more than her share of fantasizing about kissing him on the lips. She suddenly wondered if he'd ever thought of her in that way. Until recently she'd never gotten anything beyond big-brother vibes from him. Frankly, she wasn't entirely sure she trusted her instincts these days. She'd had no clue Herman was going to do something like this.

How sad was that?

She pushed away the thoughts. Obviously, her mind was attempting to compensate for the shock she'd experienced earlier. Clearing her head, she focused on Billy's movements. His long fingers flipped to a clean page in the small notepad he carried in his pocket. He readied a pen for taking notes and lifted his gaze to hers. The worry in those dark brown eyes made her wish death would stop following her. What would it be like to have a normal life? To wake up without her first thought being of the body waiting for her to pick up or to prep? She almost laughed out loud. Death would always follow her. What else could the undertaker's-daughter-turned-undertaker expect?

"Beyond your visit with Herman yesterday, did he have any contact with you?"

The question surprised her. He knew the answer. Rowan supposed he needed her response for the official statement. "He mailed me numerous letters, but I never opened them until just recently—which you know. Otherwise, there has been no contact whatsoever."

Billy nodded. "Charlotte called and asked you to come to the funeral home?"

Rowan nodded. "She said someone was here to see me."

"Did you ask who the visitor was?"

Had Charlotte told him Rowan hadn't wanted to tell anyone about the visit? Rowan moistened her lips. "I did not. I told her I was almost there. I'm sure we exchanged a few more words before hanging up. Something like 'see you in a bit' or 'goodbye.'"

Billy searched her face for a long moment. Rowan had always been quite good at hiding her feelings. Then again, Billy had known her for a very long time. If anyone could read the lie, it was him.

"When you arrived, did you go straight to your office?"

"Yes." Rowan realized then that Charlotte had not shared their entire conversation. "At some point during the call she said they were waiting in my office. But that didn't trigger any sort of warning. We generally meet with clients in my office."

"So, you assumed there was a client waiting for you?"

This time Rowan was the one doing the scrutinizing. His face gave away no indication of what was on his mind, but there was something—some point he was getting to. "Of course. Where are you going with this line of questioning, Billy? Is there something I should know?"

He exhaled a weary breath, ran a hand through his hair. "Because Charlotte was nervous as hell and couldn't seem to keep her story straight."

Rowan did laugh then. "I imagine this was the first time she has been held at gunpoint. She's not like you and me, Billy. This isn't par for the course. She was terrified. Still is. Not to mention she's known Herman forever, just like me."

Billy shook his head. "Something's wrong with this picture. The security footage shows the only person who went into Herman's room was a nurse that no one seems to recognize. We assume that same woman drove him here. Then you arrived. Was there a car or SUV, a truck maybe, in the parking lot or parked on the street that you didn't recognize?"

"Probably but I wasn't paying attention." She gestured toward the front of the funeral home. "This is a busy street. There are always cars I don't recognize."

Without saying more, he held her gaze long enough to make her want to squirm, which was exactly what he wanted her to do. It was a common interrogation technique. She'd been on the receiving end more often than not lately, but never from Billy. She didn't like it. She liked even less that she was hiding things from him again, but she couldn't help it.

"You're certain Charlotte didn't tell you it was Herman who was waiting for you?"

"Positive." It wasn't exactly a lie. Charlotte hadn't said his name.

Billy nodded. "All right, then."

Rowan relaxed as he closed his notepad and slipped it into his jacket pocket. "Is that it? If so, I have a viewing to prepare for."

Another of those long, silent stares followed. "Dressler is on his way. He wants to talk to both of us. Do you want to meet him at my office or have him come here?"

Well, hell. "He might as well come join all the fun."

With him coming to the funeral home she had the home-field advantage.

Special Agent Josh Dressler was assigned to the Nashville FBI field office. He was the same age as Rowan, with blond hair and brown eyes. Sharp dresser and pretty much full of himself. But he was good at his job. Rowan and Dressler had worked together on several cases when she was in Nashville. He had his way of doing things and believed himself to be more capable than anyone. He was also one of the lead agents assigned to the Julian Addington task force. Like most of his colleagues on that task force, he suspected Rowan knew more than she cared to share. For that reason, he and a number of others assigned to the task force had made her life miserable since Julian's unveiling as a killer.

The truth was she really knew nothing more than she had shared about Julian. It was only the bastard's accusations against her father that she had withheld. As far as she was concerned, that was none of anyone's business at this point. Her father was dead and couldn't defend himself. As much as she would love to clear her father's name, her solitary goal was to find the truth… whatever that might be.

Her last conversation with Herman was personal, as well. Nothing he had said was important enough to Dressler's investigation to allow it to get in the way of Rowan's. He could wait for the rest. Billy, too, for that matter.

Dressler paced the aisle between the rows of chairs in the viewing room Billy had used to conduct interviews. The evidence techs had finished up in her office and Rowan had called in her cleaning team to take care of the mess Herman had left for her.

Now she was the one ignoring her emotions by attempting to pretend Herman wasn't a longtime family friend. He'd been a man she had cared about deeply until recently.

A man who had betrayed her and her father.

Billy stood next to Rowan. She'd opted not to sit. Gave Dressler too much power to loom over her. She'd watched him in action numerous times, understood his techniques for pressuring a witness.

"I'm seriously pissed here, Chief." Dressler paused in his pacing and glared at Billy. "You've put me in a very unpleasant position."

"What do you want me to say?" Billy shrugged. "Sanchez died in my jurisdiction. One of my officers spotted a suspicious object in his place of residence and we investigated. That's my job. I ran his prints and here we are."

Rowan was impressed. Billy managed to make even her believe his story.

Dressler shoved his lapels back and braced his hands

on his hips. His frustration shifted to her. "I suppose you're going to tell me you had nothing to do with this."

She shrugged. "His neighbor said Sanchez left instructions to have his body sent to my funeral home. If you're asking if I was involved, I guess I was. I prepared his body for burial, but we never made it to that point since someone broke in and stole him."

Billy hadn't told him about the tattoo of—allegedly— her mother's name. Rowan was grateful. Frankly, until there was evidence her mother somehow knew the man there was no point in mentioning the tattoo to Dressler. Or the notations in her journals that seemed to allude to the man.

Dressler scrubbed a hand over his jaw. This close it was impossible to miss the weariness shadowing his face. "We have reason to believe he was involved with Addington. Not recently, but sometime ago."

Anticipation sent Rowan's heart into a faster rhythm. "Was Sanchez his real name?"

Dressler shook his head. "Antonio Santos, but even that one might not be the name he was born with. It's impossible to say. We believe he illegally entered this country from Colombia about forty or so years ago. The first crime we can connect his prints to occurred in the late seventies. Two teenage girls were raped and murdered. Unfortunately, the bodies were badly decomposed when they were found. The elements had basically destroyed any evidence except for the prints inside one of the girls' purses, which was found in the woods half a mile from the bodies. His prints were found at more than a dozen other scenes, including three we believed were committed by Addington, considering we found souvenirs from the kills in the bastard's house."

"You're saying Addington may not have committed those three murders?" Memories of that room where Julian had kept all the memorabilia he'd collected from his kills flashed in quick succession in Rowan's mind.

"I'm saying," Dressler countered, "that this guy participated somehow. To what degree, who knows."

Made a sick sort of sense in light of the fact that there was a very strong possibility that Norah and Julian were involved. Holy hell. What had her mother done?

"Hopefully we can connect the faces you found in those books made from skin to victims," Dressler said to Billy.

Rowan turned to Billy. "How many faces did you find?" Dressler asked.

"Twenty-six." His gaze held hers a moment. Clearly, he still had doubts about her and Charlotte's stories related to Herman's visit. Particularly at a moment like this, when she lied so easily.

"Since Sanchez, or whatever his name is, appeared to like keeping skin from his victims," Rowan said, addressing Dressler, "you've obviously only connected him to about half of his kills. Maybe he learned to be more careful or maybe he worked with other killers with whom he had relationships—sexual or otherwise." Serial killers most often worked alone, but it was not unheard-of to have them pair up. In fact, with the explosion of social media it was more and more common to find killing partners or even groups.

Rather than respond to her assertion, Dressler announced, "Let's talk about Addington."

Rowan frowned. "Is there something new you haven't shared with the rest of the task force?" Billy was on the task force. If he'd learned anything new, she would know. Because, unlike her, he would never lie to her.

Dressler shook his head. "I'm not the one who withholds information, Rowan."

There it was. Confirmation that he still believed she was withholding relevant information. Frustration fired through her veins. "If I had any idea where he was, I would be the first to call you, *Josh*. I'm as in the dark here as you are."

"We've been down this road again and again, Dressler," Billy warned. "She doesn't know anything that will help the investigation. Nothing. When are you going to accept that fact?"

Always on her side. Guilt heaped onto her shoulders. Would she ever be as good as Billy was? As trustworthy and loyal?

Probably not. She had far too much to lose. It was so easy to be forthright and honorable when you had no skeletons in your closet and no close family with more of the same hidden away.

Not fair, Rowan.

Dressler shook his head, that knowing grin on his face making her want to punch him. "I'm not accusing you of anything, Dr. DuPont." He swung his attention from Billy to her. "If our roles were reversed, you would be as skeptical as I am. You understand the way this works. We learn to trust our instincts, to go with our guts. That's how we stay alive, stay ahead of the game."

"Let me put your instincts at ease, Dressler," she assured him, "I haven't heard from Julian Addington since I shot him. Who knows? Maybe he's dead. But if I do hear from him, you will be the first to know."

Rowan turned to Billy then. "I have a viewing in two hours. If you'll excuse me."

Billy gave her a nod. "I'll catch up with you later."

Rowan had almost made it to the door when Dressler spoke again.

"The coroner mentioned that Sanchez had extensive tattoos. Did you photograph any of them?"

A few seconds were required before she felt prepared to face the man and his questions. "It's not standard procedure for me to take photographs."

His stare was unflinching. "Too bad. The tattoos could have provided clues to where he's lived and what groups he's associated with."

"Since we had no reason to believe foul play was involved when his body was discovered, we didn't do any sort of documentation, either," Billy offered, a blatant attempt to take the pressure off her.

Rowan appreciated his efforts, but she understood that was not going to happen. "I would be happy to describe the ones I recognized as gang-affiliated. Some were obvious prison tats."

The standoff lasted another five seconds before Dressler spoke again. He had an ace up his sleeve. He was far too cocky to be shooting in the dark. Rowan reminded herself to breathe.

"I'm just curious." Dressler turned to Billy then. "What made you run his prints, Chief? Is it standard procedure for your department to run the prints of every death by natural causes you find?"

"Like I told you earlier…" Billy began.

Dressler held up a hand to stop him. "I remember.

You said one of your officers spotted something suspicious in the man's residence. Except there's no mention of this in the initial report signed by the officer." The agent shook his head. "You should remind your officer if he's going to rewrite his report to remove the original report from the file first."

Son of a bitch.

"I asked him to run the prints," Rowan said before Billy could wade any deeper into this shit show.

Dressler shifted his scrutiny to her. "Why?"

"One of the tattoos was similar to the ones we've run into recently with a small group of extreme preppers. We had some trouble a few weeks back. I thought Billy should be aware."

Not exactly a lie but certainly not the truth.

Dressler nodded, his gaze narrow with suspicion. "I see."

The agent was far from convinced. Any attempts to change that would only make him more suspicious. "As I said, I have a viewing. Good evening, gentlemen."

Rowan didn't give Dressler the opportunity to waylay her again. She strode out the door and headed to the supply room to catch up with Charlotte. A couple of slow, deep breaths and her heart rate was back to normal. One of these days she was going to tell Special Agent Josh Dressler exactly what she thought of him.

But not today.

She ran into Charlotte in the corridor beyond the staff-only doors. "Hey. You have any trouble?"

Charlotte held up a stack of pamphlets. "All done. The floral delivery will be here in half an hour."

"Good." Rowan gave her the best smile she could muster. "Let's set up the viewing room."

Once the room was prepared and Mr. Harvey was in place, Rowan would change into more appropriate attire. Billy would likely drop by after the viewing, which meant she had a very narrow window of opportunity to do a little more investigating.

She intended to pay a visit to Herman's house. He'd urged her to do so. When she'd mentioned Herman's offer, Billy had said that he would prefer she wait until he'd had another look around first. They'd gone through the house after Herman was arrested. She didn't see the big deal. Why was he dragging his feet?

Things were happening way too fast. She couldn't risk waiting for Billy.

Dressler would see Herman's escape and suicide in Rowan's office as a reason to dissect his activities in the event he was somehow involved with Julian. By tomorrow, if not sooner, Dressler's people would likely be combing through Herman's home.

She certainly didn't want to stand in the way of the FBI doing its job…as long as she had a look first.

Seven

"You do realize she's lying, don't you?"

Billy turned away from the doorway Rowan had disappeared through and met the other man's gaze. He did not like this guy. Dressler was an arrogant ass. But he felt the same way Billy did about finding Julian Addington and he was one of the lead agents on the task force to make that happen. If Billy wanted to continue receiving updates as a member of that task force, he had to keep his personal feelings to himself. Not the easiest thing he'd ever done, but necessary all the same.

"I'm not sure I agree with your assessment, Agent Dressler."

Actually, Billy was well aware that Rowan was holding out on him. The difference between his assessment and Dressler's was that Billy understood Rowan sincerely believed she was doing the right thing. Rowan wasn't protecting Addington. She wanted him brought to justice as badly as anyone else, most likely more so. And she wanted answers. This was the part that tripped her up and Billy intended to see that she didn't get herself in over her head in her efforts to make that happen.

It was quite possible she was protecting someone, but it wasn't Addington.

"Here's what I know," Dressler said, lowering his voice as if he wanted to ensure no one beyond the room heard his words, "Addington is out there, very much alive. Rowan shot him, that's true. But whatever injury she inflicted, it wasn't enough to stop him. Was that by accident or by design? Who knows, but I think we both understand something is off, however slightly. The other certainty we can take to the bank is that if he's alive, he will be back for her—it's only a matter of time."

There was no denying the bastard's obsession with Rowan. If he was alive, Addington would be back. He would not simply disappear into the sunset without her. Whether he wanted her dead or alive was still in question, but he wanted her.

Over my dead body.

Billy would not allow the bastard to get to her.

"We have the same goal, Dressler," Billy assured him. "*If* he's alive, we want Addington found and put away for good. The difference is I don't want to use Rowan to accomplish that result." Fury roared inside Billy at the idea of how little care the agent had for Rowan's safety. Getting the job done was his singular focus.

"Five months have passed since Addington disappeared—are you still watching her 24/7?"

That Dressler ignored his blatant accusation annoyed the hell out of Billy all over again. Irritated him even more that he asked a question to which he already knew the answer. The round-the-clock surveillance had been called off months ago. Rowan wouldn't stand for it.

"I'm watching her every minute she'll allow me. She keeps her security system armed and has new locks on the funeral home. She keeps her weapon close and she knows how to use it—I've made sure. If she takes a shot at Addington again, she'll do more than injure him this time. We go to the range a couple of times a month. She's a good shot. Damn good."

Dressler shook his head. "The locks and the alarm won't stop him. I believe we both know she isn't going to shoot to kill if the situation arises again. He holds some power over her. I just don't know what it is yet."

Billy put his hand up before he said too much. "As for whether she would shoot to kill, maybe, maybe not. But I can assure you, he holds no power over her. What you need to do, Agent Dressler, is find Addington and let me worry about Rowan. I know her a lot better than you do."

Not about to be bested, the agent shrugged. "Perhaps. Whatever else you think or do, don't let your guard down because he will be back, Chief, you can count on it. Next time he'll be more careful. The man is a genius. He won't make the same mistake twice."

"Let him come." Billy didn't intend to make the same mistake twice, either. "You have my word, I will shoot to kill."

The two of them stared at each other for another three or four seconds.

"Chief, we need to talk."

Detective Clarence Lincoln's voice forced Billy to look away first. Lincoln waited in the doorway. Judging by the expression on his face, the news wasn't good.

"If you need anything else, Agent Dressler—" Billy gave him a nod "—you know how to find me."

Billy followed his senior detective into the wide corridor beyond the viewing rooms. "Did you find anything at Herman's house?"

Lincoln and two officers had been tasked with going through the man's house to determine if he'd left any sort of note there, or any clue whatsoever as to what had compelled him to flee from the hospital and then take his life. So far, they had nothing on the nurse captured on the security video footage coming out of Herman's room before he disappeared. At this point she was their only suspect. No one else except the nurse on duty had gone in or out of the room between one and four. The cop on guard duty had poked his head in through the door, seen the lump in the bed and assumed all was as it should have been. A mistake Billy imagined he would not be repeating again anytime soon.

"The place looked exactly like it did five months ago when we went through it then. No indication he'd been there. I don't think he went back to the house."

If they'd found no indication of a break-in at Herman's, then what? Oh, hell. "Did you find the unidentified nurse?"

That could be a good thing…as long as she was still breathing.

Lincoln shook his head. "We have a body—probably homicide. I'm pretty sure this one is unrelated to Herman or any of this other mess hanging over our heads."

No one was happy that Herman had escaped and offed himself or that Addington was still out there.

Billy blew out a breath. *Well, damn.* "What happened?"

"Stanley Henegar. His wife called 911. Paramedics are there now. Looks like someone nailed him to the floor and then stuffed pages from a Bible down his throat until he choked to death."

Damn. "Any chance it was his wife?" Billy had always considered Wanda a quiet, subdued woman. He wasn't aware of any trouble between the couple. Stan had been a deacon at his church for as long as Billy could remember.

"Gabrielle says she's pretty torn up. She told him that she'd been shopping with her sister. He's still trying to track down the sister to confirm her alibi. She's not answering her cell phone so he's sending a unit to the sister's house."

Billy settled his hat into place. "Well, let's go have a look." He glanced around. "I think we've done all we can here." Since the Harvey visitation was tonight, Ro would be busy here with Charlotte for a while, which made him a lot more comfortable leaving her.

Lincoln gave him a nod of understanding. "I'll make sure everyone's on the same page and then I'll meet you at Stan's house."

Billy went in search of Ro to let her know he'd be back as soon as he could.

How the hell did a fifty-odd-year-old man get himself nailed to the floor and force-fed pages from the good book?

The most likely answer was that he'd seriously pissed off the wrong person.

Stan Henegar had lived his whole life in a small brick rancher on the twenty-five-acre farm he'd inherited from his folks. From the horseshoe driveway it was easy to see the big red barn towering over the house. The barn was a good three times larger than the house. Fenced pastures spread out for as far as the eye could see. Bordering those were woods that offered shade during the heat of the summer to the cows and goats roaming the pastures. The ice-cold year-round stream that gurgled up from under the mountain provided constant fresh water and cut through the southern boundaries of the property. Henegars and Mayses had fought over those water rights for as long as Billy could remember.

Although there hadn't been any trouble recently, it was possible an incident occurred that had taken their dispute to the next level.

Billy climbed out of his truck and headed for the house. Two cruisers sat in the driveway along with the ambulance and another small sedan, probably the wife's car. Officer Joel Gabrielle stood on the porch next to the old swing, where Wanda sat clutching what looked like a Bible. Wanda was twenty or so years younger than Stan. She'd been married to him since she was a kid. This had to be tough.

As Billy climbed the steps he nodded to the woman. "Ma'am."

She swiped at her face with her free hand. "Who would do this to him? My Stan was a good man—a God-fearing man. I just don't understand."

Billy removed his hat, held it close to his chest. "It'll take a little time, but we will find out. You have my word."

She bowed her head as if she intended to pray. "I just can't believe it."

Billy walked inside the house. The living room was deserted, and the television screen was set to a Christian channel. A half-empty glass of tea, the ice melted and a slice of lemon floating on top, sat on the coffee table. The paramedics and Officer James Wiley were in the kitchen. The room ran the better part of the length of the back of the house, kitchen on one end, dining room on the other. A door exited out to the backyard. The round dining table and four chairs had been pushed aside so that Stan could be nailed spread-eagled to the floor.

A grimace tugged at Billy's face. The smell of feces was thick in the air. If he had to guess, he'd say those big-ass nails had been shot in with an air nailer. Each hand had three through the palm. Shoelaces had been wrapped around his ankles and then nailed to the floor. Blood had pooled around each injury.

Stan's eyes were round with horror, his unseeing gaze glued to the ceiling. His mouth was open, twisted with the same terror that had seized the rest of his face. Judging by the extra blood around his right hand, he had pulled loose from the floor at least once. Billy studied the palm a little more closely. Oh, yeah. At least half a dozen nail holes besides the three with nails still in them. No visible bruises on his face that would have suggested a struggle or that he had attempted to defend himself.

"The killer tore the pages from Stan's personal Bible, crumpled them and then shoved them into his mouth."

Billy looked to Wiley and then to the Bible lying on the floor a few feet from the victim. The cover was open and ragged edges were all that remained of a good portion of the pages that had once filled that space. "Have you called for the evidence techs?"

Wiley nodded. "Whoever did this wanted him dead. He wasn't playing games or just trying to scare him.

I'm guessing he was drugged or he would have fought harder to get loose."

Last month they'd had a game of chicken gone wrong. Both drivers had been certain the other would chicken out at the last minute. Both had died as a result of the head-on crash. Onlookers had assured Billy and his officers that it was only a game. No one was supposed to get hurt. Dumb asses. Like Wiley said, this was no game.

"I agree. Tox screen will tell us if that's the case." Billy glanced around the otherwise seemingly undisturbed room. "Anything else out of place in the house?" He hadn't noticed any sign of ransacking. "Did Wanda have a look around?"

"She did and she doesn't believe anything is missing. 'Course, she's pretty upset. She might notice something after she's had a chance to pull herself together."

Billy rubbed a hand over his face. "Burt on his way?"

Wiley nodded. "He should be here any minute."

Burt Johnston was pushing eighty but he had been the county coroner for the better part of the last half century. He claimed the work was far more interesting than that of the two veterinary clinics he owned. Although he wasn't involved with the day-to-day operations at the clinics, he kept his office at the larger of the two. He insisted it was too much trouble to move after all these years.

"When the evidence techs get here, have them go through the whole house just in case."

Wiley nodded. "Yes, sir."

The city only had two evidence collectors. Truth was they'd never needed more. Crime was relatively low in Winchester. At least until recently. If he brought up the subject, Rowan would swear that her moving back had set off a chain reaction of trouble. But she was wrong. Sometimes trouble just hung over a town like a cluster of storm clouds. Eventually it cleared.

Billy felt reasonably confident that whatever had happened here had nothing to do with Rowan.

This was some sort of trouble in Stan Henegar's life. Since the man had no history of criminal activity, it was a bit of a surprise. But shit happened. Sometimes it happened to guys who'd never been in trouble before.

"Let's start with a list of his friends, members of the congregation over at First Baptist and work associates, particularly those who work with power tools. Maybe he knew something someone didn't want him to tell."

"I'll get right on it, Chief."

Billy headed back outside to talk to Wanda. He would need additional confirmation of her alibi. Her sister's word would not be enough. Someone from a shop they'd patronized or a friend or neighbor they'd run into while strolling the mall. It wasn't that he believed Wanda capable of a heinous murder like this one, but as the wife she had the most to gain—or to lose—by her husband's death. It was always best to start with the spouse or significant other.

He sat down on the swing next to Wanda. She stared at her open Bible as if expecting some sort of answer to reveal itself from those revered pages.

"Let's talk about where you were today and how things have been lately between you and Stan."

She turned her red and swollen eyes to Billy. "Am I a suspect, Chief?"

"Standard protocol. Spouses, family and close

friends, they're always suspects when something like this happens. It's just a formality that we have to get past."

She swiped her face with the fingers of her free hand. "Stan and I have been married for twenty years." She smiled sadly. "Since I was fifteen years old. He practically raised me."

Billy nodded. It wasn't uncommon back in the day for women to marry so young. Wanda was a little young to fall into that category. As far as he knew she and Stan never had children together. He had two grown sons from a previous marriage—his first wife died not long after the birth of the second child. He supposed Wanda considered the boys her children.

"We have a big Thanksgiving dinner planned. The boys are coming. Stan said I should buy a new dress. Judy took me. She knows I don't like to drive in Huntsville." She exhaled a shaky breath. "We were a little later than we expected so she dropped me off and headed into town to pick up her kids."

He was relatively certain he'd never seen Wanda behind the wheel even though she had a car and was licensed to drive. "Any trouble between you and Stan lately?"

She made a face and shook her head. "Of course not. We've always gotten along."

"Any trouble with friends or coworkers? Maybe someone from the congregation?"

"Nothing that I know of. Stan wasn't the sort of man to stir trouble." She gave her head a firm shake. "He liked solving troubles. That's why they made him a deacon at church. He was a good peacemaker, my Stan."

"If you think of anyone who'd had words with Stan or any trouble at all, I want you to call me right away." Verifying Wanda and her sister were shopping would be fairly simple. At this point he saw no reason not to be confident in her version of events.

"I sure will." Her voice warbled.

"Can you stay with your sister tonight? We'll need to collect any evidence and thoroughly go over the house before you stay here again. We might need two or three days."

Hand over her mouth, she managed a single nod. It wasn't easy to grasp the reality that one's home had become a crime scene.

"Would you like me to call the boys for you?"

"It would be better if they heard this from me," she said wearily. "But I appreciate the offer."

"All right, then. We'll find your sister and get her over here to pick you up."

Burt arrived. The evidence techs were right behind him. Within minutes the house was marked as an official crime scene. Two more officers arrived to search the perimeter of the property. Billy followed Burt to the kitchen.

After a preliminary examination, Burt sat back on his heels. "He's been dead a good four or five hours. I don't see any marks on his body beyond those made in securing him."

"Do you think he suffocated, or was he dead before the pages were stuffed into his mouth?"

"We'll need an autopsy to know for sure but I'm leaning toward suffocation. It's possible he had a heart attack first." Burt turned to Billy. "But the person who did this wanted him to feel the fear."

"What do you mean?" Billy studied the body nailed to the floor. "You think he was awake while this was going on?"

"Awake but helpless. The killer took his time." He gestured to the victim's ankles. "You see those ligature marks? And the way his hands were nailed down more than once? And he soiled himself at least once. My guess is the killer tore those pages out one at a time and stuffed them into his mouth, probably deep into his throat. Stan squirmed and he did this for long enough to make those marks."

Billy leaned down and studied the marks the shoelaces had made. "I see that."

"Whoever did this enjoyed the torture."

Damn. "Thanks, Burt. See if you can get a rush on the autopsy and tox screens. I need to know what I'm dealing with here."

"Will do, Chief."

Billy pushed to his feet and went in search of Lincoln. They were going to be here for a while. If the perpetrator was in the house for as much as an hour, hopefully he screwed up and left some sort of evidence. There weren't any neighbors close enough to hope for witnesses to any vehicles that might have passed on the road.

For Billy, that was the biggest obstacle staring him in the face. Without any witnesses they were relying solely on physical evidence. A single hair or fingerprint, a shoeprint or tire print could make all the difference.

Too bad it hadn't rained in more than a week.

Eight

Rowan left the Harvey visitation early. Charlotte had everything under control. No need for both of them to stay. After the meeting with Dressler, it was clear the FBI still wasn't completely convinced Rowan wasn't in contact with Julian. It was also fairly obvious that this Sanchez—or Santos—person was somehow connected to her mother. How could she have grown up in that funeral home and not recognized that her parents were not like other parents?

Living in a funeral home had made her an oddball, a sort of outcast among the other children. Perhaps that was why she hadn't recognized how different things were on other levels. Growing up, it wasn't like she'd had any close friends other than Billy. He came to the funeral home often, but she could only recall rare instances of being at his home. A Christmas dinner once, his birthday a couple of times. With no other adults to observe on a regular basis, she'd had no firm, consistent measure of what was normal. What she lived was her normal.

Her teenage years had been filled with uncertainty and depression and self-loathing, all suffered in silence. She hadn't wanted to burden her father by sharing those dark feelings with him. It was bad enough she'd tried to take her life after the deaths of her twin sister and her mother. She felt certain that act had hurt her father far worse than anything else she could have done. But he'd taken care of her. Patched up her sliced wrists to avoid the world knowing what she'd done. He'd taken good care of her. And Billy had been there, too. Billy had been her only light during those days of darkness.

But Billy hadn't been there in college. He'd been at the University of Tennessee, far away from Nashville. She'd drifted deep into the darkness her freshman year and ended up attempting suicide a second time, with pills that go-around. She'd done her time in the psych ward and while there Dr. Julian Addington, esteemed psychiatrist and beloved member of the community, had taken a special interest in her. Over time, he'd taken her under his wing. Under his guidance she had chosen to go into psychiatry rather than returning to Winchester to take over the family funeral home the way DuPonts had for a century and a half. Once again, she had devastated her father.

She and her father had eventually moved past that disappointment. He had respected her decision and admired her work. How many times had he told her how very proud of her he was? Hundreds of times.

For the past nineteen years she had believed she was an independent woman who made her own choices in life and who had built a highly respected career.

But she had been wrong.

Julian Addington had been watching her since she was a child. He was somehow a part of the reason her twin sister had died. He was in all likelihood a part of her mother's motive for taking her own life mere months later. Rowan had spent a lifetime feeling damaged by the idea that her mother had preferred to follow her sister into death rather than to keep living with her surviving daughter. Julian was responsible for those years of agony. He had taken her mother away from her long ago and tainted any memories Rowan had of her. She would not allow him to damage the memory of her father, too. No matter the ups and downs, she and her father had experienced over the years, they had loved each other. He had been a good father. Julian would not touch those memories. He wanted her to believe that her father had killed his daughter after she murdered Raven. Rowan would never believe her father capable of such an act.

Admittedly, there were questions about the day Raven and Alisha died. One way or another Rowan intended to find the answers before someone else discovered those inconsistencies. Like Julian's ex-wife, Anna Addington. She had been in Winchester since her daughter's remains were discovered. More than once she had stated that she would stay in Winchester until her daughter's killer was found.

Maybe Sanchez had killed the seventeen-year-old who killed his lover Norah's daughter. The scenario was feasible. Rowan had worked numerous cases where a lover or close family member had killed in an act of revenge. Sanchez had been a killer. Rowan's father had not.

Rowan climbed out of her SUV and touched the car handle to lock it. Her first stop was the neighbor who had found Sanchez's body. Billy had interviewed him and, most likely, one of Dressler's people—if not Dressler himself—had done so today. But Rowan wasn't a member of law enforcement. She hadn't been since resigning from the homicide division five months ago. Quite often a person would speak more freely to someone not a part of law enforcement. People were at times intimidated by a badge. Fear that an old mistake he or she might have made would be discovered prompted him or her to maintain a low profile, including keeping mouths shut.

No one wanted to inadvertently end up incarcerated.

The block structure with the number five posted on the door was her destination. Number six, where Sanchez had resided, was still marked with crime-scene tape and a warning was posted on the door, effectively covering the *6* painted there. Rowan walked up to the door of number five and knocked. Beyond the slats of the blinds a dim light glowed, which hopefully meant someone was home and up. It was only a few minutes past eight. The man would likely still be up.

The rattle of a security chain and the slide of the dead bolt echoed in the darkness. Rowan stiffened her spine. She had her pepper spray and her handgun in her bag. She'd never carried a weapon, not in all the years she worked at Metro or before, until a few months ago. The compromise was the only way to prevent Billy from using up department resources by keeping a security detail assigned to her 24/7. She did not want her issues to create problems for him. Though the community respected him and she couldn't see the city hierarchy wanting anyone else in the position he held, money often swayed even the highest opinions. She didn't want him wasting department funds on her protection.

She could take care of herself.

A short man, presumably Owen Utter, who appeared to be in his mid- to late sixties, squinted out at her. His gray hair was mussed, his T-shirt and sweatpants worn, his feet bare. "I don't believe in God," he announced.

Rowan smiled. A reasonable mistake. She stood at his door dressed in a suit. She hadn't bothered to change into anything more comfortable when she left the visitation. "I'm not from any of the local churches, sir. I'm here to talk to you about your neighbor, Mr. Sanchez. You are Mr. Utter?"

"That's right." His gaze narrowed. "Are you another one of them federal agents? I already talked to them today. I got nothing else to say. The dead should rest in peace. Whatever old Carlos did, it doesn't matter now. He's dead. One thing I know about the Bible is that it says the wages of sin is death. Well, he cashed in his chips. Paid up. Settled his account. Whatever you want to call it."

She moved closer, getting one foot on the threshold. "I'm not from the FBI, sir. And I'm not from local law enforcement. My name is Rowan DuPont. I'm from—"

"The undertaker's daughter!" He pointed at her. "I know you. You're the one that didn't die." He nodded. "I heard you were back to take over for your daddy." He frowned. "Poor son of a bitch. I hated to hear about him dying. He was a fine man. Took care of my Suzy when she died. Sucks that your friend killed him."

Rowan took a breath, then let it out slowly to give

herself time to ensure she spoke calmly. "I appreciate your kind words about my father."

"Come on in." Utter backed up a few steps, opened the door wide. "You'll have to overlook the mess. I wasn't expecting company."

"Thank you." Rowan followed him beyond the door. Waited while he closed it. "Have you lived here long?"

She had done her research. The old motel had been turned into apartments about twenty-five years ago after a decade of being empty and abandoned. A local had bought the property at a tax auction and turned the former motel rooms into "studio" apartments. Based on what Rowan had seen, the term was being used in its vaguest and most rustic definition.

"About twenty years." He shrugged. "The wife and I moved here after we lost our house. We were both on disability and couldn't afford nothing else." He glanced around the room. "It turned out not to be so bad." His attention settled on Rowan once more. "You want to sit down?"

"That would be nice."

He cleared a space for her on a worn-out upholstered chair. "This was my wife's favorite chair. It's the only thing we were able to take from our house."

Rowan took the offered seat. "It's very comfortable."

He smiled broadly at her compliment as he settled onto the couch. "Would you like a beer?"

"No, thank you. I was wondering if you knew of any other friends or family Mr. Sanchez had."

His expression shifted back into a frown. "Did the insurance company not pay you for the embalming? He told me they would."

"I'm not here about money, Mr. Utter. I'm trying to

find out more about Mr. Sanchez. If he has any family, I'm certain they would like to know about his passing."

Utter leaned back and relaxed. "Told me he didn't have no family and I can tell you right now I was the only friend he had. He wasn't exactly the sort folks got attached to, if you know what I mean. Quiet and sullen for the most part."

"Had you known him for very long?"

Ten seconds of silence elapsed before the man decided to answer. "He only moved in next door a couple of months ago. But, yeah, I knew him before that." He shrugged. "I didn't mention that part to the cops or them feds. I didn't want to be disrespectful or anything but some things just don't need to be told."

"You can tell me, Mr. Utter. I want to help Mr. Sanchez. He deserves the same treatment from me that I would give anyone else."

Billy had not released the news about the man's body disappearing. Apparently, Dressler's people hadn't, either. This could work to her advantage.

Utter nodded. "See, I knew you'd be a kind soul just like your daddy. He never judged nobody. Treated everyone the same."

Rowan thanked him again and held her breath as she waited for an answer.

"He lived in a lean-to in the woods. There's a few homeless folks that do that, you know. It's not so bad in the summer but it's tough in the winter. I used to invite him to my place when it was really cold. He always brought a big bowl of stew he'd made himself. Best I ever ate."

Rowan's stomach churned at the idea of what might have been in that stew, considering what they had found next door. "How long were you and Mr. Sanchez friends?"

"About ten years. We ran into each other at the hospital when my wife was dying. He came to her room, brought her some flowers he'd picked on the side of the road. He knew her from before we lost everything when she waitressed at the steak house."

"You and Mr. Sanchez were friends for a long time."

He nodded. "I don't think I would have made it after she died if not for him."

"Did Mr. Sanchez have a wife or girlfriend?" Rowan held her breath again. All she needed was a starting place, a direction, something to start her on the right path.

Utter shook his head. "He said the only woman he'd ever loved died a long time ago. He had her name tattooed on his back. He never showed it to me, but he talked about her all the time."

"He never mentioned her name?"

"Never did. He was a mysterious man like that. Liked his privacy when it came to personal stuff. But he was a good friend. He kept me fed when I would have starved."

"Did he ever tell you what he did for a living or where he lived before he moved to the Winchester area?"

"No." Utter laughed. "He always said if he told me any of that stuff he'd have to kill me."

The man probably didn't realize Sanchez had not been kidding.

"One last question, Mr. Utter."

He held his hands out, palms up. "Anything I know I'll tell you."

"Could you take me to that lean-to where he lived before?"

He hesitated. "I guess so. Don't know if it's still there but we can have a look. I don't have no wheels."

"No worries—I do. I'll come by in the morning, if that's all right."

"Sure. I got nothing else to do. A road trip would be nice."

Rowan hurried back to the funeral home. She barely contained the urge to go into those woods tonight. But she doubted Mr. Utter would have agreed to an excursion in the dark. Besides, there were preparations she needed to make. The cautious side of her warned that she shouldn't go into the woods with a stranger—even an elderly one—without Billy.

Speaking of whom, his truck was in the lot when she arrived at the funeral home. Her headlights flashed across his face behind the steering wheel. Maybe there was news on Sanchez. Perhaps something Dressler had told him that he wouldn't tell her. She was, after all, a person of interest in the case, in the agent's opinion.

Billy met her at the front entrance. "Charlotte just left. She said she took care of everything for the night."

Which meant she had put Mr. Harvey back into refrigeration and the flowers into the cooler. She'd ensured the viewing room was tidied and the funeral home was emptied of visitors and secured. Rowan was immensely grateful.

"Good. You want to come in?" She unlocked the door and hurried to the keypad to deactivate the alarm. He hadn't asked where she'd been yet, but she knew him well enough to understand he wanted to do so. Part of that need was the lawman in him, the other was that overprotective big-brother thing.

Billy had a key and knew the alarm code if he'd wanted to go in before she arrived. He was far too much of a gentleman to do that. He preferred to wait for her in the parking lot and walk her inside. Some part of him likely wanted to see from which way she came. Being a cop trailed close behind being a gentleman.

He closed the door behind him and flipped the lock, then removed his hat. "You up for a couple of beers and some talk about work?"

"Sure. I'm starving, though." She headed for the stairs. "You?"

"Always."

He climbed the stairs with her, keeping his steps in time with hers. She asked, "You want me to order something or can you deal with sandwiches?"

"Whatever you've got works for me."

"Great. You take Freud out and I'll pull together something."

"Deal."

Since she had a variety of cheese and deli meats, a cold sub-style sandwich would have to work. She gathered chips and beers and put everything on the coffee table. She poured kibble into Freud's bowl and freshened his water. By the time Billy was back with Freud, their thrown-together dinner was ready.

They dug in. Ate in silence for a few minutes. Finally, Rowan asked, "What did Dressler say about me?"

Billy finished off his beer. "He's convinced Addington is still alive and will be coming back for you."

"Old news." She sipped her beer, wished it was something stronger.

"I told him not to worry, that I'm keeping a close eye on you."

"Did he buy it?"

Billy opened another beer. "Doubt it. He doesn't trust me when it comes to you."

Unfortunate but true. "Is he going to have someone watching me again?"

Billy shook his head. "He wants me to do it. I wasn't too worried about it since we have an understanding. You keep me informed and always carry your weapon. But recently I'm a little concerned. Like tonight. You disappeared and I had no idea where you were." He sent her a pointed look. "And I'm not buying the story you gave Charlotte about having some business to take care of with another client."

She sat down her beer and faced his disappointed stare. "I went to see Mr. Utter, Sanchez's neighbor."

"Oh, hell, Ro."

"I was careful, and I was armed."

Her old friend exhaled a weary breath. "I'm glad for that. What did you learn? He sure as hell didn't give me or Dressler anything useful."

"He lied to you." Rowan saw no reason to mince words. "He's known Sanchez for ten or so years, not just the short time they were neighbors. They met in the hospital when Sanchez visited Utter's dying wife. Apparently, she knew him first from her waitressing days at the steak house."

"The landlord confirmed that Sanchez had only lived there for a short time but he had no previous address. Did Utter have one?"

"He lived in the woods. Utter has agreed to take me there in the morning."

Frustration claimed Billy's face. "Were you going to tell me about this?"

"I just did." Rowan picked up a chip and nibbled it just to have something to do with her hands.

Billy shook his head. "You are the most hardheaded—"

"You want to go with me?" she asked, hoping to defuse his frustration.

"If you go," he warned, "I will be going."

"Yes, sir."

"On top of that, I have a homicide. That's why I came by. I could use your help, if you're so inclined."

"Always. Who was murdered?"

"Stanley Henegar. The file's in the truck if you want to talk about it."

"Sure." She bit her lip, decided she would push the request she'd made earlier while he was in need of something from her. Not that she would ever say no to anything Billy needed. "You should give me Herman's key, you know. He gave me permission to go through his house. I'm not happy you've been making me wait."

"We've both been a little busy, Ro. I can't have you going in there without me. Not after what he did."

Rowan knew this but she didn't have to like it and she decided not to mention that he hadn't given her the key before Herman did what he did. "Tomorrow we go right after we check this place where Sanchez supposedly lived."

"We can. According to Dressler, it's Santos," he corrected.

"Whatever. He may have buried something in the area. Like the remains of his victims." She shivered as she thought of what Utter had told her. "He made homemade stew and brought it to Utter on numerous occasions."

Billy grimaced. "You think he ate parts of his victims?"

"He did something with all those remains. Dressler didn't have a profile on him?"

"If he did, he didn't share it. He was tight-lipped on this one. Makes me wonder if there's a connection to Addington that's already been confirmed and we haven't been told yet."

"I'm guessing so." Rowan hated the idea, but it made sense. "If by no other means than an obsession with Norah. Julian's wife told me that after Norah died, he shifted his obsession from her to me. Maybe Norah was the connection between Sanchez and Addington."

You're all that's left of her, Ro, and they will all *want you.*

Herman's words echoed through her. She resisted the urge to shiver. The more she learned about her mother, the more she realized she hadn't known the woman at all. Rowan wondered if her father had felt that same way. She wished he was still alive. There were so many things she wanted to ask him.

Primarily she just missed him.

"We need to know what they're not telling us."

Billy's words drew her back to the here and now. "I can call April Jones." April Jones was a detective in Nashville who worked in the homicide division's Special Crimes Unit, where Rowan had been assigned. She was also assigned to the Addington joint task force. She had been a friend, as well. Still was. "She might be able to tell us more."

"Call her first thing tomorrow."

"I will," Rowan agreed. Then she added, "I'll call her on the way to pick up Utter. We're going into those woods first thing. Then to Herman's."

Billy looked skeptical but she wasn't taking no for an answer.

Nine

"You're sure this is the place?"

Rowan watched old man Utter consider Billy's question. His eyes were narrowed in concentration as he peered out the window at the dense woods. Rowan's hopes dropped a little lower. She'd awakened full of anticipation and in a hurry to find some sort of evidence that might help in her search for the truth. Finding Mr. Utter sleeping off a serious hangover on the sidewalk outside his place had deflated her hopes significantly. Thankfully last night's temperature had not dropped as low as the night before. Three cups of coffee and a stack of pancakes had revived him.

Still, after the fifth stop along this road with him shouting, "That's it! That's it!" and then changing his mind, she was on the verge of giving up. The man clearly had no idea where Carlos Sanchez had lived in these woods—assuming Utter's story was even true.

"This is it! I'm positive." Utter began to wrestle with his seat belt.

Rowan and Billy shared a look, shrugged simultaneously and then reached for their own seat belts. They were here. Might as well follow the man into the woods and hope they didn't get lost.

Billy had come around to the passenger side by the time Rowan was out and hanging the strap of her bag over her neck. He opened the door for the older man and helped him from the back seat of the big crew cab truck. She and Billy both wore boots and jackets. Utter wore sweats that had seen better days and sneakers, the soles of which flopped with each step he made.

"Hold on a minute," Billy said to the man. He reached into the bed of his truck and grabbed a pair of rubber boots. "Why don't you put these on over your sneakers, Mr. Utter?"

Billy had already offered him a jacket but he'd insisted he didn't need one.

When he hesitated, Billy added, "I wouldn't want you to get your sneakers dirty if we encounter any muddy areas."

The fact that it hadn't rained in several days didn't appear to cross the older man's mind. He accepted the boots and tugged them on. It took a minute and he had to lean against the truck, but he got the job done. He pushed away from the vehicle and started for the woods with renewed vigor.

"He brought me out here once to get something he'd forgotten," Utter explained as he tromped through the weeds on the side of the road. "Then he got here and remembered he'd already taken whatever the hell it was. I think maybe his memory was going toward the end."

Billy's boots were about three sizes too big but the old man managed. Rowan kept her stride in time with

Billy's, a couple of yards behind Utter. Like her, Billy kept scanning the tree line and the road. Mr. Utter was no threat since either of them could easily overtake him. But there was always the chance Julian had hired him to lead them into a trap. It was a chance Rowan was willing to take herself, but she didn't like that Billy was in the same precarious situation alongside her.

When they reached the tree line it was necessary to walk single file.

"Stay behind me," Billy said for her ears only.

Rowan didn't argue but she didn't like it.

The underbrush swiped at her jeans. The fallen leaves cushioned the ground but disguised roots and rocks, making the going treacherous. She checked over her shoulder frequently. The unnerving sensation that someone was watching or was behind them wouldn't turn loose.

Sunlight streaked down through the partially bare branches, preventing the dense woods from wrapping them in total darkness. Rowan was grateful for the light, however sparse. Somewhere overhead a crow cawed. She spotted two, three. The dark birds perched on those bare limbs sent another shiver whispering along the length of her spine.

Utter stopped suddenly and pointed to the right. He waited for Billy and Rowan to move in close behind him before he said, "That's tent city."

If she held her head angled toward her right shoulder and squinted just so, she could barely make out the tops of tents in a clearing fifty or so yards in the distance. The tents weren't large—they were the type one might use on a camping trip. Some were colorful, as dots of blue and red and green stood out among the drab grays and khaki-colored ones. Three different plumes of smoke suggested communal campfires. She inhaled deeply, noted the smell of smoke and the scent of something she couldn't quite identify cooking.

"Is this the same tent city that was once out near the park?" Billy asked their guide.

"Yeah, about ten years ago. They've managed to keep this location quiet," Utter explained. "Mostly because they ran off all the meth users. Can't trust 'em. The paranoia makes 'em do crazy stuff."

"Well, I'll be damned," Billy muttered. "I haven't heard the first peep about this."

"It's mostly folks who don't want trouble. Just don't got no other place to go."

Utter moved forward again, progressing in a slight angle left, putting distance between them and the tent-city dwellers. She wasn't much of a nature hiker, but if her instincts were on target, they were moving toward the base of the mountain. The grade of the land steadily rose ever so slightly. More than one spelunker had gotten lost in this area and had to be rescued. She'd read about a couple over the summer who'd spent days lost in a maze of caves in the area. Sanchez could have bodies and all manner of evidence hidden in this area and no one would ever find it. Her hopes deflated a little more.

Another caw drew her attention to the trees. The crows had followed them. Either that or there were three more loitering about. Her father had always said that crows had more to say than many birds because they watched more closely than most. Rowan never failed to make a trip to a cemetery without seeing one. Many people were convinced the crows were drawn to the dead, but it was more about the older trees in the cemeteries. The crows liked the security of the big old trees.

Maybe a quarter of a mile from the tent dwellers, Utter drew to a stop and pointed forward. "It's maybe thirty yards that way—or it used to be. There's some climbing involved so I'll just stay right here if that's okay."

Rather than wait for an answer from Billy, the old man plopped down on the nearest fallen tree trunk. Their winged followers had settled onto a tree limb well above where he'd parked himself.

Billy glanced at Rowan. "You could stay here while I check it out. I'll let you know if there's anything worth looking at, assuming I find more than out-of-control underbrush, rocks and dirt."

Rowan flashed him an exaggerated smile. "I'll just tag along with you, Chief."

He nodded, though his expression warned that it was with reluctance. "Suit yourself."

Rowan slogged onward, following in the tramped-down trail Billy made. The grade was rockier here and there was a bit of climbing, as Utter had said there would be. The canopy of trees seemed thicker, or maybe the limbs were simply closer to the ground. The sensation was oddly claustrophobic.

She and Billy spotted what looked like a campsite at about the same time. It was well hidden, against the mountainside and surrounded by trees and under-brush. If not for so many fallen leaves, they wouldn't have noticed it at all. The top of the primitive shelter was made of cut tree limbs, three layers deep with the center layer placed in the opposite direction from the others. Beneath the canopy of long, dead limbs was an area about eight feet by eight feet that was mostly overgrown with brush and saplings. No sign of human inhabitation. No old fire ring, no discarded cans or other tools or utensils. If not for the canopy of limbs, it could be a naturally formed animal haven.

Disappointment speared Rowan. All this trouble for nothing. If Sanchez had slept here, that was all he had done.

Billy crouched down and inspected the ground and mountainside in the small alcove. Rowan glanced around. She supposed Sanchez could have brought his victims here, one by one. If there had been any goods or tools kept around, they were obviously long gone or tangled in all that underbrush.

"There's a small access to what might be a cave."

Billy's voice dragged Rowan from the frustrating thoughts. "A cave?" Her pulse reacted to the news. This could be what they were looking for.

"Maybe."

Cutting through the underbrush, she moved to his side and crouched down next to him. "Can you see anything?"

"You have a flashlight in that bag of yours? It's a long walk back to the truck." He pulled out his cell phone and turned on the flashlight app. "This could work, but it's awkward to hold it when I need to get down on my hands and knees."

She reached into her bag and pulled out the flashlight she'd taken from her bedside table and offered it to him. "I have a bottle of water and a protein bar, too, if you're interested."

Billy flashed her a grin as he accepted the flashlight. "You always were prepared."

He was right. She'd carried Band-Aids, tissues and breath mints in her purse for as long as she could remember. In school, he'd always snag a mint from Rowan when he wanted to flirt with one girl or the other.

"Let's do this, then," she suggested.

"You follow when I give you the go-ahead," he reminded her. "Not before."

She gave him a little salute. "Aye, aye, Captain."

He shook his head and got into position on his hands and knees. Once he'd crawled beyond the small opening, he disappeared. Rowan sat on her haunches and waited impatiently.

What was likely only a minute but felt like an hour passed before he called her name. Rowan crawled into the hole, anticipation whirling inside her. Three feet in and the hole in the mountainside yawned open. Billy offered his hand and helped her to her feet.

He roamed the beam of the flashlight over the walls. Not much over six feet in height and four feet wide, but the tunnel or whatever it was disappeared into the darkness beyond the reach of the flashlight. This was definitely a cave. It could go on for miles.

Billy settled the glow of the light onto the ceiling above their heads. "I don't know how safe it is to be in here and what we can expect beyond this point." He moved the beam over the walls and floor once more. "I'm not seeing anything we can take with us or even any sign there's ever been another human inside here."

"I imagine Sanchez was the kind of man who knew how to cover his tracks." A man didn't haul around twenty-six faces and books made from the bodies of his victims without careful planning.

"No doubt," Billy agreed. "But I'm not prepared to go any deeper until we have this cave or tunnel—whatever the hell it is—checked out by someone smarter than me when it comes to caves. We're not adequately prepared."

As much as Rowan wanted to keep going, he was right. "Do you know someone who can do a quick inspection? Hopefully today?"

"I do. When I get back to the office I'll call and see how quickly he can check it out so we can get a team in here to look around."

Even if it took a few more days, it wasn't the end of the world. She had waited this long; what was a few more hours?

Outside, she got to her feet and dusted off her knees. Instinctively, she looked around and glanced up. Those damn crows had followed them and watched from high overhead. How strange was that?

Rowan studied them a long moment, then shook off the eerie sensation their presence elicited.

Ten minutes later they found Utter sitting on the same tree trunk as where they'd left him.

"Find anything?" He looked first at one of them and then the other.

Rowan was happy to allow Billy to handle that question. Her instinct was to keep the tunnel a secret until the authorities had thoroughly examined the area. Besides, there was something knowing about the man's expression. As if he already knew the answer.

"Not one damn thing," Billy said, apparently on the

same page as her. "But we appreciate the tip. You never know which ones will pan out."

Utter gave no appearance of being surprised.

As they moved back through the woods, Rowan couldn't help straining to see more of the tent city Utter had pointed out. She wondered if she knew anyone who lived there. Homelessness wasn't age- or race-specific. Anyone could end up losing everything with nowhere to turn.

When they reached Knight Street to deliver Mr. Utter to his home, the feds were in Sanchez's place. Rowan thanked the older man again and Billy helped him from the truck. He seemed so pleased with the too-big boots, Billy let him keep them. They watched until he was back inside his home. Rowan noted that along with hers, Billy's attention shifted to the ongoing activity, as well.

"Dressler said they're taking the place apart—literally."

Rowan turned to Billy. "Wouldn't be the first time a killer has hidden evidence in the walls or the ceiling or crawl space."

Billy nodded. "Yeah." He rolled away from the curb and put the neighborhood in his rearview mirror.

"Did you bring the key to Herman's house?" Rowan had made it very clear she wanted to have a look today. Billy had put her off long enough. She hoped he wasn't going to put her off again.

"I did." He braked for a traffic light, sent her a sidelong look. "We'll have a look and then we'll talk."

Talk. "I see. You think Herman said something else to me that I haven't shared with you." Dressler had most likely planted that seed of doubt.

It was true. Herman had, and she was. But nothing she had withheld from Billy was relevant because she had no clue what it meant. As soon as she understood what Herman had been trying to tell her, she would share that information with Billy. No question.

"What is it you're looking for in his house?"

"I don't know. He wouldn't tell me. He just said I needed answers and I should look in his house. He mentioned that Estelle had been a stickler for keeping things. I'm hoping that means there are photographs or something along those lines."

"You would tell me if there was more." Billy glanced at her.

She managed to resist looking away. "I would tell you anything relevant. You have my word."

"Relevant." He turned onto High Street. "Define *relevant.*"

Good Lord. "You know what I mean. Jesus. If we find anything in his house, we'll both know what he meant. If I wanted to hide something from you, I would be demanding to do this alone."

Billy parked, opened his door and climbed out. Rowan breathed a sigh of relief and exited the vehicle. She didn't like keeping anything from Billy. There was just too much she didn't know to determine how to share what she did know. Billy was the closest thing to family she had left. She wanted to protect him just as much as he wanted to protect her. But he would never understand that reasoning coming from her.

When it came to protection, he had that "do as I say, not as I do" mentality.

They climbed the front steps together and Rowan thought of the last time she'd sat on this porch, drinking sweet tea with Herman, her father's lifelong friend. How was it possible that he'd betrayed her and her family? She'd known Herman her entire life, thought of him as an uncle—almost a second father.

She had given him grace since he had been desperate to help his dying wife. Desperation on that level could make a person lose perspective and all sense of boundaries. But this thing with Julian, it was different. There was no excuse.

Billy dug the key from his pocket and reached for the door, then he stopped and went for his cell phone. He passed the key to Rowan as he took the call. He listened for several seconds before responding. Rather than unlock the door, Rowan watched his expression go from expectant to grave. His body language warned there was trouble.

"I'll be right there." He ended the call and slid his phone back into his pocket. "There's been another murder."

"Like Stanley Henegar?" She thought of the crime-scene photos Billy had shown her last night. Something about that scene felt familiar, but she just couldn't place the memory.

"Not the same, but strange like Henegar's. I'd like you to have a look, Ro."

There was no help for it. Exploring Herman's house would have to wait until later. Rowan trailed Billy back to his truck. As soon as they were buckled in, he rushed away from the curb.

"Is the victim anyone I know?"

Although she'd lived in Nashville for the past twenty or so years, she had grown up in Winchester and her father had always kept her informed about who passed on and newcomers to the community.

"Barney Thackerson."

"The old man who ran that little store over near the park?"

"That was Barney's father, Barney Senior—most people called him Buster because he beat up anyone who tried to steal from him. The old store is a gas station and mini market now."

Rowan didn't know the son. He was ten years or so older than she and Billy. She did recall as a kid seeing him in the store with his daddy on Saturdays.

"Wife? Kids?"

"No wife, he's a widower, one grown daughter. He lived alone in the back of the store. An employee found him."

Rowan wondered if her body would be found by Charlotte or someone on the cleaning team. All these years she had lived alone she had never once considered who would find her body when she died. At least she would be in a funeral home already. That was something, she supposed.

The drive to the Thackerson Mini Market took only about ten minutes. Two Winchester PD cruisers sat in the small parking lot. Burt Johnston arrived at the same time Rowan and Billy did. Burt and his assistant, Lucky Ledbetter, climbed out and waited at the front entrance for Billy and Rowan. Black cats and bats reminding all who entered of the upcoming holiday hung in the plate glass window.

"I hear we've got another strange one," Burt said.

"That's what I hear. I guess we'll see." Billy opened the door for Rowan to precede him.

The uniformed officer standing guard at the door nodded to Rowan, then said, "'Afternoon, Chief. The body's back that way." He hitched his thumb toward the rear of the building.

Moving between the aisles, they all pulled on gloves. In the storeroom, another officer waited at the door to the entrance of the living quarters. From the street the store looked fairly small. The building made up for its small width with depth. It went on and on. Like Rowan's home, Thackerson's residence was an extension of his work space. Saved a bundle on living expenses.

Thackerson's body wasn't in the kitchen area, as Henegar's had been. He was tied to the bed. His arms and legs had been spread out wide and secured with nylon rope. He wore boxers, a T-shirt and socks. Like Stan Henegar's face in the crime-scene photos Rowan had viewed, Thackerson's expression was frozen in horror. His head was tilted back slightly and his mouth was open perhaps wider than was natural. Bars of what appeared to be soap had been shoved inside.

The scene nudged that same sense of familiarity in Rowan. Where had she seen this before? Not precisely this, she decided, but something that struck the same chords.

"Evidence techs are here," someone said.

"Good." This from Billy.

Rowan walked to the other side of the bed and studied the victim from the opposite angle. "We should run this MO through the database. There's something familiar about it. I think I've seen it before."

Billy nodded his agreement. "We're doing that with Stan, too. The killer leaves no note or message. No indication of how the victim wronged him. Nothing missing at the Henegar home."

Rowan thought about that for a moment, but a moment was all it took. "He wants us to figure it out." She met Billy's gaze. "He wants to see if we're smart enough to solve the mystery."

"He could be watching." Billy glanced at the door. "The parking lot for the park is across the road. He could be watching from any one of those vehicles."

"He probably is." Rowan thought of all the small houses along this road and of the vehicles in the lot Billy mentioned. Binoculars at the right spot in the park would allow him to see the store and the official vehicles now surrounding it. Watching the buzz of activity would stimulate him.

Burt leaned over the victim and started an examination.

"We need to know what he had in common with Stan Henegar," Billy said.

"Or who," Rowan countered. "Someone who was very unhappy with the both of them. Someone who wanted to torture and murder them but didn't want anything in their possession."

"He's been dead well over ten hours. Rigor is almost set."

"That would put time of death after the store's closing time," Billy said. "Since the doors were locked when the employee showed up and we've found no sign of forced entry, the killer was waiting here for Thackerson when he locked up last night."

"Either that or it was someone he knew and opened his door to," Rowan countered.

Thackerson's wrists and ankles bore the ligature

marks that told the story of how desperately he had attempted to escape. The bed had an old iron headboard and footboard, and the killer had tied him securely so there was little chance the man was going to escape, however hard he fought.

Billy suspected Henegar had been drugged, which cut short his attempt to escape his killer. Had Thackerson been drugged, as well? If so, how had he managed to sustain his battle? He was a far larger man than Henegar. Perhaps the dosage of whatever drug had been used had not been sufficient for his size.

Over the course of the next half hour, the lack of forced entry was confirmed. The door had been locked from the inside when the employee had attempted to check on Mr. Thackerson. When Thackerson hadn't come out into the store by lunchtime, the employee had grown concerned. He'd had to use the spare key hidden under the register's money tray to let himself in. He'd called 911 immediately. The paramedics had established Thackerson was dead and called the cops and the coroner.

By the time the body was removed from the scene, the victim's daughter had been called and had arrived. Once she had regained her composure, she walked through the living quarters and corroborated that nothing appeared to be missing. She also confirmed there was no wife or girlfriend or children except her.

Thackerson had lived alone while Henegar had a wife. The men were approximately the same age, but entirely different. Henegar had been a religious zealot, a farmer who lived a quiet life. Thackerson was a little saltier. He sold booze and kept a weapon under the counter. He'd shot his fair share of would-be robbers.

On the surface, the two had very little in common beyond the fact that they had both been murdered.

Rowan walked over to the dresser and studied the framed photo of the daughter. But life was rarely as simple as it looked on the surface.

No one knew that better than Rowan.

Ten

Rowan parked on the street in front of Herman's house.

Billy would be at the Thackerson crime scene for hours yet. He'd had one of his officers drive her home. She had taken a moment to let Freud outside and pour kibble into his bowl, and then she'd come here to do what needed to be done.

She couldn't risk waiting until morning. It was a miracle Dressler's people hadn't assumed control of this property already. Billy had given her the key to Herman's house when they'd left earlier to go to the Thackerson crime scene. Maybe that had been his way of letting her know he was okay with her doing what she needed to do. After all, Herman had told her to have a look.

Images of Herman pulling that trigger flashed one after the other in her head. Rowan squeezed her eyes shut. Herman's death was not her fault. He'd made the decision to take his life. She might never know whether it was the thought of spending the rest of his life in prison, or guilt for all that he had done, or the idea of living without Estelle. Then again, perhaps it was fear of what he recognized was coming next—some horror only he understood.

Sitting in her SUV debating the unknowns and the possibilities wasn't going to change what she needed to do right now. Wasting time was not in her best interest. With that in mind, she climbed out and glanced down the street in both directions, then headed up the walkway toward the porch. She'd been to this house endless times as a child. Her parents had played Rook with Herman and his wife on Thursday nights. The get-together hadn't happened every week. The schedule generally depended upon what was happening at the funeral home. Of course, like everything else in her life, that routine had gone away after Raven's death and their mother's suicide.

Life in general had changed for both her and her father. He'd become more focused on work. She had lost interest in most things, rarely left the house other than to go to school, or to visit the cemetery or the lake where her sister had drowned.

The key slid easily into the lock and Rowan gave it a twist. The door opened, and she took a deep breath before stepping inside. A flip of the nearest wall switch filled the room with light. A closed-up smell lingered in the air despite the fact that someone from Billy's team had gone through the house to ensure Herman wasn't in hiding, or hadn't taken anything readily noticeable. Back in May, in addition to the process of scouring the property for evidence, a reasonably thorough inventory had been taken after Herman was arrested.

Rowan hesitated before moving through the room, decided to lock the door behind her. For the purpose of this excursion, she'd tucked her handgun into the waistband of her jeans at the small of her back. Her bag was too small to add the size and weight of the weapon. The already overcrowded shoulder-strap purse felt like a collection of rocks hanging around her neck as it was. No matter that evidence techs had already swept the home, she tugged on a pair of gloves. No use leaving her prints all over the place for the feds to find.

The living room was tidy. Though the furniture's upholstery was well-worn and a bit out-of-date, it was clean and welcoming. Rowan had curled up on that sofa dozens of times as a kid. Her sister would snuggle close as they watched a trending movie or television show. They had giggled and whispered about their latest celebrity crush. Those shared moments were the kind only sisters, especially twins, could appreciate.

But that was before. Before puberty. Before Raven had gotten herself murdered in the murky waters of the lake that had thrived around them their entire lives. Before their mother had hung herself in the house where they had grown up. The carefree days of Rowan's childhood had vanished in a bone-jarring instant on the heels of those painful tragedies.

Piece by piece, Rowan searched the furniture in the living room. No doubt the police had done this already, but she still checked beneath the couch and chair cushions. Struggling, she managed to push each piece of furniture onto its back so that she could look underneath for anything hidden. The drawers were next. Both end tables had drawers. A console table near the front door had two small drawers. She checked each item inside the drawers and then checked the bottoms of all. Nothing beyond keys, old receipts, appointment cards and pocket change.

Room by room, Rowan inspected everything from dinnerware to sock drawers and stacks of fluffy towels. Since Herman had mentioned photographs, she saved the books and photo albums lining the shelves in the hallway for last.

First, she flipped through each book, then shook it to ensure there were no notes or photos hidden inside. Herman had acquired a nice collection of first editions. Nearly all were hardcover and well read. The loose spines made her search easier. The distinct smell of vintage pages reminded her of elementary school and then the hours and hours of burning the midnight oil at the university library.

With the books done, she stacked the photo albums on the floor and settled cross-legged amid the piles. Herman was right about Estelle's penchant for documenting their history. The woman had more photo albums than any collection Rowan had seen. Family members of clients often invited Rowan to their homes to help select attire for the funeral. She couldn't walk through a person's house without noticing the photographs and books. There was something innately intimate about preparing a body for its final disposition in this world. Doing so made Rowan feel to some degree responsible for that person's welfare until they were buried, or their ashes turned over to the families. When Herman's body was released, she would prepare him for burial next to his wife. She would check with his extended family to see if anyone was interested in a memorial service, though she doubted she would find much enthusiasm.

The first stack of albums contained the most recent photos Estelle had tucked into plastic sleeves. It wasn't until Rowan reached the third stack that the pages revealed the years before Raven and Norah were gone. A shiver swept through Rowan as she was forced to acknowledge how very much she looked like her mother had at her age. The resemblance was eerie.

Barbecues, picnics at the lake, celebrations at the funeral home—endless moments were captured and stored within the pages. Her parents had smiled a lot then. She and Raven were always dressed alike and appeared happy. Of course, all that had changed when Raven decided she didn't like being a twin anymore. Many photos included other people; some Rowan recognized, others she did not. She decided to take the photos from that era home with her. Billy or his mother would likely be able to help identify the faces Rowan couldn't.

There were far more photos of her mother than of Rowan and her sister or her father. The photographer appeared usually to be her father or Herman, sometimes Estelle. Norah was never behind the camera—she was in every photo. People were drawn to her.

Rowan's fingers stilled after turning the next page. The air caught in her lungs.

Sanchez—or Santos, whatever his name was—stood next to Norah. There were four other people in the photo—none of whom Rowan recognized. Her heart pounding and her fingers trembling, she removed the photo from its sleeve and turned it over.

Nothing. No date, no names.

Rowan forced herself to breathe.

This was definitive evidence that her mother and her

father had known the guy. The photo had been taken at least thirty years ago. Was it possible Sanchez/Santos hadn't been a killer in those days?

Rowan pushed away the hope. Her mother had written about him in a way that suggested she had known exactly what he was. Rowan held the photo close, peered at the man's face. His hair had been too long to see his ears. Damn it. She studied the other faces. Wondered if they were killers, too. Had her father known what this man was? She scrutinized the man's fingers on her mother's left shoulder. His arm was draped around Norah. His fingers were loose against her skin, not digging in possessively. Was that because Rowan's father was close by or because Sanchez/Santos and Norah had only been friends?

"Which would absolutely explain the tattoo on his back." Rowan rolled her eyes at the foolish denial to which she had dared to cling. Norah and the man had clearly been lovers. To pretend otherwise would be foolish.

Had her father known?

She frowned, trying to recall if she had seen Sanchez/Santos at her father's funeral. If they were friends, wouldn't he have been there? If for no other reason than to celebrate the death of the man who had stood between him and the woman he loved or wanted or whatever?

Slowly, methodically, Rowan reviewed each photograph. Removed each from its sleeve and checked the back. If the photo appeared relevant to her search for the truth, she placed it aside rather than putting it back into the album. By the time she had finished she was exhausted and it was late. Really late. She checked her phone. No text messages from Billy.

It was a miracle. He generally kept up with her more closely. Surely he was finishing up at the Thackerson scene by now.

After gathering the photographs she had set aside, she walked through the house once more to ensure she'd left all as it should be. One thing she did not want to do was to give Dressler something else to complain about or to give Billy trouble over. This was her problem and as much as she appreciated Billy's help, she didn't want to drag him any more deeply into this mess.

Outside, she stood on the porch until her eyes adjusted to the darkness. The block was quiet. Cold air whispered around her, making her wish she'd worn a coat instead of a sweater. She checked the door a second time to ensure the lock had engaged properly. Satisfied the house was as secure as she'd found it, she made her way down the steps and to the street. A dog barked in the distance, maybe on the next block or on the street behind this one. Leaves drifted across the sidewalk in front of her as she instinctively quickened her pace.

She didn't breathe easy until she was settled behind the steering wheel and all the doors of her SUV were locked. The nearest streetlight was at the end of the block, at least twenty yards from where she was parked. She placed her weapon on the console and started the engine; the headlights automatically illuminated. Her skin prickled. She glanced in the rearview mirror, then scanned the street in front of her. The distinct feeling that someone was watching her spread across her skin, raising goose bumps.

"Just drive," she ordered, her right hand going to the gearshift.

Rowan checked the rearview mirror repeatedly as she drove across town to the funeral home. Tonight was one of those times she desperately wished she had a garage. She parked beneath the portico, where the hearse sat during a funeral, before it would lead the procession of family and friends.

Her right hand clutching her weapon and her left holding the house key, she climbed out and hurried to the side door. A few seconds later she was inside and disarming the security system. Freud greeted her, allowing her to relax and to dismiss the creepy feeling of being watched.

"How about a potty break, boy?" She scratched his head and made her way through the lobby and into the rear corridor. Freud trotted along beside her, glad to have his mistress home.

At the back door, she leaned against the open door frame while Freud raced around the yard and did his business. Leaves had gathered against the fence that surrounded the rear yard. Her gardener was scheduled to come back on Thursday. He would mulch the leaves and do the usual fall cleanup. This would be the first time since she was a child that Rowan plunged her fingers into the dirt for the purpose of planting bulbs. The gardener had mentioned that the tulips around the front porch looked a little sparse this past spring. It was time to plant new bulbs. Rowan had picked up the bulbs weeks ago and stored them in the refrigerator as suggested. After the first good freeze, she would plant them. This home was her responsibility now. She might as well start with the tulips.

"There's a first time for everything," she murmured. Her father would laugh and remind her to be careful or she'd ruin her image as a hotshot advisor.

"Not such a hotshot anymore, Daddy."

Julian Addington had damaged her reputation far too badly to recover. Didn't matter, she supposed. The family and friends of her clients didn't mind that she couldn't spot a killer right under her nose as long as she could make their recently deceased loved ones look nice in the casket.

That she could do.

Freud finally pranced up the steps and across the deck. Rowan stepped aside for him to come inside, then she locked up and reactivated the alarm. Trudging up the back stairs with Freud on her heels, she realized she hadn't eaten since grabbing fast food at lunch. She wasn't sure what was in the fridge so a peanut-butter sandwich might have to do. The old reliable had become a mainstay of her diet since returning home.

She dug the key to her door out of her bag. The last time the locks were changed Billy insisted she needed a different key for her living quarters. Given all that had happened with Julian and her former mortuary assistant, Woody, she had agreed.

Freud bounded through the door in front of her and hurried to his water bowl. Rowan locked the door and sagged against it. It was good to be home. All through her teenage years she had dreamed of little else beyond escaping this funeral home and this town. Now she was glad to be back. Grateful for the familiarity amid the turmoil in her life.

She dropped her bag on the sofa and dug out the photos she had taken from Herman's house. Photos in hand, she made her way to the kitchen and spread them out on the counter.

While she smeared peanut butter on a slice of bread, she studied the photos. Who were these people? Why was Sanchez/Santos so cocky? His expression loudly proclaimed his arrogance and self-confidence. He certainly hadn't looked so arrogant spread out on her mortuary table.

"Who are you?"

A killer. A friend of her parents? Her mother in particular?

"Too bizarre."

The muffled sound of her cell reached out to her from the other room. Rowan hurried to the living room and dug it from her bag.

Billy.

"Hey." She walked back into the kitchen. "You get things wrapped up at the Thackerson scene?"

"Pretty much."

He sounded tired. Understandable. "Anything new on who wanted him dead or how he and Henegar are connected?"

"Nothing yet." He sighed. "You find anything at Herman's place?"

Rowan shook her head. She should have known. She set the phone to Speaker and placed it on the counter so she could finish preparing her sandwich. "Do you have someone watching me again?"

She hadn't meant for the question to come out like an accusation, but there it was. He did not need to put himself out on a limb like this. How would she get that through his head?

"No, ma'am. I do not have anyone watching you. Why? You feel like someone's watching you?"

"Besides Julian, you mean?" She suppressed a shiver and reached into the fridge and grabbed a cola. "We both know he has eyes on me somehow." To believe otherwise would be foolish.

"You know what I mean, Ro."

The sound of his truck door closing told her he'd hopefully made it home. It was awfully late for him to be going back to the office. But that was the life of a cop at times.

"There was a moment when I was leaving Herman's," she confessed. To ignore her own instincts would be unwise.

"Ro—"

"Before you say anything," she said, interrupting what she suspected would be one of his overprotective lectures, "be advised that I was armed and paying attention to my surroundings."

Another of those weary sighs. "Good."

She smiled—couldn't help herself. "I'll take that as a compliment."

"I'd prefer you didn't go prowling around so late at night."

A laugh popped out before she could stop it. "You sound like my father."

A soft chuckle whispered across the line. "You at home now? Doors locked? Alarm activated?"

"Yes. Yes. And yes."

"We'll talk more about this tomorrow. 'Night, Ro."

"'Night, Billy."

She stared at the phone for a long moment after the call had ended. She suddenly wished he were here.

This damn place got lonely sometimes.

Eleven

"Stay."

Freud glanced up at Rowan, his eyes telling her he really, really wanted to take off after whatever had torn through the underbrush not ten feet from where they stood. Like the well-trained animal he was, he stayed put despite his instincts urging him to give chase.

"Good boy."

Rowan gazed out over the lake. The underbrush was thick in this area. Trees towered overhead, their limbs bare for the winter. Five months ago she had come back to this spot for the first time in years. Her father had been murdered only weeks before and she'd been settling into life as the undertaker. Adjusting to living in Winchester again, as well as the funeral home, where she'd grown up. She'd dreamed of her sister every night, so coming here was a natural extension of the turmoil that was her emotions.

This was where her sister's body had been found twenty-seven years ago. This was also where the remains of Julian's daughter, Alisha, had been discovered. During her visit to this place on that early-spring day, Rowan had dropped her cell phone and, when recovering it, she'd found the bones tangled among the weeds and roots. The investigation that ensued had determined that Alisha had died on the same day as Raven. The only unanswered question was who had killed her.

Julian would have Rowan believe her father had killed the seventeen-year-old after learning she had murdered Raven, but Rowan did not believe him. Julian wanted her to doubt her father and she refused to allow him to undermine the memories of the only real family she'd had from age twelve until a few months ago. Well, she'd had Billy. He had always been like family to her, but her father had been her only living blood relative.

Rowan walked closer to the water's edge, something she rarely did. After Raven's death, she had been terrified of the water—of even taking a bath. She had grown up believing her sister had accidently drowned in this lake. The fear of meeting that same fate had been a growing, pulsing nightmare that consumed her life. Rowan had dreamed of being dragged into the water with her dead sister. That fear had kept her away from pools and beaches. But now she knew her sister hadn't accidentally drowned. She had been murdered by Alisha Addington. Lured to this place and held under the water until her lungs filled with water and the life slipped from her small, thin body.

Anger tightened in Rowan's belly. Their mother had brought Julian Addington into their lives. Raven's death was *her* fault. Was that why she killed herself less than five months later? Had the guilt eaten at her like a cancer? Had their father known?

So many questions. So few answers.

A low growl issued from deep within Freud's throat. Rowan tensed. The sound of leaves crunching and dried grass cracking pierced the quiet morning air. Rowan's right hand went to the small of her back. She'd gotten in the habit of tucking her weapon there whenever she carried it. Hours of practice had enabled her to draw it smoothly from that position and to fire with lethal accuracy.

She turned slowly and spotted the form weaving through the trees.

Female.

A wisp of blond hair peeked from beneath the black scarf wrapped around the woman's head, and dark glasses shielded her eyes. But it was the sleek blouse and elegant trousers that first identified the woman for Rowan.

Anna Prentice Addington.

Freud recognized her scent about the same time Rowan visually identified her. His stance went from ready to lunge, to relaxed but guarded.

Rowan had tried to make it a point not to run into the lady. She hadn't expected to have her show up here, but really she should have. Her daughter had died here. Like Rowan, she had questions. She wanted answers.

"Good morning, Dr. DuPont." Anna paused a couple of yards away. "I didn't anticipate running into anyone out here on a Sunday morning."

Rowan supposed that was a reasonable conclusion. Most folks were in church by now or at their favorite Sunday-morning breakfast spot. Beyond setting up a funeral in one of the local churches, Rowan hadn't been to church since her father's funeral. Before that, she couldn't even remember the last time she'd walked through the doors of a house of God. She'd scuttled that relationship long ago. She and God hadn't gotten along since Rowan was twelve. She didn't see that standoff changing anytime soon.

"I guess I had the same idea." Rowan glanced back at the water. She was closer than she preferred to be and her nerves were vibrating, largely due to the presence of this woman. Instinctively, she moved away from the water's edge. Anna's husband was a killer; her daughter had been a killer. Who knew what she was capable of.

"Your mother was afraid of the water, too."

The unexpected announcement jerked Rowan's attention back to her. "How would you know that?"

"I read many interesting facts in her file."

Oh, yes. The woman claimed to have found certain files that had belonged to her ex-husband, including Norah DuPont's file. If Anna Addington could be believed, Norah had been Julian's patient before becoming his lover. She had suffered from multiple personality disorder.

Rowan did not believe this woman any more than she trusted her motives.

"Enjoy your visit, Mrs. Addington." Rowan walked past her, taking a wide berth.

"He's not dead, you know."

Rowan hesitated and turned back to her despite wanting to keep walking. There was no need to ask who she meant. Julian. Rowan had shot him. Right here, in this very place. "How can you be certain?"

The lady wanted a reaction, but Rowan wasn't giving her what she wanted, and was instead turning the question back on her.

"He's moved certain resources. Very recently."

Careful not to show her surprise, Rowan held her gaze. "How do you know this?"

"We had an overseas account—actually we had many, but this one I had forgotten about. My CPA called to tell me it was emptied and closed recently. Since I didn't close it, he must have. There is no other explanation."

Still refusing to show interest, Rowan asked, "Have you informed the FBI?"

"Of course. I called Agent Dressler on Friday. Didn't he tell you?"

Rowan resisted the urge to laugh. "I'm sure you're aware that I am a person of interest in the case. I am the last person Agent Dressler would inform of any new developments in the investigation."

"I thought you might feel more comfortable knowing that he's in Switzerland."

"Your husband—"

"Ex-husband," she corrected.

"Ex-husband," Rowan replied, acquiescing, "could have had someone handle the transaction for him. I'm sure he's aware that the FBI is watching carefully for the use of his passport, as well as for his face to be picked up on international facial-recognition software."

Anna's gaze narrowed. "Agent Dressler said the same thing. Are you sure he didn't tell you about the account?"

"Goodbye, Mrs. Addington." Rowan gave the woman her back once more. She had no desire to play her games.

Addington's driver, Garret something or other, waited at the car. Rowan wondered why he hadn't accompanied his employer down to the water. She was well over sixty, and trudging through the underbrush wasn't exactly a leisurely Sunday-morning stroll.

When Rowan reached the funeral home, Billy was waiting for her. He'd said they would talk this morning. Usually he called before driving over. Apparently, he'd wanted to surprise her. She hoped the bag in his hand meant he'd brought breakfast. She hadn't even bothered with a coffee before driving to the lake this morning.

"I swear you have someone spying on me."

He held up the bag. "Because I brought your favorite breakfast sandwich?"

She made a face. "No coffee?"

He grinned that lopsided tilt that had the strangest effect on her pulse lately and passed her the bag. "I'll grab the coffee."

She unlocked the door while he grabbed the drink carrier from the cab of his truck. Freud trotted inside as she deactivated the alarm. Billy waited for her to lock up and then followed her upstairs.

"I have some photos to show you," she said. "This is what I found at Herman's house." She figured she might as well tell him before he bothered to ask.

"Can we eat while we look?"

She grinned. Growing up, he'd always been hungry. "We can."

Rowan gave Freud his breakfast while Billy arranged their food and coffee on the kitchen counter. The coffee was hot and strong, and Rowan savored it for a moment before nibbling at her sandwich. Billy did the same, only he surveyed the photos she had spread on the counter as he ate.

"Holy cow," he muttered. "So the dead guy did know your mother."

"My father, too, evidently." The bites of sandwich hardened in her belly like rocks. Would her father have knowingly associated with a killer? Did he understand how this man had felt about his wife?

Not possible.

Billy hummed a questioning note. "There's always the chance neither of them knew what he was."

Wouldn't she love to learn that was the case? But Rowan had already been faced with too many disillusionments to go down that path. "I stopped believing in Santa a long time ago, Billy."

"Then you've already decided your parents are the bad guys."

When he put it that way, her conclusions sounded harsh. "My mother, not necessarily my father, and I'm only going on the evidence in front of me. It's fairly difficult to deny."

There was no ignoring the photographs.

"Things are not always what they seem, Ro."

The man was preaching to the choir. "I'm well aware but I doubt we'll ever know for sure."

Herman was dead. She refused to trust anything Julian told her. Who else was there to ask? No one she had found.

"I have some news."

She searched his face. Had Dressler called him with an update or was he talking about his two homicides? She hadn't been able to reach April Jones. Instinct nagged at Rowan again where those two cases were concerned. "What sort of news?"

"The engineers checked the cave—we can go inside. I was thinking after Mr. Harvey's funeral we could go have a look. The evidence techs are doing a sweep this morning."

Anticipation chased away the frustration she had felt after this morning's confrontation with Anna Addington. This was very good news. "I would very much like to see if there's anything useful in that cave."

It wasn't that she was looking forward to clambering around beneath the side of a mountain, but if Sanchez/ Santos had left any evidence there she wanted desperately to find it. Anything to clear up at least some aspect of this mystery.

Billy set aside his coffee cup. "Have you given any thought to how far you want to go with this?"

"What do you mean?" The way he studied her made her uncomfortable.

"Your parents are gone, Ro. Will it change anything if you find all the answers?"

She had wrestled with that question more than once. "Does it matter if my mother was involved with one or more killers?"

He waited while she considered her own question. She kept the biggest one to herself. *Will it change how I feel if I learn my father killed another human?*

"Not really," she confessed. "Norah has been dead for a very long time. I've already come to terms with the idea that it was her involvement with Julian that took my sister's life, that turned mine upside down and killed my father."

This was the hard part. Allowing her mind to go

back to when she was a child. How could her life have been such a lie? All the stories, all the research trips—all of those excuses were lies. Norah evidently lied most of the time. A carefully constructed cover for her heinous extracurricular activities.

"But I need to know for me." It hurt that she couldn't tell him what Julian had said about her father killing Alisha. She desperately needed to prove that was wrong and she couldn't bear the idea of Billy considering the idea that her father might have been a murderer.

Was she wrong not to share that painful possibility with Billy? Would he understand her reasoning when she did tell him? She was undecided about the answer to the former, but the answer to the latter was an absolute no. Billy would not understand her inability to trust him with anything.

"If that's what you want and the answers are out there," he assured her, "we'll find them."

Rowan had never been more grateful for Billy's support than she was now. He was the one person she could rely on.

Then why not tell him?

"I went to the lake this morning."

The expression on Billy's face loudly announced his disapproval.

She ignored the unspoken rebuke. "While I was there, I ran into Mrs. Addington. Did Dressler tell you Julian had moved certain resources?" She had a feeling he had not. Either way, the question took the immediate pressure off her other worries. "The ex-wife claims her CPA caught the movement. I reminded her Julian could have had someone else acting on his behalf. Closing an account in Switzerland doesn't mean Julian is there by any means."

Billy shook his head, irritation flaring in his eyes. "Dressler didn't mention any new developments."

"Maybe Dressler's not convinced it was Julian, either."

"I'm not sure Addington would allow that much distance between the two of you."

Billy's point was a reasonable one, if one she'd rather not hear. "He's not going to walk into any situations where he might be trapped. As much as he wants me for whatever reason, his freedom means far more to him."

"He's waiting for the right opportunity."

Rowan didn't argue. Billy was right.

Before this was over, there would be a final show-down of sorts.

Twelve

The Harvey funeral and burial went off without a hitch. Charlotte was happy to take care of closing up at the funeral home while Rowan dressed to go into that cave with Billy. She wore a pair of skinny jeans that fit more like leggings, with tube socks and high-top hiking boots that would help ensure no critters managed to wiggle their way into her pants leg. A T-shirt and a heavy pullover sweatshirt, along with a pair of gloves stuck in her back pocket, and she was good to go. At the last minute she decided to braid her hair.

She gave Freud a goodbye pat, slung her bag over her shoulder and hurried downstairs. She would have loved to take Freud along but it was a potential crime scene. Having her dog digging around could be a problem.

Billy pulled into the parking lot as she set the alarm and locked up. Charlotte and the cleaning team were gone already. It was Sunday. No one wanted to hang around any longer than necessary.

She climbed into the passenger side of Billy's truck. "Did the evidence techs find anything?"

He hadn't called, but then she supposed he hadn't wanted to interrupt her during a funeral. Her seat belt was snapped into place and he'd rolled onto the street before he answered, sending her tension level over the moon.

"I have to call Dressler."

His resigned and weary tone told Rowan it had been a long day and it was far from over.

"You found something." Her heart was pounding before the words were out of her mouth.

"There are bones, Ro. Lots and lots of bones."

Bones. Oh, Jesus. "Okay. I suppose it makes sense that the bones go with the faces and those bizarre books he made of skin."

"That's what I'm thinking. Under the circumstances I assume Dressler's people will want to do the exhumation and lab work."

"Of course." A massive undertaking such as this one would consume tremendous resources. Rowan was grateful Billy's department wouldn't be saddled with that responsibility. The flip side was that he would lose control over the evidence and would be at Dressler's mercy where information was concerned. Still, as a member of the Addington task force, he would be briefed on the findings. At some point, anyway.

"Meanwhile I have most of my department focused on those two homicides."

Once again she felt responsible for the enormous weight on his shoulders. She had brought nothing but trouble his way since her return. Hopefully these latest two murders weren't a part of the trouble she had ushered to his door.

"Anything new?" she asked.

"None of Henegar's friends or family can imagine anyone killing him, especially in such a depraved manner. Same with Thackerson. No one knows of any enemies either of them had. No trouble we've been able to find."

"What about the autopsies?" There was always the possibility that the bodies would provide some sort of evidence besides time, cause and manner of death.

"Won't have the preliminaries back until tomorrow or Tuesday. Tox screens will take even longer. For now, we've got a lot of nothing."

"Insurance policies?"

"Henegar had one. One hundred and fifty thousand. The wife's the beneficiary, of course." Billy made the turn that would take them out of downtown Winchester.

"What about Thackerson's daughter?" Money was a powerful motivator.

"No insurance policy but the man had a couple hundred thousand bucks in his safe. And the store, of course."

"Any other heirs?"

Billy shook his head. "Not for Thackerson. Henegar has grown sons but the wife is the only beneficiary on the insurance policy."

Rowan felt certain Billy had already considered this but she asked, anyway. "When did the insurance policy go into effect?"

"Ten years ago. One hundred and fifty thousand would be a lot to Wanda. Stan believed in living frugally. There may be money in savings, as well."

"Any marriage issues?" Wanda was considerably younger than her husband. It was possible she'd gotten involved with someone else. "Wanda has no children of her own. Maybe that had become a problem."

"We're still looking into the more personal dynamics of their relationship." He glanced at Rowan. "Folks don't like to speak out of school about a deacon or his wife."

Some things never changed.

"What's the Thackerson woman's name?" Rowan tried to recall if she had gone to school with a Thackerson but she didn't remember anyone by that name.

"Sue Ellen. She's thirty."

Which would explain why Rowan didn't remember her. "Married? Kids? Money problems? Job worries?"

The more questions she asked, the guiltier she felt for taking any of Billy's time. Homicide cases could be overwhelming. For a department as small as Billy's to have two at the same time… Well, it was no party.

"Married and divorced a couple of times. No kids. She was in and out of trouble as a teenager. Petty theft, possession of marijuana. A couple of DUIs, one speeding ticket and another marijuana charge as an adult. She lives in that trailer park over on Mingo Road. Drives a clunker. And she's unemployed at the moment."

"They both have potential motives."

"They do. But they also have alibis for the times of the murders."

"Do they know each other?" One was thirty-five, the other thirty. Maybe they remembered each other from school. What was she thinking? This was Winchester. Everyone knew everyone else. But then, she didn't remember either one. Giving herself grace, she had blocked many things from those years.

"No connection that we've found. Wanda dropped out of school when she was fifteen so they weren't in school together." Billy eased to the side of the road. "But bear in mind that we're just getting started. We still have a lot of questions to ask and a lot of fact-checking to do."

Rowan didn't envy him the process. "I will bear that in mind, Chief." She flashed him a smile. "And you know I'm always happy to assist."

"I'll probably take you up on that offer more often than not, Dr. DuPont."

"I look forward to the challenge."

As she emerged from his truck she noted the official vehicles already on-site. Two patrol cars and the crime-scene-unit van. She recognized the fourth vehicle as the coroner's. "Burt's here?"

"He's having a look." Billy glanced at her. "Mostly out of curiosity, I think."

"Like me." Dressler would not appreciate Billy allowing her onto *his* crime scene.

"This involves you, Ro. I see your being here as a necessary part of what I have to do to conduct this investigation."

Always on her side. "Thanks."

With all the official folks who had gone through, the path was tramped down to a degree, making the going somewhat easier. Rowan craned her neck to get a look at tent city as they passed the gap in the trees that allowed a glimpse. At least a dozen tents stood in the clearing. She hoped the inhabitants had sleeping bags. The nights were getting colder all the time.

A crime-scene perimeter had been set up well before they reached the cave entrance. Three...no, four crows sat high in the trees. A cold, shrill caw pulled her attention to another tree where two more crows were perched. One cawed again, his head swiveling at the activities going on below. Rowan stared at the dark-eyed creatures and resisted the urge to shiver. She'd never been the superstitious type, but seeing the crows still hanging about made her wonder if some of those old tales she'd heard as a child were true. How did the story go? One crow meant bad luck, but six? Six meant death was nearby.

Maybe there was something to that old saying.

An officer Rowan didn't recognize was maintaining the perimeter. Billy spoke to him as they crossed beneath the yellow tape. At the lean-to-style campsite, another officer was stationed at the entrance.

"Chief." He gave Billy a nod. "Ma'am," he said to Rowan. She smiled and gave him a nod.

"I'll be right behind you," Billy assured her.

Rowan hunkered down and made her way through the opening. Inside, she straightened and sidestepped to give Billy plenty of room to join her. Burt's voice echoed from somewhere deeper in the cave. Battery-operated lights had chased away the darkness, revealing the rocky floor and walls.

"This way."

Billy moved forward and Rowan followed. It was necessary to watch each step. There was no level ground. After rounding a bend in the cave, she spotted a larger room where more lights had been stationed. Burt and the evidence techs were deep in conversation.

Beyond the men gathered in the center of the space, Rowan's gaze settled on the images on the cave walls—stick figures had been drawn all the way around. Some were standing, others appeared to be lying on the ground. There were symbols and notations not readily translatable.

"Have you photographed the images?" She would need to study those in order to determine the meaning. A couple looked vaguely familiar.

"We did." He gestured to the mounds all the way around the space, like a circular burial ground. "At first we thought it might be some sort of ancient Native American burial ground, but pieces of clothing were found among the bones and those items were newer so that scenario was ruled out."

Burt turned toward them. "I'm guessing there are at least two dozen, maybe more, sets of remains here."

"This could be his dump site," Ro said, more to herself than to anyone else.

"Makes sense." Billy scrubbed a hand over his jaw. "Also makes me sick."

It was difficult to learn that a serial killer had been living in your midst and taking victims—wherever they'd come from. Since Billy had no unsolved missing-persons cases, the victims were obviously from some other town, maybe even from a different state. Dressler could very well be able to identify a large number based on the files he had on this previously unidentified serial killer.

Hopefully the find would at least provide closure for the families of the victims.

Rowan leaned close to Billy and, for his ears only, asked, "Have they found anything related to Norah?"

Billy shook his head. "Not yet. I can't put off Dressler beyond tomorrow morning. Once he takes over, we won't be allowed anywhere near this place."

"I understand. I'll have a look around now."

"I'll catch up with my techs." Billy gave her a nod

and then joined the huddle of evidence techs. Two Rowan recognized, the other she did not.

Rowan walked around the perimeter, careful to stay off the mounds. Had he degloved his victims here? Perhaps skinned them entirely before he buried them. Used other parts for his special stew that Mr. Utter had enjoyed so much? She glanced around the space, then studied the images on the wall. The drawings were very simplistic. She counted them. Twenty-six. Oh, yes. This was his dump site. Most likely every one of those preserved faces went with a set of remains buried here.

What would her mother—her parents—have in common with this man? The idea made no sense at all.

What was Julian trying to show her? What did any of this even mean?

Another half hour and Rowan was ready to go. There was nothing more she could learn here without exhuming the remains and that wasn't going to happen. Dressler's people would be moving on that step.

When they reached his truck, Billy hesitated at her door without opening it. "I know this is difficult, Ro, but we will figure it out."

"I really hope so, Billy. Every time I think I have some aspect of my parents' secret lives figured out, something else crops up." She shook her head. "It's like I didn't even know them."

"He wants you to feel that way," Billy reminded her. "He wants you to feel disconnected and lost. But you are not disconnected and you're damn sure not lost." He reached out, trailed the fingers of his right hand down her cheek. "He can't take the memories you have away from you unless you let him."

She smiled, appreciated the warmth in his touch.

She clutched his fingers with her own and gave them a squeeze. "You're right. I will not allow him to take the good memories from me. My father loved me. I know he did. I don't know as much about my mother but that's okay. I've learned to live without her."

"There you go." He opened her door. "When he figures out he can't tear you down, maybe he'll let you go."

Rowan climbed into the seat. She hoped Billy was right. But she knew Julian too well to believe he would ever give up on anything he really wanted. He was not a very good loser. Julian liked to win—he wanted to be right in all things.

She scanned the woods. The partially barren trees surrounded by the underbrush so thick one could hardly walk through it. Two of the crows had followed her and Billy to the road. They sat on a bare branch a few yards away, watching, warning. This was not a good place.

She thought of the poor people living in that tent city and wondered how many had disappeared from there.

"Do you think the people who live in that tent city would talk to you?"

"Lincoln and another of my detectives are working on that. I don't know if they'll learn anything useful. But we won't know until we try."

She wondered if Julian had been to that cave. Did he know about all the victims? About Sanchez/Santos? Was he a part of this?

Billy slid behind the wheel and closed his door.

Rowan studied his profile as he drove back toward Winchester proper. She thought of the way he'd touched her only a moment ago. Over the past five or six months things had changed somewhat between them. Nothing significant, only subtle nuances. A certain look. A special touch, like him tracing her cheek moments ago. Without even thinking, she had curled her fingers around his whenever he reached to help her. Had he noticed the slight shift? The whole idea terrified her.

As much as she would love to explore something more with Billy—God knew she had lusted after him from the time she first understood what a real kiss was—how could she risk the relationship they already shared? More important, how could she risk drawing him further into this insanity with Julian? He would be jealous of Billy just as he had been of her father. Julian would have already noted the subtle deepening of their relationship. He never missed a thing.

Billy glanced at her as if he'd felt her watching him. She pushed away the worries about whatever was happening between them.

"I have some things to follow up on," he said, "but if you're free later, we could talk about the case some more. Maybe go over the crime scenes together."

"Sure." Anything to take her mind off all those remains and that photo of her mother with the man who likely killed them. Apparently, she needed to keep her mind occupied to prevent following paths she had no business going down.

"If you wanted to disappear for a while. You know, just get away from all this," he explained, "the people who care about you would understand."

Rowan stared at that handsome profile again. "Are you suggesting I dump the funeral home on Charlotte and go somewhere to hide until this is over?"

He didn't answer her for a long time. Then he said,

"Yes." He braked to a stop at an intersection. He turned to her, looked her straight in the eye. "You would be safe that way, Ro. Every new discovery confirms one thing for me—you are not safe as long as he knows where you are."

She looked away first. He didn't look away until he rolled forward, beyond the intersection.

"He would wait me out. He's persistent that way."

"You're that convinced he won't give up or lose interest."

She didn't look at Billy this time. "Probably not. He has nothing left to lose now. To his way of thinking, I ruined everything. All of this is my fault. He might as well have his revenge and whatever else it is he wants."

"I see."

Rowan stared at him, those two seemingly innocuous words making her uneasy. "You see what?"

"What you're saying is that you won't be safe until he's dead."

He had pulled up in front of the funeral home and pushed the gearshift into Park before she gave him the only answer there was to give. "Probably not."

"That settles it, then."

She was afraid to ask what he meant with that statement, but then he told her.

"If I get the chance, I'm killing him."

Thirteen

Rowan rarely used the dining room. The only company she ever entertained was Billy and they generally ate in the living room. *Entertained* was a stretch. They kept each other company. Talked about work and who was doing what around town. They were comfortable.

Tonight dinner had been one of their mainstays, pizza. Delivered by the family-owned diner downtown. The remains of the delicious oven-roasted veggie pie were still in the box on the coffee table. Why bother with a formal setting like the dining room when it was just the two of them? Billy was like family, not company.

But the big family table was perfect for spreading out crime-scene photos and reports. The perfect conference room. Cases had been discussed in this room all summer. Though the local crime rate was usually quite low, she couldn't deny a surge of exhilaration whenever Billy mentioned wanting to discuss a case. Particularly since, until now, none of them had involved her since the encounter with Julian all those months ago.

She passed Billy a beer and tapped the first photo

from the Henegar murder scene. "This one is different from the other one."

Billy shrugged. "Henegar was nailed to the floor and Thackerson was tied to the bed. The end result is the same." He took a swallow of cold beer.

"True, but you said the nail gun used on Henegar wasn't at the scene. In fact, he had no power tools beyond a Skilsaw and a drill driver in his garage."

"That's right."

Rowan gestured to the photos of Thackerson. "He was tied to his bed with nylon rope—none of which was found on the property."

"The killer brought the supplies he needed to secure his victims. It happens all the time."

Rowan pointed a finger at him. "True. But more important, the actual weapons he used to kill his victims were something at the scene. The Bible at the Henegar scene and the soap at the Thackerson scene."

Billy's gaze collided with hers. "Both were personal to the victim. Stan's own Bible was used. The soap was the only kind in Barney's bathroom so we know it must have been his preferred brand. The killer knew these items would be there. More important, he was aware they meant something to the victims."

"Precisely." Rowan felt the surge of adrenaline that came when a case started to come together. "Which would suggest that we're looking at either a single perp or two perps who worked as a team. Either way, the killer or killers knew the victims. But that deduction alone doesn't explain why the scenes were treated so differently. The first scene was relatively clean. He didn't leave the nail gun or anything else he brought with him. Most people have watched enough TV crime

shows to know that anything they leave behind be-
comes evidence. And," she said when Billy would have
spoken, "everyone knows the purchase of goods can
often lead the police right back to him or her. We've
confirmed the nylon rope was newly purchased because we found the packaging in the backyard. That
was a foolish mistake."

"What we presume to be the packaging," Billy corrected.

Rowan gave him that one. "The perpetrator also
knew where the security camera system was in Thackerson's store. The videotape had been removed. Further proof that he either knew Thackerson well enough
to have some idea where the security equipment was
housed, or he was a pro who knew to look for cam-
eras." She tapped another photo, this one a close-up
of one of Thackerson's wrists restrained by the nylon
rope. "If you study the photos of the wrists and ankles,
you note that the knots are not the same. The first two
are different from each other, but by the third one he'd
figured it out so three and four are the same."

Billy looked from one photo to the next. "The killer
was nervous or new at tying up a victim. He hadn't
done this before."

Rowan counted off what they had so far. "We can
safely say that the killer or killers were acquainted with
both victims. He—they—knew the victims, knew their
homes and understood certain things that were important to them. Though we can't be certain the relevance
of the soap, we know it was the only brand Thackerson purchased."

"We're on the same page so far," Billy agreed.

"Now, let's look more closely at the victims. Henegar didn't fight the way Thackerson did. My guess is he either suffered some physical reaction to the stress—a heart attack or stroke, which disabled him to some degree—or the perpetrator drugged him." Rowan realized as she said the words the reasoning for this. "Whatever Henegar's crimes, he didn't deserve the torture the same way Thackerson did. Thackerson needed to feel the pain and fear. Or the killer needed him to. Another indication that the killer or killers were somehow involved in the victims' lives."

Billy's brow furrowed. "I hadn't considered that aspect, but it makes sense."

Something about the two scenes still niggled at her. "I think the overall difference in the scenes confirms that we have two different perps. This one—" she tapped a photo from the Thackerson scene "—was far more confident. He wasn't afraid Thackerson would best him. He must have known about any frailties he had."

Billy looked from the photos to Rowan. "Burt told you about his MS? I meant to tell you but it slipped my mind."

So, she was right. "No. I wasn't aware Mr. Thackerson had multiple sclerosis. The muscle weakness may have prevented him from effectively fighting his attacker, though he would be able to try to resist his restraints since he obviously wasn't to the point of needing a wheelchair yet."

"He was diagnosed only recently. Even his daughter said she didn't know."

"But someone did, or knew him well enough to understand his physical limitations whether he was aware of the reason for those limitations or not."

Billy reached out, touched a photo of Henegar's face and all those crumpled Bible pages shoved into his mouth. "I'm with you on the theory of two killers. I can't argue with a single conclusion you've made."

Rowan leaned forward, looked from the photos of one scene to the next. "The feel of these scenes is familiar to me somehow. The soap and the victim being tied to the bed doesn't ring any bells for me, but the pages from the Bible and being nailed to the floor..." A memory nudged her again and the air trapped in her lungs. "Oh, Jesus. This could have been Julian."

No. No. No. She didn't want two more murders to be about her. She couldn't bear to keep bringing this nightmare down on Billy.

Billy's gaze locked with hers. "You remember something he said or did?"

"Possibly. I couldn't download any of the Addington files from the system in Nashville, but April allowed me to have a look. Dressler certainly wasn't sharing. I do remember there were two victims, maybe three, a long time ago. Perhaps twenty years. Julian had constructed makeshift crosses with two-by-fours. He nailed the victims to those crosses and poured rock salt down their throats." She shook her head. "I should have remembered. This very well could be him. It's possible he wants me to see that he can still reach into my life even with everyone around me looking for him."

Five months. He had been gone for five months. She had thought that maybe—just maybe—he was dead. She pushed out of her chair, scrubbed at her aching forehead. Her brain was tired of thinking about him. Defeat tugged at her. Of course he wasn't dead. She should only be so lucky. He wasn't dead and he wanted her to know it.

No reason for her to be surprised. Julian wouldn't go down so easily. But now two people who likely didn't know Rowan any more than she knew them were dead because of her and Julian's need to prove something to her.

"He killed more than a hundred people, Ro." Billy stood, stretched his back and came around to her side of the table. "How could you hope to remember all the different MOs and the way he staged each scene?"

That much was true. Julian had changed the way the world viewed serial killers. He had used numerous MOs. But she should have remembered. She knew him better than anyone except maybe his ex-wife. The killing rampage he'd started five months ago in Nashville was somehow her fault. And it was her responsibility to stop him.

No matter what Billy and Dressler believed.

This was about her and she had to find the way to end it.

Focus. First and foremost, she needed focus and objectivity. Her education in the field of psychiatry and her experience in homicide had taught her well. She needed to think, to analyze his full intent and to determine his method. Emotion was her enemy. The feelings of anger and regret and guilt would only get in her way.

Keen focus, now, starting this minute, was essential.

"Whether he's behind these murders or not, he isn't the one who did this." She gestured to the table and the photos spread there. "The inexperience and uncertainty are obvious. The person or persons who executed these two men will have left evidence. You only have to find it."

"If we find that person or persons, maybe we'll find a trail to Addington."

"Perhaps. But he won't make it easy." Julian was far too brilliant to be caught so effortlessly. She decided to keep that conclusion to herself. Billy wouldn't appreciate hearing her deduction about Julian's intelligence level. She hated to admit it, but it was true. Damn him.

Moving on, she said, "Tell me about the next of kin in each of these murders." They had talked about this before but Rowan needed to hear any new details and it wouldn't hurt to refresh her memory on the older details. So much had been going on she wasn't so sure she trusted her recall ability just now.

"Wanda," he began as he guided Rowan into the living room, away from all those photos, "was a quiet girl, according to the family and friends we've interviewed. She was anxious to start her own life and to have children of her own so she married at fifteen."

"A man two decades older who already had two sons and apparently didn't want any more." Those details had struck Rowan from the beginning. There was always the chance Wanda simply hadn't been able to conceive. Either way, she had grown up raising another woman's children. A worthy accomplishment, without doubt, but had doing so made her happy…made her feel complete?

Rowan curled up in her favorite chair while Billy settled in her father's chair, with nothing but a small table between them. He reached for a leftover slice of pizza. She watched him eat. It wasn't like she'd never seen him eat before. But there was something immensely comforting about sitting here with him eating pizza. Comforting and *comfortable*. He was the one person in the world who made her feel completely at ease. Utterly relaxed.

There was a time when Julian had made her feel that way. Something else she would not share with Billy, though she suspected he was aware of how very close she and Julian had once been.

Rowan looked away to avoid Billy glancing at her and reading the thought in her eyes. She had felt nothing for Julian other than respect and admiration. She had adored him as a dear friend and mentor. There was never anything even remotely sexual between them. What she felt for Billy lingered on the fringes of sexual. Deep down it always had. She realized that now. As a girl she'd lusted after him like every other girl in school. But they had always been merely friends. Good friends, like family, but nothing more. In the past few months that closeness had gradually deepened. Felt more important, more intense. Neither she nor Billy had set out to prompt that attraction—at least she didn't think he had. It had come naturally.

They danced so close to that line—the one that stood between friendship and something more, something deeper, more physical and emotional at the same time. But crossing that line could damage the amazing friendship they had shared since they were children.

Could she take that risk?

"None of her friends mentioned Wanda having any issues with her husband."

Rowan blinked, pushed away the troubling thoughts. "Maybe she was afraid to talk about it. Are most of her friends also members of the church where her husband was a deacon?"

He nodded slowly, as if contemplating the implications of that question in terms of how much Wanda might share with those particular friends. People had different levels of friendship. Church friends were rarely shown the dirty laundry.

"All her friends are church friends."

Rowan smiled. "All the ones you know about are church friends. There will be at least one other, even if they've drifted apart over the years. Someone with whom she dared to share her deepest, darkest secrets."

His gaze lingered on Rowan's lips, then he said, "What about you, Ro? Who's privy to your deepest, darkest secrets?"

At one time she would have said Julian. The reality of how very foolish she had been twisted like a knife in her chest. "You. Who else?" The smile that stretched across his face told her the answer had made him happy, though it wasn't entirely true—at least not recently. She couldn't bring herself to share certain thoughts and feelings. "What about Sue Ellen Thackerson? She's single. Young. She probably has quite a few friends."

"A few," he agreed. "They all said the same thing— she never got along with her daddy. He didn't like her lifestyle so he cut her off financially after her last divorce."

"Really?" Interesting, and brimming with motive.

Billy finished off his pizza and chased it with a swallow of beer. "She was a bit of a wild child growing up and she didn't change a whole lot after she hit adulthood. No violent crimes. No domestic issues to my knowledge during her marriages."

"She's the one who lives in the trailer park." Billy had mentioned she was unemployed and drove a clunker. More motive.

"According to the landlord, she was served an eviction notice a couple of days ago."

Motive and serious stress in her life. "Do you mind if I talk to one or both? I'd like to see their reactions to certain questions."

"You're the expert. I didn't deputize you for nothing." He grinned. "Besides, I've offered you a position in the department about three times now."

Her arms went around her waist, an instinctive need to camouflage herself. "I like helping you, Billy. And I'm happy to do it anytime. But I don't trust my instincts enough to go official with this arrangement beyond a case-by-case basis."

"Your instincts are as sharp as ever, Ro. Don't allow Addington to keep you doubting yourself forever. Five months is long enough to punish yourself for making a mistake."

That mistake had cost the lives of many people, including her father. But she understood Billy wasn't minimizing the enormity of what had happened with Julian. He just wanted her to trust herself again and to move on. He didn't understand she couldn't move on until Julian had paid for what he'd done.

Until she had the truth.

"I'm working on it," she said, mostly to make him feel better.

After a half minute of silence, he asked, "Are you

thinking that Addington used Wanda and Sue Ellen the way he did Logan Wilburn's sister?"

Wilburn's sister, Juanita, had been a member of the funeral home's cleaning team. Julian had used her to gain access to the funeral home, to Rowan's living quarters. He'd tortured and murdered Juanita's brother to remind her of what was at stake.

"It's possible, but frankly, I can't see the point. I don't know either of these women. They're not involved with me or the funeral home, but it feels exactly like it was one or both of them."

"The other side of that is that they both have alibis," he reminded her. "And, like you said, neither of them is associated with you the way Juanita was. No matter how I look at or shake the pieces, it all comes back to those two and that brick wall called an alibi."

"One thing we can be certain of—if this is Julian, he has an agenda. If not to access me in some way, then to distract one or both of us for some reason not discernible just now."

Billy finished off his beer. "Our tattooed man and your mother." He looked at Rowan then. "He doesn't want you to find the truth. It's possible there's more to learn about Addington through Sanchez or Santos, whatever the hell his name was."

"What could he possibly want to hide that's worse than what we've already uncovered about him?" Rowan shook her head, frustration making her want to kick something.

Billy chuckled but the sound held no humor. "Considering what we found at his place, I think I'd be afraid of the answer to that question."

She sighed. "Good point."

"I should get going." Billy stood. "I'm supposed to meet Lincoln to go over a few things."

It was late but a homicide investigation wasn't limited to anyone's schedule. Rowan got to her feet, felt incredibly heavy with the weight of all she didn't know and desperately needed to. "Thanks for the pizza and the company."

He grabbed the pizza box and his empty beer bottle. "I'll take this down as I go." He held up the box, which was way too large for the trash can in her kitchen.

"Thanks. I'll gather up the crime-scene photos for you."

While she shuffled the photos together and packed them into the appropriate file folders, he deposited his beer bottle into the trash in the kitchen and interacted with Freud. The dog loved him.

Rowan loved him.

She stopped, her fingers on the manila folders. The feeling was strong, like the love she'd felt for her father and her sister. But different. She hadn't analyzed the realization too deeply in the past. Honestly, this was the first time the thought had fully formed in her brain. Ideas and conclusions so very close to that thought had bobbed to the surface of the ocean of others flooding her life lately. No matter, it was becoming more and more difficult to deny that her feelings for Billy were strong. He felt something similar. She saw it in the way he looked at her. A lingering glance or touch.

She imagined he was afraid to cross that line, as well.

They would need to talk soon or risk making a mistake during a frantic moment.

She followed him to the door. He settled his hat

into place and she tucked the folders under his arm. "Drive safely."

"Always." He nodded. "'Night, Ro."

"Good night."

She watched him walk down the corridor and then disappear around the corner. The air seemed to change with him gone. Loneliness filled the space she called home, closing around her.

A long hot bath and a good night's sleep was what she needed.

Maybe tomorrow she would help him figure out how two men who hardly knew each other and certainly had little in common got themselves murdered in such a similar manner.

If Julian was involved, what did he hope to gain?

And why hadn't he called her if there was some pending move coming?

Being a fugitive had never stopped him from doing what he wanted before.

Maybe he was dead…or maybe there was a copycat out there trying to gain notoriety using the media frenzy surrounding Julian.

Her cell rang and she had to think a moment where she'd left it.

"Kitchen." She hurried there and picked it up before whoever it was hung up. There was no time to check the screen to identify the caller. "Rowan DuPont."

Silence greeted her.

She stilled, listened for the sound of breathing.

A single breath, so soft she barely heard it. Her jaw hardened. "What do you want?"

More of that burgeoning silence.

"I'm waiting," she said, anger fueling her now. "I'm

sick to death of your games and your hiding. Stop being a coward, Julian. Come out, come out, wherever you are."

A distinct click announced the call had ended.

She shivered. She checked the screen. *Unknown caller.* Bastard. She went to the keypad by the door and checked the security system. Billy had set it downstairs as he left. She double-checked the dead bolts, and then went to the front window to ensure Billy's truck was no longer in the parking lot. He was gone.

Probably a good thing. If he'd still been down there, she might have called him back. If she had called him back, she wasn't sure she could have trusted herself not to use these new feelings as a distraction.

Angry and frustrated, she snagged a beer from the fridge and headed to her room.

That bath was calling her name.

Fourteen

His chair leaning back and his feet propped on the conference table, Billy considered the case board Detective Clarence Lincoln had created. He'd done a damn fine job. Billy was fairly certain even someone like Rowan, with years of big-city homicide experience, would be impressed.

"I've added the points you and Rowan discussed," Lincoln said, gesturing to his latest additions to the board. "We'll be reinterviewing friends and family again starting tomorrow. We've narrowed down a sizable lot of trace evidence—hairs, cloth fibers—but none that have pointed us in a particular direction. I talked to Yance again. He says there had to be more than two hundred thou in that safe."

Yancey Quinn was the assistant manager at Thackerson's Mini Market. He was reopening the place tomorrow and would be running it until the estate cleared probate. "Did he actually see the money or is he guessing based on things Barney told him?"

Lincoln sat down across the table from Billy. "He claims he helped him count it one night and there was three hundred and twelve thousand dollars. That was maybe a month ago. It's his life savings. What his daughter didn't go through, anyway."

Billy shook his head. "Why on earth would Barney keep that kind of money in his safe?"

Lincoln shrugged. "He didn't trust banks. He had a bank account—the checkbook was in his desk. I guess he had to for operating his business. Think about it, it wasn't like anyone was going to carry off that safe. Hell, it's six feet tall and four feet wide. No telling how much it weighs."

"Sounds like he was trying to avoid paying Uncle Sam his fair share." In Billy's experience, when a business owner avoided the bank, he was evading tax liability and/or trying to hide criminal activity.

"That could be but Yance didn't mention tax evasion."

"Could he have given some to his daughter in the past month?"

Lincoln shook his head. "Yance said he swore he wasn't giving her another dollar until she got her act together."

Billy ran his fingers through his hair, rubbed at his forehead and the ache that had started there. It was late. Too late for Lincoln to be working on this case or any other. Too late for him. This level of exhaustion prompted mistakes. They didn't need any mistakes. "If Yance is right, someone removed a little over a hundred thou and left the rest. Why would a robber who'd gone to all the trouble of torturing and murdering Barney leave two hundred thousand in the safe?"

"Maybe one who took only what he felt was owed to him."

Billy chuckled, couldn't help himself. "An honorable, murdering thief, huh?"

Lincoln rubbed his eyes and then reached for his coffee. "I should go home. Get some sleep and talk to Yance again tomorrow. See if his story changes after he's had a night to sleep on it."

"We should look more closely at the daughter and at Stan's wife." Rowan was right about those two.

Lincoln nodded. "Those two certainly had the most to gain. They got airtight alibis, though."

"They do," Billy concurred. "Can't argue with an alibi. But we both know it's always possible they hired someone to do the deed."

"There's a thought," Lincoln said. "What about Rowan's suggestion that we might be looking at more of Addington's handiwork?"

"If that's the case all we have to do is figure out who did his dirty work for him. Ro says the kills were far too sloppy to be Addington's personal efforts."

"Sanchez, or Santos, could have friends around here." Lincoln shuddered. "Who knew we had a serial killer living right under our noses? There could be more."

"Makes you think twice about the neighbors you think you know."

"No kidding," Lincoln agreed. "What about that neighbor of his? Utter? You think Sanchez/Santos would have let this guy see where he kept his souvenirs if they hadn't done some serious bonding?"

"That is a very good question, Lincoln. I think you should talk to the man again and see if he's got any skeletons of his own buried around here somewhere."

"Will do. Mrs. Addington came by again today."

Billy finished off his coffee. He winced. "She bring her private detective with her?"

Cash Barton was a retired homicide detective from Los Angeles. He had been following the case of Addington's missing daughter for twenty-seven years. Now he and Addington's former wife were staying in Winchester in hopes of learning who killed the girl. And maybe to be here if Addington showed up again. Billy suspected they would both love to see him take his last breath.

Billy wouldn't mind seeing that himself. In fact, he hoped he had the opportunity to make it happen.

"Nope. She says he's out of town following up on that assets liquidation Dressler told you about."

"He's in Switzerland, I guess." Evidently Mrs. Addington had the resources to send him halfway around the world at the drop of a hat.

"Guess so." Lincoln picked up his coffee cup, made a face and set it aside once more. "She wanted to know if her husband was involved in these two recent murders, considering that we rarely have homicides happen in our quaint little town. She thought he might be playing games with us again."

"Interesting that she would even wonder." Billy sat up, dropped his feet to the floor. "Did she mention anything about the MO seeming familiar?" The news and the local paper had been running stories about the bizarre murders. Far too many details had leaked for Billy's liking.

"No," Lincoln replied. "She was just dropping by for her weekly update. Maybe she threw that question in for good measure."

The woman came by once a week come hell or high

water. Billy recognized his feelings about the former wife of Julian Addington might not be objective, but she was a strange one. He'd hoped that when she took her daughter's remains back to LA for burial that she wouldn't return to Winchester. Less than a week later she was back, staying at the same B & B and checking in with his detectives once a week.

"I know you have a lot on your plate—" Billy almost hated to put this on Lincoln, too, but he was his most trusted and experienced detective "—but keep an eye on her as best you can. I'm not entirely convinced of her motives for staying. For all we know, she could be reporting to Addington. She could be watching Rowan for him. I don't quite know what to make of the woman."

"I got it, Chief." Lincoln cocked his head and looked Billy straight in the eye. "This is going to sound crazy, but is there any chance she could be a killer? With the help of that creepy driver of hers or that former detective?"

"We both grew up here, Linc. Went to university right here in Tennessee, so I realize I'm not like Agent Dressler in that I haven't seen the kinds of things he has, but after listening to Rowan talk about the cases she has been involved with, I'm here to tell you anything is possible. I say we watch her, for no other reason than the possibility that she might be leaking info to Addington."

Lincoln gathered his notes and stood. "I need some sleep."

Billy pushed to his feet. "See you tomorrow. Really good work, by the way."

Lincoln grinned. "Thanks, Chief."

Billy walked back to his office and locked up. He gave a little salute to the cleaning team as he exited the building. He settled his hat into place and descended the steps that fronted city hall. Every time he'd passed this building as a kid he'd told his mom he wanted to be a cop. His father had tried to dissuade him. What parent wouldn't fear for their child's safety? After a few pretty serious injuries on the football field at UT, his parents had decided if he could survive four years of college ball and all those rodeos back home during the summer, he could probably handle being a cop.

Besides, this was Winchester, not Nashville.

He'd had a few close calls, mostly with the drug dealers and manufacturers who cropped up now and then. A hit of the right kind of drug made a man dumb as hell, but damn fearless.

Billy hit the fob and unlocked his truck, climbed in. As he rolled around the square, he was thankful for the peace and quiet despite the rows of cars parked in front of the few cafés that were still open on a Sunday evening. Before heading home, he drove past the funeral home.

The second-floor lights were still on. Rowan was probably pouring over notes about the two murders or sifting through her mother's ramblings in hopes of finding something more that would help her find the truth.

His fingers tightened on the steering wheel. The idea that she would never be safe until Addington was stopped gnawed at him. Who the hell knew what this Sanchez/Santos bastard had been about? Whatever connection he'd had to Rowan's mother, he certainly hadn't bothered Rowan before he died and she'd moved back to Winchester nearly six months ago. He'd had the opportunity. This whole thing was just completely wrong.

Keeping Rowan safe was his top priority and she didn't like to cooperate. Yeah, she was armed and he'd made sure she could use her weapon. She had the best security system available and she had that big-ass dog.

But Addington was smart. Too damn smart. What Billy really wanted was eyes on her at all times.

She would not have it, though. To some degree she was right. His resources at the department were already stretched thin with these two murders.

But he had another resource, one he preferred not to use unless it was absolutely necessary.

No question. This was necessary.

Going out on that particular limb wasn't without its hazards, but he was willing to take the risk.

Fifteen minutes were required to reach his destination. The man he needed to see lived in an old hunting shack halfway to Huntland. The woods on either side of the road were dark and thick. If he hadn't known the area he would have been utterly lost. He took the left that was impossible to see until you were right on top of it.

The gravel road was narrow and all of a mile long. A dim glow filtered past the edges of the curtains on the front windows of the shack. Someone was home. Whether it was Eddie Culver or one of his friends, Billy wouldn't know until he knocked on the door.

He parked, shut off the engine and climbed out. He reached under the seat and palmed his .38. Eddie was a mean bastard these days. Getting booted off the force had changed him. Couldn't trust him completely. But the two of them had an understanding. Eddie owed him and Billy was about to call in one last favor on that marker.

The snap of a shotgun barrel locking into place made Billy freeze. His grip tightened on his .38.

"What the hell do you want?"

Eddie. Billy relaxed. "I have a job for you, Eddie."

Eddie Culver stepped directly in front of Billy, blocking the distant glimmer of light from the shack. "And why would I give one shit about a job from you? I don't work for you anymore, Chief."

"Maybe we should go inside and talk, Eddie. We have some catching up to do."

The silence expanded and the air went way too still.

Finally, Eddie stepped aside, clearing the path to the shack. "After you."

The hair on the back of Billy's neck stood on end as he walked toward the shack with an armed man walking behind him. Never a good scenario.

An ex-cop. A *dirty* ex-cop.

It had been Billy's first year as chief of police. He'd suspected that Eddie and his partner were abusing their power as officers of the law before he was selected as chief. He'd mentioned it to Luther Holcomb, the former chief, once. But Luther had blown off Billy. Five months into his stint as chief, Billy discovered what Eddie and his partner were up to. The partner, Bruce Stratton, ten years Eddie's senior in age and time on the force, was strong-arming certain business owners and demanding money for protection. Eddie went along and took his share. Billy was never able to get one of the business owners to talk, so taking steps to correct the situation was impossible. The shop owners were too afraid of Stratton. Stratton had killed a man not once but twice. Both were righteous kills, but dead was dead and the idea that he might kill one of them terrified the shop owners. Finally, Billy decided his only choice was to watch the two and catch them in the act.

Catch them he did. But things didn't turn out the way he'd expected. Billy had anticipated charges against Stratton, maybe immunity for Culver if he talked. Didn't happen.

Stratton, a widow with no children, put a bullet in his own head. Billy concluded that the man's career was all he had and he had no intention of watching it fall apart. Since the shop owners had all confirmed that Stratton was the main one behind the strong-arming, Billy decided to make Eddie a deal. With twenty years of service in the job under his belt and no other black marks, Billy gave him a choice: resign and clean up his act, or be suspended and face charges.

Smarter than he acted at times, Eddie had taken him up on resigning and cleaning up his act. So far, Billy was reasonably sure the man had stuck by their deal. But he hadn't been happy about it. His luck with finding a new career hadn't exactly panned out and he spent more time unemployed than employed. His grandfather had left him this old shack and the spot of land, which allowed him to squeeze by on little or no income. Once in a while, Billy called upon him for assistance and he always complained. In the end he did the job and did it well, and took the pay. But those rare occasions were their only interactions. Eddie had basically turned into a hermit.

When they reached the shack, Eddie stepped in front

of Billy and opened the door. He didn't speak again until they were inside with the door was closed.

Apparently, Eddie was between jobs again. His beard was full-grown and he looked as if he hadn't seen a bathtub or a shower in at least a week.

"What job?" he snapped.

"A security assignment. I have someone I need you to watch."

Eddie grunted. "And why would I be interested?"

"If you do this, we can call it even. You won't owe me anything else. Clean slate."

The other man's gaze narrowed. "How do I know this time will be any different from the other times I did you a favor?"

"Did I ever tell you that we'd be even on any of the other assignments?"

Eddie stood his shotgun against the wall. "What's so different about this time?"

"This time is personal."

Eddie's eyebrows shot up. "I'm listening."

"I need you to watch after someone. Twenty-four/seven. If there's trouble, you call me. Intervene if you have to. I want her protected at all costs."

"Her?"

"Rowan DuPont."

A grin hitched up one side of his wooly face. "The undertaker's daughter." He laughed. "I guess she's the undertaker now. I heard she brought some trouble with her from up in Nashville. I thought that was over."

Billy shook his head. "Not yet."

"She going to have a problem with me hanging around her all the time?"

This was where things got tricky. "She can't know."

A rusty laugh hitched out of his throat. "So, she doesn't want protection, is that it?"

Billy tamped down his frustration and dredged up a little more patience. "That's it. You up for it or not?"

"I'll need expenses."

Billy nodded. "Fifty bucks a day."

Eddie shrugged. "A hundred works better. You did say day and night."

"A hundred." Billy wasn't going to haggle. He wanted Rowan protected and she wouldn't let him do it.

"Plus any expenses I incur beyond basic sustenance. I may need a rental car. I'll have to swap out regularly to prevent her from getting suspicious."

"All right. Anything else?"

"Depends how long this takes. I'll let you know."

"Don't push me, Eddie. I'm a nice guy but I have my limits."

He laughed more of that rusty sound. "You are a nice guy, Billy. Maybe too nice sometimes. I'll make sure she's safe. You know I'm good at that. When do you want me to start?"

"Tonight. The sooner the better."

Eddie nodded. "Then we'll be even."

"You do the job right and you have my word on it."

"I guess I'd better clean up. I imagine you can see yourself out, Chief."

Billy started to turn back to the door but hesitated. "I appreciate it, Eddie."

The other man grunted and gave a nod.

Sometimes Billy wondered if he had done the right thing making Eddie give up his career, but in the end, he was good with his decision. Eddie had certainly been influenced by his older partner, but he was also an experienced lawman and a willing participant.

A man had to own his deeds.

Billy climbed into his truck and headed home.

Rowan wouldn't be happy if she found out what he'd done, but he could live with that. What he couldn't live with was her getting hurt or worse.

Rather than drive straight home, he went by the funeral home again. The lights were out this time. There had been a moment tonight when he'd felt her attraction to him. He'd wanted to lean across that narrow table and kiss her, but he didn't want to rush whatever this was.

She was too important to him to allow anything to ruin what they already had.

There were other women he could ask out, but there was only one Rowan.

Fifteen

Three days until Halloween.

Charlotte had decorated the main entrance of Du-Pont Funeral Home with pumpkins, cornstalks, a couple of hay bales and pots of chrysanthemums. Across the street there were skeletons rising from the ground in the flower beds. All over town the holiday themes were happily displayed with eager mischief. After such a long, hot summer, folks were particularly glad to snuggle into fall, and gearing up for all the holidays was a good way to get into the spirit. On Thursday, one business and three residences would be awarded plaques for having the best Halloween decor.

When Halloween arrived, Rowan would put out a bucket of candy next to the hearse for the kids who came by on their trick-or-treat trail. Her father had always made sure there was plenty of candy for all who dared come to the funeral home. She intended to carry on as many of his traditions as possible.

She finished off her yogurt, drained her coffee cup

and tidied up the kitchen before going downstairs. The nursing home had called and there would be a client arriving before noon. Charlotte would handle the intake and then Rowan would do the preparation and embalming. Since she had an errand or two she wanted to run this morning before meeting with the family of the new intake, she'd dressed in business attire just right for the season. Orange skirt and blouse with matching pumps.

There was paperwork to be done first. As the month came to an end, there were reports and forms to prepare. Inventory to complete and orders to be placed. She had checked last year's calendar and this was also the month that the heating units were to be serviced, as well as numerous other maintenance checklists to be covered. She'd added the list of items to her electronic calendar with reminders.

On her way out, Rowan stopped at Charlotte's office and let her know she would be back in a few hours. Freud plopped down on the rug next to Charlotte's desk and curled up. She opened a drawer and retrieved a treat for him. The entire staff spoiled the dog. Rowan was glad. Things had been a little rocky for both her and Freud in the beginning.

The morning air carried a crisp bite. Rowan shivered, wished she had grabbed a coat rather than just a sweater. But she refused to complain. After the summer they had endured, cold was good. If it snowed all winter she was not going to complain.

The parking lot was empty as she climbed into her SUV. The Henegar crime scene had been released by the evidence techs, so Wanda had been allowed to return home. Rowan drove directly to the Henegar home. There was only one car in the drive and hopefully it belonged to Wanda, though by her own account she rarely drove. Rowan parked and exited the car. It was quiet. She hoped the new widow was home. Alone, preferably.

Rowan knocked on the door and waited. Silence on the other side had her worrying her lip with her teeth. With the recent loss of a loved one, she could be taking care of any number of preparations. There was all sorts of paperwork and arrangements. Family to notify. A good funeral director was always happy to help, which gave Rowan the perfect excuse for showing up at her door.

The door opened and Wanda Henegar looked as if she'd been expecting someone else—anyone besides the person she found at her door. She blinked, not quite quick enough to wipe her face clean of the surprise. She wore a plain white T-shirt and a pair of jeans. Her feet were bare.

"You're the undertaker's daughter." She shook her head. "I mean, the undertaker."

"I am." Rowan smiled and thrust out her hand. "Rowan DuPont. I'm so sorry for your loss, Mrs. Henegar. May I come in?"

Wanda hesitated for five or so seconds, then said, "Sure. It's a mess. I'm going through…things, Ms. Du-Pont."

"I understand completely. Please, call me Rowan."

Wanda backed up and Rowan stepped inside, then waited while she closed the door. When Wanda looked to her again, she said, "I know what a difficult time this can be. There are so many decisions to be made. So much to do and it's just plain overwhelming."

"It is." She glanced around, gestured to the living

room. "Would you like to sit down? I just made a fresh pot of coffee."

"How kind of you. I hate to be a bother."

"No bother." She took a big breath, as if her nerves had settled. "Cream or sugar?"

"Black is fine." Rowan didn't really want any coffee but she would gladly take a cup if it bought her some extra time.

"Have a seat and I'll be right back."

She hurried toward the back of the house and Rowan turned all the way around, scrutinizing the room. A framed photograph of Wanda and her husband hung above the fireplace. A smaller framed photo of two young men—the twentysomething sons, she presumed—sat on the mantel. Alongside that photo was another of the older son with a woman and a small child. His family, Rowan supposed. The sofa and chair were well-worn. The television was a small box set, no doubt two decades old. A braided rug kept the wood floor from being completely bare.

The decorating was minimal at best. There were no embellishments sitting around or hanging on the walls beyond the picture over the fireplace. No plaques or paintings or anything unnecessary. Rowan seated herself on the sofa. She thought of the woman in the other room. Her dark hair was long and straight. Hazel eyes were uninspired and weary. Of course, her husband had just been murdered. She wasn't supposed to be bright-eyed and dressed to party.

Rowan shivered, noted that the inside temperature seemed to be colder than the outside one, which hadn't hit fifty yet. The curtain over one window shifted. Another look confirmed that the windows had been raised.

No wonder it was so cool in here. To clear the air, she supposed. There wasn't really a noticeable smell of death in Rowan's opinion, but she imagined to someone who didn't smell that particular odor every day, it was overpowering no matter how faint.

Wanda reappeared, coffee mugs in each hand. "I like my coffee strong. I hope that's okay with you."

"Strong is good."

"Sorry it's kind of chilly in here. I needed to air the place out. I couldn't bear the idea of…"

Rowan nodded. "I understand."

Wanda placed a cup in front of Rowan and then sat down at the other end of the sofa. She stared at the vacant chair before picking up her coffee. The chair had been her husband's, Rowan suspected, and she didn't feel comfortable sitting there even with him dead.

Rowan launched her prepared spiel. "I checked the files and I noticed that Mr. Henegar's parents were both taken care of at DuPont, as was his first wife. Would you like me to put together a couple of options for his services? That way, you'll be prepared when his body is released."

Wanda held the cup inches from her mouth, as if Rowan's announcement had rendered her incapable of moving it the rest of the way, much less taking a sip. "I—I hadn't really thought about it." The cup shook and she quickly lowered it to rest against her thigh. "I was actually considering cremation."

Cremation was something DuPont rarely did but they were a full-service funeral home. The option was certainly available. "Then I'll put together a preliminary agenda for a cremation and a small memorial service, if that's what you have in mind."

She nodded slowly. "How much would that cost?"

Billy had said there was a reasonably large insurance policy. Perhaps there were other considerations that warranted her need to be particularly thrifty with her husband's final arrangements despite the insurance proceeds to come.

Rowan gave her a ballpark figure. "That would include a memorial service in the chapel and memorial pamphlets in remembrance of Mr. Henegar."

"How much if we leave off the pamphlets?"

"I'm sure we can find a number that will work for you, Mrs. Henegar. At DuPont we're very flexible with our services."

"Wanda. Call me Wanda."

Rowan smiled. "Wanda. Do you have an urn you'd like to use or would you prefer we provide one?"

"Is that extra, too?"

"Yes, but not so much. We have a nice selection of very affordable urns. There's also a box that is no additional cost."

"I'll bring something."

"We'll work with whatever you want to use."

She nodded. Looked away.

"When we can firm up a schedule, would you like us to take care of the announcement in the paper and on the radio?" This was a service they always provided, but she was guessing Wanda wasn't aware. According to Rowan's research, both her parents and grandparents were still alive. She hadn't lost any siblings. There was no reason for her to be experienced in the final arrangements of a loved one.

Another blink of uncertainty as to how to answer. "I guess so."

Rowan sat her cup on the coffee table and reached into her bag. She rounded up a pad and pen. "I'll need to ask you a few questions. We can start with Mr. Henegar's full name. The full names of his parents and those of his sons."

By the time she had called off all the names, she'd sat her cup on the table at the end of the sofa and was wringing her hands in her lap.

"Thank you, Wanda. This is painful, I know."

She nodded and stared at her hands.

"Would you like to invite anyone in particular to participate in a eulogy? One or both of his sons? A close friend? A minister?"

"His sons don't like me very much. They're not even speaking to me right now."

Interesting. "I'm so sorry to hear that. Oftentimes, a tragedy like this will temporarily fracture a family. I'm certain it's not really personal, just an emotional reaction to their loss."

"Maybe so." She answered without meeting Rowan's gaze.

"Do you need me to contact the insurance company?" This was also common practice.

Her attention snapped to Rowan. "No. No. I've already taken care of that but they won't pay out until after the body is released and I have a death certificate. Is that a problem? Can you still cremate him even if I can't pay you until the insurance comes through?"

"Of course, that's absolutely doable. There won't be any delays. I assure you."

Obviously, Henegar's sons blamed her for some reason. This was why they weren't here consoling their stepmother and helping to make arrangements for their father.

"Good." She nodded adamantly. "I want this over."

Her eyes widened and her breath caught as she realized what she'd said aloud.

"No one enjoys this process," Rowan offered in hopes of putting her at ease. "Most want it over as quickly as possible. It's only natural." Which was not necessarily true. There were many who wanted to prolong the process. Saying goodbye was too difficult, too painful. They wanted to hang on to their loved ones as long as possible. On the other hand, there were those who practically had to be dragged to the funeral home. Denial was a powerful emotion.

"It sounds awful of me, but I just want to put this nightmare behind me." Her hands relaxed, stopped twisting together and lay limply in her lap.

"Completely understandable." Now they were headed in the right direction.

She shook her head. "It's bad enough I have no place else to go and have to stay in this house after he was killed here." She shuddered. "It still smells like death in here. I feel it in my lungs, hanging there."

"I have a solution for that." Rowan jotted down the vinegar-and-baking-soda aromatic potion her father had sworn by and passed it to the woman. "That should take care of it."

"Thank you." She stared at the words written on the paper.

Rowan decided to push a button and see what reaction she got. "Should I coordinate a date for the memorial with the Thackerson family?"

Her wide-eyed gaze snapped to Rowan's.

"The bodies should be released around the same time," Rowan explained. "Winchester is a small town. I'm sure you have friends in common. We do have one viewing room large enough for a memorial service if we need to do them at the same time."

The color drained from the younger woman's face. She stared at Rowan, her mouth agape, but no words were coming out.

"If you're not certain, I could call Mr. Thackerson's daughter and check with her."

Her head started to move from side to side. It wagged that way until Rowan was certain she would give herself whiplash. "No. I don't want the services to be at the same time. I don't want… No. No. No. No. We'll do ours separate. Completely separate."

"Of course." Rowan scribbled a note on her pad. "I'll make sure the services are not on the same day."

"Thank you." Wanda cleared her throat. "Is there anything else?" She stood. "I have a lot to do."

Rowan pushed to her feet. "I'll call if there's anything else. Do you mind if I put your cell number in my phone?"

"Okay."

Reaching into her bag once more, Rowan retrieved her phone. "I hope you'll call if you need help with anything else, Wanda. I'm happy to assist you with whatever issues or difficulties that arise during this painful time. It's what I do."

They exchanged numbers and Wanda saw her to the door. When Rowan was in her SUV and headed back to Winchester proper, she called Billy and set up a meeting with him and Clarence Lincoln. Clarence was the lead detective on the case. Whatever had happened, Wanda Henegar had done something or knew something relevant to her husband's murder.

Rowan wasn't surprised at all.

Twenty minutes later she was climbing the steps to city hall. She smiled for Officer Wiley as she placed her bag on the table for the necessary security check. "The chief is expecting me."

"Yes, ma'am, he let me know. How are you today, Dr. DuPont?"

"I'm great, James. How are you?"

"Just wonderful, ma'am." He passed her bag back to her. "Go right on in."

Rowan thanked him and hurried to Billy's office. Her heels clicked on the marble floor. When she reached the corridor that led to the police department, the marble was replaced with commercial-grade carpet, softening the sound of footsteps and allowing her to walk even faster without the worry of slipping. She really was out of practice walking in heels. In Nashville she'd worn them every day. Now that she was back in the funeral business she only wore them for meetings with the families, viewings and funerals. The rest of the time she was a hard-core jeans, T-shirt and sneakers girl these days.

"In here, Ro."

Billy called to her from the conference-room door. He and Clarence had created a timeline and murder board in the room, though Billy preferred to call it a case board. *Murder* wasn't his favorite word.

Clarence was hunkered over the conference table, reports and photographs fanned out in front of him. "Hey, Ro." He gave her a nod.

"I spent some time with Wanda Henegar." She sat down. Her feet were aching. She almost sighed. The big-city girl was disappearing completely. Not that Rowan missed her that much. There was a lot to be said for casual and comfortable.

Billy pulled out a chair and straddled it, propped his arms on the back of it. "She's sticking by her story and so's everyone who saw her that day."

"Do she and Sue Ellen Thackerson have a history?" Rowan looked from Billy to Clarence. "Maybe they were friends or enemies at some point in their lives."

Clarence was the first to answer. "I don't think so. Wanda went to Huntland School, lived over in the Pleasant Grove area. I'm not saying they didn't know each other, but they lived in different zip codes and had different friends. I've talked to folks all the way back to elementary school and didn't find a connection."

"You pick up on something when you talked to her?" Billy asked.

"I did." Rowan knew grief. She had seen it over and over growing up and in her work in Nashville—not to mention during her internship in psychiatry. What Wanda Henegar displayed was not grief. It was fear. Relief. Maybe even a little resentment. But it wasn't grief by any stretch of the definition. She explained this to Billy and Clarence. Then she said, "She wants him cremated. As soon as possible."

Billy made a face. "Was their marriage on rocky ground before he got himself murdered?"

"I didn't get that from any of the friends or family members," Clarence pointed out, "but I haven't talked to Henegar's sons yet."

Rowan said to him, "There's a problem with his

sons. They're not speaking to her. Why haven't they agreed to talk to you? Are they not in town yet?"

"They've only all just arrived in town as of late yesterday," Billy said. "One lives in Texas, the other in New Mexico."

Under the circumstances, it was reasonable they hadn't been interviewed just yet. "There's trouble between the young wife and the sons. I don't know the reason, but there's something off there."

"Insurance policy only has her name on it," Clarence warned. "I'm sure that didn't sit well with his sons."

"That could be the sticking point," Billy agreed. "What about the house and land?"

Clarence checked his notes. "All the property—house, land, truck, furniture—goes to his sons."

"I can see how he would want the farm to stay in the family," Billy noted.

Clarence asked, "Why did you ask about a history between Wanda and Sue Ellen?"

"I was fishing," Rowan explained, "so I mentioned that the two men, Thackerson and Henegar, might have services on the same day. Wanda was having no part of that. She made it clear that they could not be in the funeral home on the same day. When I suggested I could call Sue Ellen to coordinate dates, she was adamant that the services had to be separate."

"Maybe there was bad blood between Stan and Barney." Billy looked to Clarence. "You found no connection between those two, either?"

"Nothing. Based on what I've gotten, they knew each other but nothing more."

That nagging instinct that told Rowan when she was onto something wouldn't let go. "Could Wanda have had an affair with Barney?" She couldn't see Sue Ellen with Stan. Besides, by all accounts the man had been far too pious to have an affair.

But then, sometimes people lied, kept secrets and did bad things that no one knew about until they dug deeply enough or turned over the exact right rock. Her family was the perfect example.

"I have my doubts about that," Billy said, echoing her initial thoughts. "Barney was not the affair type. After his wife died, he never dated anyone else. Just focused on that store."

"No man is until it happens the first time," Rowan reminded him.

He shrugged. "Valid point."

"What about Stan and Sue Ellen?" Clarence turned his hands up in question. "It wouldn't be the first time a member of a church hierarchy crossed the line."

"True. We need to nudge all the possibilities, no matter how unsavory," Billy pointed out. "If there was any connection between the Thackersons and the Henegars, we need to find it and define it."

"It's possible the sons will be able to provide some insights." Rowan wasn't completely on board with the affair scenario either way, but there was definitely something and that something was pertinent to the murders.

"Then again, none of this is relevant if Addington is behind these murders," Billy countered.

He wanted it to be Julian. Rowan couldn't blame him. Blaming Julian was better than believing his community had suddenly sprouted one or more killers. Winchester was a small, sedate town. Everyone knew everyone else. No one wanted to believe they knew a murderer without *knowing* it.

Been there, done that. Several times over, apparently.

"No question," she agreed because he was right—if that proved the case.

"We've got our work cut out for us," Clarence admitted.

"We absolutely do," Billy confirmed. "But we'll get it done."

"I would love the opportunity to talk to Sue Ellen Thackerson," Rowan confessed. "No matter that they have alibis or whether Julian is involved, I feel like these two women are key to what happened."

"This is your lucky day, Ro," Clarence announced. "Sue Ellen will be here in—" he checked his watch "—half an hour to answer a few questions."

"Perfect." She had some time before she had to return to the funeral home and begin prepping the new client. "Since we're here—at city hall—I'm happy to simply watch rather than ask questions, but I can offer some suggestions, if you'd like."

It would be really nice to be able to help Billy close these two cases. He had done so much for her, she owed him a tremendous debt.

"We would appreciate any and all suggestions, Ro." Billy gifted her with a nod of appreciation. Clarence echoed the sentiment.

For the next several minutes she watched as he and Clarence went over the points they wanted to broach with Sue Ellen. She offered suggestions from time to time. They were close on this one.

She could feel it.

Sixteen

Sue Ellen Thackerson was dressed to the nines today. No tight jeans and revealing top like she usually wore. Nope. Today she wore modest black pants and a black high-necked sweater with pearls, no less. Her hair and makeup were slightly tamer than usual, not so over-the-top. She looked exactly like a woman in mourning.

Billy wasn't entirely convinced but he gave her kudos for the effort.

He and Rowan watched from the observation booth, which was really a former storage closet that had been repurposed for observing ongoing interviews in the only interview room they had—which was a former office. Unlike the booth, the interview room was particularly well lit.

Lincoln sat with his back to the mirror that allowed Billy and Ro to see into the room. The interviewee—in this case, Sue Ellen—sat on the opposite side of the table facing the mirror. With the low lighting in the observation booth she couldn't see them but they could see her. Soundproof walls prevented those in the interview room from hearing anyone in the booth, while a speaker system allowed the reverse.

"I can't give you a definite date for the release of your father's body," Lincoln said in answer to her question, "but we're hopeful it won't be too many more days. I'm sure you and your family would like to make arrangements for his funeral."

She shook her head. "We're not having a funeral. Daddy never wanted to be laid out on display like that. The funeral home in Tullahoma is going to cremate him. That's what he wanted. He always hated the idea of lying in a casket being looked at. His friends can stop by the mini market and pay their respects."

Rowan exchanged a look with Billy. "I told you Wanda wanted her husband cremated. They planned this. I'm certain of it. You can't exhume bodies for additional examinations if they no longer exist. They don't want to leave any loose ends."

She was right. There were some things that could be tested for once a body was ashes, like poison, but who knew if they would even keep the ashes. Lots of people spread the ashes. Basically, once the bodies were burnt, there would be nothing more to learn.

"We need one of them to talk," Billy muttered, frustrated. "To find out who they hired to do the job." The two had airtight alibis. They were in the clear unless he could find the person or persons they hired. "To tell you the truth, whoever did it will likely brag eventually. Someone will hear about it. I just don't want these two walking around scot-free until then."

"Wanda is the weaker link." Ro watched the woman beyond the glass. "Sue Ellen is far more confident. She's probably been planning this for years. Maybe not an actual plan, but dreaming of being rid of her father and having his money. The store, probably." She turned to him. "She has known what she wants for a long time and he has always been in her way. Telling her how to live and what she did wrong."

Billy liked it when the psychological analyst came out in Ro. She was good. He was lucky to have her willing to advise on cases like this one.

"Maybe the autopsy results will give us something to work with." He could hope. It was difficult to try one method of coercion or the other if you didn't have a single piece of evidence on which to base an accusation.

Rowan suddenly smiled. "Give them some time to believe they're safe. Allow their confidence to build and their guard to fall. Then strike with something stunning, like the autopsy results."

"You're saying, to make one or both believe we have evidence based on the autopsy whether we do or not."

"Yes. Start with Wanda. She's the most likely to break. This one—" Rowan turned back to the mirror "—won't be quite so malleable."

"All right. It's a good plan. This is why I need you in this department, Ro. You would be a tremendous asset."

She made a soft sound, a dry laugh of sorts. "I didn't tell you anything you didn't already know." She flashed him a look. "Let's not pretend you're so naive, Chief. Remember, I've known you a very long time. I know how smart you are."

"It's always good to have a second opinion," he countered. Apparently going the "we can't do this without you" route wasn't going to work. He'd decided in the past few months that his best chance of being able to keep Rowan safe was to have her working alongside him. So far she hadn't been convinced to take him up on the offer. Her confidence was still stinging from the way Addington fooled her. Didn't matter that he had fooled everyone else, too.

"I'm happy to assist on a case when you need me, Billy. I don't have to join the staff. How would I take care of the funeral home if I was here all the time?"

"Charlotte is really good at her job."

Rowan sighed. "You just want to be able to keep an eye on me."

He bit back a grin. The woman knew him far too well.

On the other side of the glass, Lincoln asked, "Are you aware your father had spoken to an attorney about his estate recently?"

Billy watched shock and then indignation claim Sue Ellen's face. This was one of Rowan's suggested interjections into the conversation. No attorney had said any such thing, but the goal was to see the daughter's reaction.

"I spoke to our attorney already. He didn't mention anything about Daddy talking to him recently. He said Daddy's will is unchanged. Everything goes to me. That's what he has always wanted. Anyone who says different is a liar."

"Are you expecting anyone to contest the will?"

She made a face. "Of course not."

Lincoln glanced at his notes and moved on. "Were you aware that a large sum of money is missing from his safe?"

Surprise flared before Sue Ellen could prevent the

reaction. That question had been one of Billy's contributions to the interview. He'd hit a nerve.

"How do you know there was money missing? Daddy didn't even let me in the safe."

"He and his assistant manager counted it recently."

She waved a hand in dismissal. "You can't believe anything Yancey Quinn says. He'd tell a lie when the truth would serve him better."

Lincoln shook his head. "Mr. Quinn didn't tell us anything. We found the accounting slip where your father noted the amount and the date it was counted. He signed it and he had Mr. Quinn sign it, as well. That was just a day or so before he was murdered."

She flinched at the word *murdered*. Billy studied her face. Was that guilt he saw? Regret?

"Then he must have deposited it or paid bills or something. This time of year he could've paid taxes and insurance. Going through a hundred or so thousand when you operate a business isn't such a big deal."

"She has an answer for everything," Rowan noted. "But she always says too much."

Rowan was right. Lincoln hadn't said how much money was missing. Sue Ellen couldn't have known an amount so close to the actual count unless she had taken the money.

"How well do you know Mr. Quinn?" Lincoln asked the question with just the right amount of suspicion in his voice.

Sue Ellen's strained expression relaxed and she jumped at the chance to turn the spotlight on someone else. "I've always thought he was taking advantage of Daddy. I mean," she said, shrugging, "think about it. How many other signed receipts did you find? If Daddy counted money and had Yancey sign it, he must have been suspicious, too. He probably had been stealing from Daddy for years. You know, he was over in Afghanistan for a while." Sue Ellen tapped her temple. "Came back a little crazy, they say. He might be capable of anything."

Rowan glanced at Billy. "Any truth to that?"

Billy shrugged. "He served, that's true. I never heard any rumors about the other."

Sue Ellen said, "He probably took that money when he found Daddy dead on the floor."

Rowan shifted, stood straighter. "She had the perfect opportunity when her father's body was found to suggest that Quinn killed him." She turned to Billy. "But she didn't until now."

Billy braced his hands on his hips and studied the woman again. "What are you up to, little lady?"

"If I were Wanda Henegar," Rowan said, "I would be worried."

"She'd be a handy scapegoat." Billy had assigned officers this morning to surveillance on both ladies. He didn't want either of them disappearing or ending up dead.

"Sue Ellen," Lincoln said, "is there anyone else besides Mr. Quinn who knew how much money your father kept in the safe?"

She scrunched her brow as if concentrating hard on the question. "He didn't have a lot of close friends. He spent all his time at the store. There were a few pissing buddies, I call them, who hung out at the store on weekdays. Retired old farts who stopped in for bad coffee and to brag about what they'd bought or done.

Especially during hunting season. They liked trying to outdo each other."

"Would you be able to give me a list of those names?" Lincoln asked.

"Clarence is good," Rowan commented. "You've trained him well, Billy."

Pride swelled in his chest. A compliment from Ro was a big deal to him. "Thanks. He's a quick study. The best detective in the department."

"I'm waiting for that other shoe to drop," Rowan said.

Billy turned his attention back to the interview. "Any minute now."

"Sue Ellen, just one more question." Lincoln turned to a new page in his notebook.

"I'm all ears," she said with a roll of her eyes. "This is becoming monotonous."

"Not to worry," he assured her, "this is the last one, I promise."

She turned her hands palms up in a "what?" gesture.

"Is it true that six months ago you and your father had a very public argument about him cutting you off financially? Witnesses say you said something to the effect that you'd see him in hell before you let him do that to you."

"Yancey probably told you that, too," she snarled. "He's a total piece of shit. He doesn't know anything. Yes, I said a lot of stuff. I was angry. People do that when they get pissed off. I didn't mean any of it. You don't think I haven't wished a thousand times I could take that back?" Her voice wobbled and she blinked repeatedly before the tears started to flow. "I hear myself saying those awful things to him every night in my dreams. I have to live with that for the rest of my life. But we got past it. Daddy loved me and I loved him. And now he's gone."

Her hands went over her face and she sobbed loudly.

"Well." Rowan folded her arms over her chest. "She should receive an award for that performance."

Lincoln passed her his handkerchief. "Let me just check with the chief and see if you can go home now, Sue Ellen. I'm as sorry as I can be for upsetting you like this."

She accepted the handkerchief but didn't respond other than the pitch of her sobs growing louder.

Lincoln left the room, closing the door behind him. He joined Billy and Rowan in the booth.

"What do you think?" he asked, looking from Billy to Ro and back.

"She's hiding something," Billy said. "No question about that."

Rowan didn't answer. She watched the woman alone in the interview room. Billy and Lincoln did the same. Sue Ellen Thackerson dried her cheeks with Lincoln's handkerchief and then tossed it onto the table. She heaved a breath and sat there, her face clean of emotion beyond the impatience radiating from her thin shoulders.

"She's patting herself on the back for passing this latest test," Ro said. "Give her enough rope and she's going to hang herself."

"Yep," Billy agreed, the word bitter on his tongue.

Whether Sue Ellen killed her father or not, she had something to do with it.

"How long should we leave her like that?" Lincoln asked.

"Ten, fifteen minutes," Ro suggested. "It will feel like an hour and she'll grow angrier with every passing minute."

The door to the booth opened and Cindy Farris, Billy's assistant, poked her head in. "Chief, that FBI agent is here to see you."

Rowan's gaze shot to Billy's. "Dressler?"

Cindy nodded. "That's the one. He's in your office and demanding to see you."

Well, hell. "I'll be right there."

Before Cindy could step back and close the door, Dressler, the pushy bastard, appeared behind her.

"There you are, Chief."

He pushed into the room, forcing Cindy to step aside. The booth was hardly big enough for the four of them but that didn't stop Dressler.

"It's all right, Cindy," Billy said, noting her horrified expression.

She nodded and closed the door. Billy turned his attention to the federal agent. "What's this about, Dressler? I usually prefer appointments. Like you, my time is valuable."

Dressler gestured to the woman in the interview room. "I'm here to see Ms. Thackerson."

"Is that right?" Billy reared back, assessed the man. "And why would you need to see Ms. Thackerson?"

He knew Rowan wouldn't have called Dressler about her concerns related to one of Addington's MO being similar to these murders. And he sure as hell didn't call. He had planned to later today, but he hadn't called yet.

Dressler shifted his attention to Rowan. "Are you working for Chief Brannigan now? I thought you were sticking with burying the dead."

"I'm here as an advisor," Rowan said, "much the way I was in Nashville for Metro. I'm sure you recall the numerous times I corrected your profiles."

Billy's lips quirked with the need to smile. "What's this visit about, Dressler? I was planning to call with an update this afternoon. You couldn't call me before driving down from Nashville? I hate to see you waste your time and taxpayer dollars."

The fed swung his gaze back to Billy, the frustration lining his face visible even in the meager lighting. "Actually, I was surprised you hadn't called me already, particularly after the call from Ms. Thackerson."

"Is that right?" Billy asked when what he really wanted to say was "What call?"

"Ms. Thackerson called me with some serious concerns and I came directly here. She's worried that your department might be overlooking the facts related to her father's murder."

"What facts?" The two words were out of Billy's mouth before he could stop them.

"She saw a man who fits the description of Julian Addington talking to her father on two occasions in the past month and now her father is dead. When she described the murder scene, I was stunned you hadn't called me, Chief." He shot a look at Rowan. "The Thackerson and Henegar murder scenes could have come directly from Addington's playbook. There are some stunning similarities."

"First," Billy said, "I wouldn't call the similarities stunning." He kept the part about not knowing one damn thing about some guy who matched Addington's description being seen by Sue Ellen to himself.

"Similarities nonetheless," Dressler argued.

"It's the chief's job to confirm hearsay," Rowan pointed out, "before making a call to other law-enforcement authorities. You're aware of this, Josh. It's standard protocol. The Bureau certainly wouldn't want to be called out every time a cop in some town *thought* they had a connection to a federal case. What a waste of resources that would be."

Anger gripped the federal agent's face then. He glared from Rowan to Billy as if he wasn't sure which one had made him more angry. "I'd like to speak to her now, Chief. Unless you have reason to deny my request."

"We're only too happy to have you assist on this one, Agent Dressler." Billy gestured to the interview room. "She's all yours. I will have my lead detective observe, however."

"Excuse me. I have to take this." Rowan had her cell phone in her hand.

Billy's attention was divided between Ro and the man now bellowing about being left out of the loop one too many times by Billy and his department. But it was the worry dancing across Ro's face that concerned him. He couldn't care less about Dressler's complex. Ro wouldn't have taken a call in the middle of this if it wasn't important.

"Excuse me," Dressler said to Lincoln as he exited the booth.

He entered the interview room, closing the door behind him. With all the arrogance of the fool he was, he introduced himself to Sue Ellen and took a seat.

Rowan put away her phone and lifted her gaze to Billy's. "That was the security company. The alarm is going off at the funeral home. I have to go."

"I'll take you." Billy's cell vibrated against his hip as he spoke. He answered without taking his eyes off Ro.

"Chief, this is Officer Sails. I think maybe you might want to come to DuPont Funeral Home. Someone has broken in through the back entrance. There's a body, Chief. I've never seen anything like it."

Well, hell. "Be right there."

Seventeen

Rowan watched the landscape go by a little faster than was comfortable. She glanced at Billy. He was driving like a bat out of hell. Whatever the officer who had called told him couldn't have been good. If he attempted to send another text while driving so madly, she might just make a citizen's arrest. She'd called Charlotte to ensure she was okay. She wasn't supposed to be at the funeral home, but Rowan had needed to be certain.

"The officer who called, he's sure Freud is okay?"

"Freud's in the backyard."

Thank God. That was the downside to allowing him free rein when she was gone. If someone broke in, they might hurt him to prevent him from attacking, as was his instinct. That he was in the backyard and safe begged the question of how someone managed to get him out while they got in?

Unless Freud recognized the intruder.

Rowan's heart rose into her throat. Would Julian dare come back here?

Billy took the left onto Second Avenue way too fast.

Her stomach flip-flopped. Staring forward, she tried distracting herself by thinking of Sue Ellen Thackerson sitting in that interview room weaving her elaborate lie to Special Agent Josh Dressler. Rowan shook her head. Hopefully he would see through it before he wasted too much time. Then again, as long as he followed that lead maybe he would leave Rowan alone.

Like that was going to happen.

Of course, it was possible Julian was here, but why would he approach Sue Ellen's father? Julian was far too careful, far too calculating. Thackerson was not connected to Rowan in any way. What would be the point? Julian would never waste his time in such a way.

Billy cut into the parking lot in front of the funeral home and she grabbed the armrest to steady herself. He squealed to a stop and Rowan took her first deep breath since he'd put her SUV in Drive. There were a number of other questions she had considered asking him, but with the way he drove she didn't want to distract his focus.

"Thank God," she muttered as she climbed out. He didn't seem to notice her discomfort.

Two police cruisers sat in the parking lot, lights throbbing.

That certainly couldn't be good. Freud's frantic barking echoed from beyond the funeral home. The sound allowed her to relax marginally.

"I should check on Freud."

"Freud is fine. You need to come with me."

She glanced at Billy as they hurried forward, crossing the parking lot in a near run. "Is there something else I need to know?"

Oh, hell. The nursing home had left a client. If the body had been stolen…

She grabbed Billy by the arm and pulled him to a stop. "Tell me another body hasn't been taken."

She needed to hear those words. Now. *Right now.*

If the dark expression on his face was any indication, the news was perhaps worse than she had imagined. "What, damn it?" she demanded.

"Nothing was taken," he said, his voice dangerously low.

His tone sent a new streak of adrenaline searing through her. "If nothing was taken, what did happen?"

"Whoever broke in left a body. That's all I know."

She supposed that was better than the other way around. Wait, no. Not if someone had been murdered. "I don't understand."

Billy started moving again. "The perp broke in through the back so we'll go in through the front. No need to trample on any possible evidence. Crime-scene unit will be here ASAP. Burt, too."

At least now she knew to whom those texts he'd sent while driving had gone.

As soon as they entered the lobby, the smell assaulted her senses. Rowan covered her nose with her hand. The stench of a decomposing corpse was unmistakable. The embalming process didn't stop the decomposition process; it merely slowed it down. Exposed to room temperature and the very air everyone breathed, the process was going to do what it would.

Moving through the doors marked Staff Only, they didn't get far before Rowan spotted and recognized the body.

Carlos Sanchez, or whoever he was, was lying on

the floor not five feet from the back door. His face was the only part of him that was recognizable. From the neck down his body appeared to have been skinned.

"What the hell?" Billy crouched down near the body to get a better look at the face.

Rowan sank to a crouch next to him. "The perp skinned him very precisely."

"To destroy the tattoos?"

She nodded. "Most likely. The tattoos told a story. Whoever removed them didn't want us to know that story." She moistened her lips. "Julian skinned three victims." She gestured to Sanchez. "Like this, leaving the faces intact."

To the officer hovering at the back door and looking as if he might lose whatever he'd consumed last, Billy said, "Tell Detective Lincoln to pick up Owen Utter and bring him over here."

While Billy reviewed the area in and around the point of entry, Rowan studied the body. His lips had been sliced apart. Since she had glued them in place, that would have been the only way to access his mouth. The wire she'd used to keep his jaw closed had obviously been removed. She leaned closer still. There was something in his mouth. Paper?

"Billy." She looked up as he turned back to her; dark, worried eyes searched hers. Her chest constricted. Something like this could happen to him…

Billy might die trying to save her…

She blinked, banished the horrifying thoughts and forced air into her lungs. "I need gloves. I think there's something in his mouth."

He was at her side in three long strides. He pulled a pair of gloves from his jacket pocket and handed them to her. She tugged them into place as he pulled on a pair of his own. She reached for the dead man's jaw, levered his mouth open. The corner of paper protruding from his teeth was part of a small page tucked into a plastic sandwich-size bag.

Her heart thumped hard against her sternum.

Julian.

He had left her notes in this manner before.

Carefully, she withdrew the bag, then removed the page from the bag and unfolded it. That she did this without her hands shaking was a flat-out miracle.

They're here, watching you. Be careful, Rowan. They all want you. Julian

"Is that his handwriting?"

Rowan nodded. The bold strokes were unmistakable.

"You have any idea what he means?"

She shook her head, nausea preventing her from opening her mouth.

"Has he ever said anything like this before?"

The tension in Billy's voice rose with each word.

"No." She moistened her lips. Forced out the rest of what she needed to say. "But Herman did."

Billy stared at her, the heat of it burning her profile. She met his gaze. She hadn't told him about Herman's final words to her. She'd intended to when the right time came. The right time had come and she'd been behind the curve.

"Explain that to me, Ro."

The disappointment in his words tore at her. She shouldn't have kept this from him.

"Before he pulled that trigger, he said, 'you're all that's left of her and they will *all* want you.'"

Betrayal flashed in his eyes and it was like a kick to her side. When he spoke, his voice was low and harsh. "Any thoughts on what he meant by that statement?"

She shook her head. "None."

"Anything else you haven't told me?"

"No." Her answer might be another lie. Right now, she wasn't sure of anything. What she'd told him, what she hadn't. Who said what.

She thrust the note at him and stood. "I need some air."

Her legs felt wobbly as she moved away from the corpse. Her hands shook as she tore off the gloves. She thought about going outside, but the newshounds would be gathering out front. There would be more cops. The backyard and porch needed to be preserved. She couldn't go outside.

She made a left and went to her office. She closed the door, sagged against it and shut her eyes. Voices and images whirled in her head. Her mother smiling at her. Her father's warm smile. Billy's grin. Julian praising her work. Herman bringing her breakfast and laughing in that jolly way of his. The sound of the bullet exploding from the gun and tearing his head apart burst in her brain.

Rowan opened her eyes and stared at her desk and the chair where Herman had been sitting that day.

You're all that's left of her, Ro, and they will all *want you.*

"What the hell does that mean?"

She crossed the room and collapsed into her chair. The *her* was obviously her mother, Norah—the woman she apparently hadn't known at all. It was the *they* that she couldn't classify or quantify.

Worse, how could she have loved and trusted her father—lived with him until she went off to college—and not known that things were not right somehow. He had to have recognized that something was wrong, particularly after Raven's death. And Herman. They had been friends, like family, for as long as she could recall. How could he have kept secrets from her? Lied to her?

A soft knock on her door forced her to her feet. She righted her sweater, pushed her hair behind her ears and rounded her desk. With a deep breath, she opened the door.

Billy stared at her for a moment before he asked, "You okay?"

A sound burst out of her, not quite a laugh. This was a conversation they'd had before and her answer was much the same as the one she'd given the other time. "Are you out of your mind, Billy Brannigan? No, I am not okay. I doubt I'll ever be *okay* again."

The fact that tears welled and burned her eyes made her all the more furious. She gave him her back and walked to the bookshelves that held the books her father and his father and grandfather before him had collected. Most were about death, preparing bodies and comforting survivors. Rowan closed her eyes. Her entire life had revolved around death and she was so, so tired of the darkness and the tragedy.

"Ro."

He stood right behind her now when she hadn't even realized he'd moved.

"I'll be fine. Just give me a minute." She was overwrought. It happened. Even to those fully trained in handling emotions. She might be an educated psychiatrist and an undertaker, but she was still only human.

"All I want is to protect you."

His voice was so soft and yet it hurt to hear the words, they pressed too heavily on her heart. She closed her eyes against the ache.

"I can't do that if you keep me in the dark. Please." His hands rested on her shoulders; despite the sweater and the blouse she wore, his palms burned her skin. "Please don't shut me out."

Anger—at herself, at Julian, at all of this—fired through her. She whirled to face him, forcing his hands to fall away.

"I didn't shut you out, Billy. I lied to you. We all lie. We all keep our little secrets. Pretend it's perfectly normal not to tell certain thoughts or conclusions." Surprise, then regret, flickered in his eyes and she could hardly bear to look. "Survival and all that. It's human nature. Instinct. No matter how well you know someone, they will still lie when the need arises."

He nodded, the move so faint she might not have noticed if she hadn't been staring so intently at him.

"I've lied to myself and to you for a long time," he said.

Startled, she tried to summon the right words to respond but nothing came. Billy never lied. He was the good guy, the knight in shining armor. The hero. The person she had looked up to since she was old enough to understand the concept of role models and emotional attachments.

"I don't understand." Her throat felt raw simply saying the words. The damn tears dared to brim over her lashes. As they slid down her cheeks, she felt like a fool.

Except his eyes were bright as well, as if he, too, were struggling to contain the same emotions she felt. He lifted his hands and cupped her face, wiped away her tears with the pads of his thumbs. And then he kissed her. So tenderly. So slowly and yet it was over far too quickly. Her heart felt as if it might fracture all the way through.

He drew away but only far enough to look into her eyes. "I have wanted to do that since junior prom, when I begged you to dance but you refused." He laughed softly. "You told me to dance with my date, but you were the person I wanted to bring, but I knew you'd say no if I asked. I should have told you a long time ago. But I lied to myself and to you. You're my best friend, Ro, but that isn't enough. I want more."

"Chief!"

Rowan jerked, her mind yanked through the decades, back to the here and now. Someone was calling Billy. They couldn't do this now…

Whatever *this* was…

Billy flinched but he didn't take his eyes from hers. The fingers of one hand found hers, squeezed. "Say something, Ro. Say anything."

"Chief!"

There wasn't time. Instead, she went up on tiptoe and kissed his lips, quickly but firmly. And then she rushed away, didn't look back. She ran headlong into Dressler in the corridor.

"Whoa." He grabbed her by the shoulders and steadied her. "What do you know about this note Addington left for you?"

Rowan fought to slow her racing heart. Her lips were on fire. Her head was spinning. "The same thing you do. What are you doing here, anyway?" Irritation overrode the other emotions. "I thought you were busy wasting your time interviewing Sue Ellen Thackerson."

"I was until I stepped out of the interview room for water and heard one of the officers mention the missing body that was returned to DuPont Funeral Home. Have you had any other bodies go missing, Rowan? Since I was reasonably certain you haven't, I realized the body dropped at your door had to be mine."

Rowan produced a smile. "You'll need to speak to Chief Brannigan, but as far as I'm concerned you can have that body. You're welcome, Agent Dressler."

She moved around him and went in search of Burt. He should be there by now. Behind her, Dressler's outraged voice echoed, followed by Billy's calm, low voice. She shivered at the sound.

How was it possible he had felt the same way she had all these years and she hadn't known?

Didn't matter. She shook herself. They were friends. They couldn't be more than that. Especially right now. Julian was still close, and he would pounce on the opportunity to hurt her. She could not—would not—allow Billy to be hurt, or worse, because of her.

I assure you, when I'm done, you will want to end the agony of living with all the guilt.

Julian had said those words to her.

Forcing her focus back to the moment, she noted that Burt and his assistant, Lucky Ledbetter, had already bagged the corpse.

"You've got quite the mess on the rug, Ro." He nodded to the vintage Persian runner on the corridor.

Fluids and tissue were stuck there from the way he had been skinned.

"No problem. This is why I employ the best cleaning team in the state." She would call Rhonda McCord, the head of the cleaning team, next.

"We'll ship him off to the lab unless Agent Dressler instructs me otherwise."

Ro glanced back—Billy and Josh were in a heated debate. Though they weren't shouting, their body language told the story.

"Those two look as if they're about to tear into each other," Burt noted.

They were standing close, nose to nose practically. She supposed it was a miracle they hadn't come to blows already.

"Cops can be territorial," she offered. She refused to consider any part of what she was witnessing might be personal. She and Josh had never shared so much as a meal outside work. Not for his lack of trying, but the bottom line was the same. There was no reason for whatever was going on a dozen yards away to be about her.

Yet, she knew that it was.

"I need to check on Mr. Kramer. He was dropped off earlier today."

Charlotte had sent a text confirming the delivery. With all the commotion, she hadn't even thought to check and see that he was still safe and sound in refrigeration.

You are losing it, Ro.

"We'll finish up here so the evidence techs can do their jobs," Burt promised.

Rowan flashed him a smile and hurried away. She

made sure to go wide around the two men still in each other's faces. She walked into the refrigeration unit, breathed a major sigh of relief at the bagged body lying on the single gurney in the room.

"At least no one bothered you, Mr. Kramer." She walked over to the gurney and unzipped the bag far enough to confirm the elderly man was the one who'd been delivered.

Earnest Kramer had been her fifth-grade math teacher. To a little girl, he'd been ancient even back then. She worked up a smile. "I'll get you squared away tonight, Mr. Kramer. I'll make sure you look your very best."

She closed the bag wondering when she had so thoroughly become her father? He had always chatted with the clients. She vividly remembered walking into the embalming room and hearing him carrying on a conversation with the person on the mortuary table. As a teenager she had thought it was completely bizarre.

It was true, she supposed. You did become your parents.

Too bad she seemed to have no idea who her mother really was.

When she stepped out of refrigeration, Billy and Josh were nowhere to be seen. Rowan wasn't sure whether to be relieved or more worried than ever.

She made her way back to her office and called Rhonda to get the cleaning team over later this afternoon. The evidence techs would need time to finish up. It was possible the cleaners wouldn't be able to do the job before tomorrow. Rowan sure hoped she didn't have to wait that long. Thankfully there was no visitation

scheduled for tonight but there was one tomorrow—
Mr. Kramer's.

She wandered back into the lobby. Somewhere out
back Freud barked. She should go out the exit on the
west end and bring him inside and up to the living
quarters. The evidence techs wouldn't want him running around out there, anyway.

Outside, the wind whipped through her hair as she
hurried beyond the portico and around to the gate that led
to the backyard. An officer she recognized—Gabrielle,
if she remembered correctly—was throwing the Frisbee
across the yard, keeping Freud entertained.

"Thanks," she said to him. "I appreciate you taking care of him."

"No problem, ma'am."

Freud greeted her, Frisbee in mouth. "Drop." He did
as she ordered. "Let's go, boy."

He followed her to the west entrance and to the
lobby without deviating from her path. At the stairs,
however, he heard Billy's voice and hesitated.

"Come, Freud."

Reluctantly, he followed her up the stairs. She unlocked the door, urged him inside and returned to the
first floor. Dressler would likely be gone by now. Not
necessarily a good thing since she was not looking forward to any time alone with Billy in the near future.
She had to figure out her strategy for defusing this new
development first.

"Ro."

Too late. He waited at the newel post for her.

Her traitorous heart took an extra beat. "Is Dressler
still here?"

Billy nodded, his eyes searching her face for some

indication of her feelings. She hated—*hated*—the idea of leaving him confused and wondering.

"He's in your office on the phone with Wanda Henegar."

"Did he give you any idea about the subject matter?" Why would Wanda be speaking to Dressler?

"Dressler wants you to join him." The anger that sparked in Billy's eyes told her he wasn't happy about it.

"Well, let's not keep him waiting."

They walked side by side across the lobby and down the silent corridor that led to her office, the lounge and public restrooms. She wasn't sure what terrified her more: the idea that Billy would bring up that kiss and reiterate that he wanted more, or that he would apologize for it and call it a mistake.

By the time they reached the door to her office she was so grateful for the reprieve of Dressler's presence that her knees almost gave out on her.

"I just spoke with Wanda Henegar, the wife of the other murder victim—"

Rowan's patience was far too thin already. "I know who she is, Josh, get to the point."

"She says that after your visit with her she started to think about all the news around your return to Winchester this past spring."

Rowan refused to allow him to see her confusion. Instead she stared at him, waiting. He was sitting in *her* chair behind *her* desk. "Well, I was in the news, like, nightly for quite some time. I would be flabbergasted if she hadn't noticed me."

Josh scrutinized her where she stood. She had no

desire to sit and she was aware Billy stood behind her, close enough for her to feel the heat from his body.

"She claims a man matching Julian Addington's description approached her husband just two weeks ago. He was quite upset when Mr. Henegar refused to entertain his offer of purchasing his farm."

Rowan laughed. Couldn't help herself. "I'm sorry, but you did say farm, didn't you?" *Julian* and *farm* in the same sentence was utterly incongruent.

"He insisted he was thinking of moving here to be near his *family*."

Rowan flinched before she could restrain the reaction. "What family? Was he referring to his ex-wife? If so, perhaps you should be speaking to her."

Dressler stared at her a long moment. "I think he was referring to you."

"Really?" She crossed her arms over her chest, another move she should have controlled. "You actually believe that Julian would purchase property here? In Winchester? He's not a fool, Josh. But you are if you believe the nonsense Sue Ellen Thackerson and Wanda Henegar are telling you."

"He's playing a game, Rowan." Dressler stood. "He wants to make you wonder. To keep you off your game because he realizes that if anyone can help find him, it's you."

Now the man just wanted to earn himself a few brownie points. "You let me know how that scenario pans out for you."

She turned, stepped around Billy and walked out of her office. She had a client waiting.

Dressler had hit the mark with one aspect of his conclusions. Julian was here or, at the very least, close by. The handwriting was his. But he was not the one who had killed Henegar or Thackerson. He was far too much of a perfectionist to do such sloppy work. Not to mention, he would have had a point to his efforts. Wasting his time murdering two locals with no discernible reason was not his style. He had no patience for such trivial pursuits. He often said that when one reached a certain age, they didn't waste time or effort—it was far too precious.

The real question was why would he risk being here at all? What did he want? If he wanted to kill her, why didn't he make a move? He'd said that he wanted her to feel the pain. Well, she was feeling it, all right. He wanted to continue playing his game, was that it? Maybe Dressler had concluded correctly on that part, too.

The question was a rhetorical one. The game was what he wanted. Until he tired of playing. Then what? The answer to that question was what gave her nightmares.

Rowan was not going to play Julian's game. If he wanted to tell her something, he should do it. Come to her door. Call her. Meet her somewhere.

She was ready to see him.

To finish this.

Eighteen

Rowan tossed the hair dryer onto the bed and brushed out her hair. She needed a trim. She frowned and leaned closer to the mirror. Was that a gray hair?

She made a frustrated sound. "It was only a matter of time."

Gray hair was the least of her worries. She had never felt so tired in her life. When she'd finished preparing Mr. Kramer and settled him into refrigeration, she'd cleaned up the mortuary room and finally come upstairs and hit the shower.

The evidence techs were still collecting whatever they could find and the cleaning team had arrived and were standing by. The corpse of suspected serial killer Sanchez/Santos had been hauled away to the lab. The FBI now had control of the body. No surprise there. Anything related to Julian was their jurisdiction, their case. Billy and his department could only react to what happened in their jurisdiction. Once any aspect of a case proved potentially related to Julian, Billy had a duty to notify Dressler.

Rowan dropped the brush onto her dresser and

closed her eyes. If, really big *if* in her opinion, Henegar and Thackerson were victims of Julian's—via some killer he hired or prompted to act—then the body count related to her return to Winchester had risen by two.

How many did that make?

Six? Seven?

No matter how she rationalized the facts, those deaths were on her. Billy and everyone else involved had told her repeatedly that none of this was her fault, but deep down she knew. She knew Julian had followed her here. She knew Julian had selected each victim specifically to get to her or to send her a message. The family and friends of those victims no doubt felt she was the reason they were dead.

No matter that the actions of Julian and his minions were out of her control, the end result was the same—the victims were dead and she was ultimately the reason.

Weary of all of it, she dragged on a pair of sweats with her T-shirt. It was too cold in this old house to sleep only in a T-shirt, as she had all summer. Before she called it a night, she should eat something. Her breakfast of yogurt and granola had been a long time ago. Not that she was actually hungry, but she realized food was essential, just as sleep was. She needed to be able to focus and to think straight. She blinked her raw eyes. The contacts had to go, too. She'd forgotten to take them out last night and now her eyes felt gritty. The usual drops weren't cutting it at this point.

First, she had to eat. Nothing heavy or complicated, she decided. Cheese toast or cereal would do. Freud followed her; settled onto the kitchen floor and watched as she peeled cheese off the block and placed it on the bread. She tucked the cheese-topped bread into the toaster oven and decided to prowl the fridge in search of something to drink. Her fingers curled around a can of soda. She pushed the door closed, leaned a hip against the counter and waited for the oven to ding.

The memory of that kiss—Billy's kiss—trickled into her thoughts and warmed her unreasonably.

Not smart, Rowan.

But she had waited since she was twelve or thirteen years old to be kissed by him. Billy had been her hero. As a kid, she'd firmly believed he would be the man with whom she would spend the rest of her life. Shaking her head at the foolish adolescent memories, she decided a few more seconds wouldn't matter and plucked the toast from the oven. As she placed dinner on a plate, the oven timer dinged, rubbing in the fact that she should have been just a tiny bit more patient. Plate and soda in hand, she made her way to the living room and sat down. It was the first time today she'd attempted to relax.

As she nibbled on the cheese toast, she considered the plausibility of Julian selecting the Henegars and Thackersons to somehow send a message to her. She couldn't see the connection or what he hoped to gain or accomplish.

Because there was nothing to see. This was wrong. She got up, took her trash to the kitchen. Julian wasn't using Henegar or Thackerson. *They* were, somehow, using him. All she and Billy had to do was find who the two had hired to commit murder. There was more than one hundred thousand dollars missing from Barney Thackerson's safe. Hiring someone to commit murder for six figures wouldn't be so difficult. It was keeping that hireling quiet afterward that would be the problem.

Unless they had sought out a professional hitman, the killer would talk, brag about what he'd done. Particularly if he was a novice, and whoever had killed those two men had certainly been a novice. But, as Billy said, working up the confidence to brag would take time.

She wondered if the two women, Sue Ellen and Wanda, had gotten together and come up with the idea to use an MO similar to one Julian had used. Since neither of them had mentioned Julian before, Rowan guessed that they had waited to see if the police would make the connection first. When that didn't happen, they suddenly remembered additional details.

Rowan doubted the two women had any idea how transparent their motives were.

A soft knock at her door shifted her attention there. She glanced at the clock. A few minutes past nine.

"Ro? It's me."

Billy.

Who else would it be at this hour? Bracing herself, she unlocked the door and opened it. "Hey. Your people all done downstairs?"

His hat in his hand, he nodded. "We are. The cleaning team has almost finished. You'll need a new back door and frame. I think this one is beyond repair at this point. We've boarded up the door, secured it as best we can."

"I appreciate that." She suddenly felt terrible about having eaten cheese toast while Billy took care of business downstairs. "Would you like something to eat? I could make you a grilled cheese." His mother made the best grilled-cheese sandwiches.

"Don't go to any trouble, Ro. You're tired. I'm tired. Food isn't exactly on my mind right now."

"I had cheese toast." He had to be starving. "Have a seat. I'll toast you a couple of slices with extra cheese. You want a beer?" She'd considered having one herself, but she'd never enjoyed drinking alone. Maybe she'd have one now.

Rowan didn't wait for his answer—she padded back to the kitchen and preheated the toaster oven. She had just placed the cheese slices on the bread when Billy wandered into the room. Pretending not to notice, she placed the toast into the oven and moved on to the fridge. She grabbed a couple of beers and took a deep breath before closing the door and turning around.

She couldn't pretend the kiss hadn't happened. If she were lucky, he wouldn't bring up the subject. It happened. No big deal. Except in her adolescent memory.

Keep telling yourself that, Ro.

"Here you go." She passed him a beer, opened her own and downed a swallow.

"Lincoln says Dressler finally allowed Sue Ellen and Wanda to go home."

Rowan shook her head. "I told him he was wasting his time."

Billy nodded. "He's like a dog with a bone. You can't shake him loose once his teeth are locked on. I think he wanted them to see each other at city hall. Escalate the stakes. One of them is bound to break. He's hoping one or both have actually seen and spoken to Addington."

"You're not leaning in that direction, are you?" If he was, she was going to be seriously disappointed.

"Hell, no. Dressler is an idiot. I basically told him so but he evidently didn't listen to me, either."

Rowan wondered what else she had missed while she was down in the mortuary room and then up here hiding out. The toaster oven dinged and she moved the toast from the oven to a plate and passed it to Billy. "You need anything else? I might have pineapple slices if you'd like some."

"No, thanks." He stared at his plate rather than look at her.

Rowan grabbed her beer and led the way back to the living room. "I was afraid to turn on the news." She glanced at the dark television screen. "If Sue Ellen or Wanda have spoken to a reporter, all of Winchester probably believes my presence has brought two more murders to the community."

"There were a few speculations on the one report I saw. But don't worry about it, we'll have a press conference to clarify what really happened."

"Assuming you can find what you need to prove those two are lying."

"We'll find what we need."

Rowan sipped her beer while Billy polished off his toast. She was grateful this day was over. Clashing with Dressler was always draining, particularly since this had been going on for months and it was, unfortunately, personal. He and his colleagues at the Bureau believed she was keeping information about Julian from them. That she was somehow in communication with him. Not true, on either account. She was keeping certain information about her parents from everyone, including Billy, but none of it was relevant to finding Julian.

Dressler was no fool. He was likely picking up on the fact that she was hiding something. She was good at hiding her feelings, but she wasn't completely unreadable. Dressler was a highly trained field agent.

Billy had seen through her easily enough. Even now she felt his disappointment on that score.

Breaking the silence, he asked, "You think Julian arranged for Sanchez's body to be stolen just to skin off all those tattoos?"

"Yes. I think he wanted the tattoos gone to prevent Dressler from deciphering whatever there was to decipher. I don't think the symbols mean anything earth-shattering any more than his daring act to remove them does. I believe it was a way to buy time by distracting Dressler and slowing him down."

"You mentioned that you photographed the tattoos."

"I did." She finished off her beer and set the empty bottle on the coffee table. "I haven't put all the pieces together because there hasn't been time, but I will. Though I don't really believe they are relevant to anything that will help us find Julian."

"I'd be grateful if you filled me in as you go."

She nodded. "I will, and I won't leave anything out. You have my word."

"This has been a tough year, Ro. You've gone through a lot. Feeling isolated by all the shocking secrets you've uncovered and the need to conceal information that feels too personal is understandable."

She laughed, the attempt a little weak and pathetic. "You sound like a psychiatrist."

"I've spent a lot of time lately with a really good one. She's rubbed off on me."

He looked so tired and yet he smiled, and she loved that about him. Billy Brannigan was a good man. He deserved a lot better than the insanity she could offer him. No matter how she'd fantasized about him when she was growing up, he needed someone with far less baggage.

Rather than allow the lapse in conversation to drift into awkward territory, she asked, "Did Dressler mention all those bones?"

"He said they were still working on the exhumations. I drove by there and he has an entire team of folks out there. The tent-city squatters moved to a new location—too much official activity, I think."

"Did you locate Utter?" Rowan abruptly remembered him ordering Clarence to find Owen Utter and bring him in.

Billy shook his head. "He's MIA. I'm betting he moved with the tent-city folks. We'll find him. Like everything else, it'll just take some time."

Rowan picked up his plate and stood. "You still hungry?"

He held up a hand. "I'm good. Thanks."

She carried her empty beer bottle and his plate to the kitchen. She should probably take Freud out again before she went to bed. They could walk down with Billy. When she returned to the living room, she said as much.

"About that..." Though he stood, his hat in his hands, he made no move to start toward the door.

She waited for him to continue, holding her breath. He was stalling for some reason. She really hoped he wasn't going to bring up the kiss.

The *kiss*.

Warmth spread through her before she could stem the reaction.

"I don't feel comfortable leaving you here alone tonight."

Well, it wasn't about the kiss, but it was almost worse. "Are we really going there again?" She did not want to argue with him, particularly this argument. They'd had it a dozen times already. "I thought we were past that issue."

"We have a pretty good reason to believe Addington is here, Ro. The funeral home isn't completely secure after the break-in. I'd feel better sleeping on your couch. Just for the night."

No. Very bad idea. "That's not a good idea, Billy. I'm fine. I have my weapon. I have Freud and the security system is online. We'll be fine."

"Why is my being here not a good idea?" He was frustrated now, maybe even a little annoyed. "Is it about what happened in your office?"

He couldn't even say it. "We've had this same discussion many times before today, Billy. This isn't about what happened in my office."

Another little lie—the part about what happened today, at any rate.

"I kissed you because I wanted to, and I damn sure hope to again. If that's a problem, you need to tell me now."

He wasn't letting this go and part of her yearned to just get it over with. To throw her arms around him and invite him to her bed.

But she couldn't do that. Not now. Maybe not ever. The closer he was to her, the more dangerous Julian was to him.

"This is not a step I can take right now." She somehow managed to draw air into her lungs. "Until this... whatever it is with Julian is over, I'm not free to make those sorts of decisions."

The surprise on his face at her words shifted to disbelief. "So, you'll allow him to control your life? That's what he wants. If you give him that power, he wins, Ro. He wins."

Rowan closed her eyes and fought the urge to lean into him. "Lock up as you leave, please." She met his gaze. "Good night, Billy. I'll see you tomorrow."

"Fine. For now," he warned.

Guilt heaped on her shoulders for allowing him to go without explaining her fears. But this was the right thing to do...*for now.*

Closing the door behind him, she pressed her forehead there. She was so very tired, but she doubted sleep would come. Like most nights, she would likely spend hours going through her mother's journals and writings in hopes of finding something she had missed. Something that would answer all the questions.

Then, when she did sleep, she would dream of her sister or maybe her father or her mother.

But none of it would help her find the answers she needed.

Nineteen

"Sue Ellen and Wanda have lawyered up," Lincoln announced as he walked into Billy's office with two steaming cups of coffee.

Billy tossed the evidence report he'd been attempting to read onto his desk. "Well, damn. Who did they hire?"

"Sue Ellen hired Wesley 'Weasel' Wiseman."

Billy groaned. *Weasel* was the nickname anyone who'd had the misfortune of going up against the man had given him. Wiseman would lie, cheat and steal—whatever was necessary—to win his case. "What about Wanda?"

"She went in the other direction and hired Floyd Becker."

At least Becker was a decent man and a fairly good attorney. "What time are the Henegar sons coming in?"

Steven, the oldest, had called first thing this morning and set up an appointment. David, the younger brother, would be with him. They had both moved away—Steven now married and in Texas, David un-married and in New Mexico. Neither one came home often. One of Stan's hired hands from back when he farmed his land claimed there had been a falling-out over Wanda. He couldn't remember the details but he'd heard more than one fight between father and sons. Stan kept the trouble quiet but there was definitely trouble. With him dead—murdered—hopefully the sons would be willing to share that trouble. Any insight into Stan's life could potentially be useful to the case.

"At nine." Lincoln handed one cup to Billy and took a seat.

"Thanks." Billy tested the coffee. Not too hot, which was surprising since that damn coffee machine had a bad habit of heating it to the point of scorching tongues. He swallowed a sizable gulp of the liquid caffeine, then said, "We have a few minutes. Any update on the au-topsies or when the bodies will be released?"

"Just got an email from Cates." Lincoln set his cup aside and opened the email app on his phone. "Cates says the autopsies are happening later this week, but the preliminary exam basically confirms what we al-ready know. Both men appear to have died from as-phyxiation. No tox screen results yet."

"Thank him for me, would you?" Norton Cates was a top-notch technician at the state lab. He was par-ticularly good about keeping local law enforcement informed. Even when there was no particularly earth-shaking news, Billy appreciated having a status report.

"Doing that now," Lincoln said, his fingers tapping away on his phone.

Billy reviewed the list of points he wanted to go over with the Henegar brothers while Lincoln went to the conference room to update the case board. Culver had given Billy updates every couple of hours last night. No activity around the funeral home. Today Rowan was preparing for the Kramer visitation, so she and Charlotte were basically on-site for the day. Knowing where she was and that Culver was watching her allowed Billy to concentrate on things here.

He rubbed his hand over his jaw and lips. Tried not to think about that kiss. Maybe the reaction had been a foolhardy one, but he'd done it and he didn't regret it. The jury was still out on whether Rowan did or not. He didn't think she did. After all, she'd given him a peck on the lips before she ran out of her office. Still, he wasn't entirely sure. It was all too damn confusing, and this was about the worst possible time to be going there. Truth was, part of him was terrified of what the future held. Addington wouldn't hesitate to kill one or both of them. It didn't feel right to take for granted their time together.

Lincoln ducked his head through the door. "The brothers are waiting in the lobby."

"Let's do this here since we have the case board set up in the conference room." His office wasn't that large, but he wasn't trying to impress anyone. He just wanted to get the facts as the two boys knew them.

Scarcely half an hour later and the Henegar brothers were done. They both were mad as hell at their father for leaving the insurance policy to Wanda. The house, farm and most every other worldly possession that had belonged to their father was now theirs—or would be at the end of probate. They disliked their stepmother immensely, apparently due to an event that occurred when the oldest, Steven, was in high school. He swore to his father that he saw Wanda fooling around with his football coach behind the locker rooms. Wanda adamantly denied the accusation and Stan had believed her. Wanda and Steven had been estranged since. David never liked her because she wanted to be their mother. Since the coach was dead, Billy couldn't check out the allegation. None of the family's friends or acquaintances had mentioned infidelity on the part of either of the Henegars.

All that said, neither one of the brothers felt she was capable of killing their father. Was it possible she had hired someone to do the job? To that question, they both answered with a resounding *maybe*.

Billy and Lincoln were back where they'd started before the long-awaited interviews with the sons.

While Lincoln followed up with Sue Ellen Thackerson's most recent ex-husband, Billy had another lead he wanted to track. Not really a lead, but a hunch. He shook his head as he drove across town. What he had was a desperate need to find something—anything—that would help with Rowan learning the truth about her mother. He hoped that truth would help take down Addington.

He drove to Luther Holcomb's place. He'd basically taught Billy everything he knew about being a good cop. After retiring, Luther had walked away from civilization. Walked away from his wife, too. He spent most of his time hunting and fishing and just being alone. Maybe he'd seen too much or just gotten tired. Whatever the real reason, he'd turned into a hermit.

His truck was parked in front of his cabin, which hopefully meant he was home. Then again, there was always the chance he'd gone into the woods to prepare a tree stand for deer season. This time of year hunters were gearing up for the closest thing to big-game hunting that existed around these parts.

Billy had never been into hunting. Tracking down criminals provided all the excitement along those lines he needed.

He climbed out of his truck, shrugged his jacket higher around his ears. It was cold as hell today. Already, the old men who did their whittling on the bench in front of the courthouse during warm weather insisted there would be lots of cold and snow this winter. Billy didn't mind snow unless someone got lost out in it, or drivers forgot to slow down during a blizzard.

"Wild Bill!" Luther lumbered out onto the porch. "What brings you out and about this morning?"

"I'm hoping you've got a fresh pot of coffee in there."

"Always. My daddy taught me it was a sin to take a drink of alcohol until after twelve noon. Coffee's the next best thing. Can't live without it."

Billy followed him inside and had a seat on the shabby sofa that occupied the wall facing the door. Luther still used the recliner he'd brought from his office. He was the only person Billy had ever known to use a recliner at his desk. Back trouble, he always said.

Luther strolled back into the room carrying two mugs of coffee. He passed one to Billy and took his seat. "You found that serial killer yet?"

Billy tasted his coffee, then shook his head. "Not yet."

"He's a crafty one, is he?"

"Yeah. He's something, all right."

Luther sipped his coffee, content to sit in the quiet.

"There's a good possibility he was having an affair with Norah DuPont," Billy said. "You ever know of her to mess around on Edward?"

"She was an odd one, that's for sure." Luther cradled his mug in both hands. "I guess it would be hard to say one way or the other since she spent so much time traveling. She was always leaving Edward and the girls at home while she went off on one trip or another."

"You never heard of anyone around town she might have gotten involved with?"

Luther shook his head, then frowned. "I don't think so but let me ponder on it. Unless she committed a crime, she wasn't really on my radar. The biggest thing I remember is when she hung herself." He grimaced. "God Almighty, that was a bad day."

Billy nodded. "It was."

"I remember that little girl, Rowan. She was torn all to pieces. Her daddy was in the basement in the mortuary room. He didn't even know anything had happened until he heard her screaming."

The thought of how badly Norah had hurt Rowan made Billy sick, even now.

"Norah didn't have a lot of friends," Billy said. "We've learned she was evidently acquainted somehow with this guy, Carlos Sanchez. Turns out that wasn't his real name and he was a serial killer himself. Guess you heard about that."

"Yeah. I recall seeing Sanchez around. Kept to himself. Lived off the grid before living off the grid was a trend."

"I suppose he never showed up on your radar since

none of his victims came from around these parts." At least none who had ever been reported missing.

"Nope. Whatever he was up to, he was quiet about it. Did his dirty work in some other jurisdiction, I imagine."

"You never saw the two of them, Norah and Sanchez, together?"

Luther's brow furrowed in concentration. "Not that I can recollect. But I don't know many men who wouldn't have been happy to have some of that if she offered."

"She was a good-looking woman."

"Rowan looks just like her," Luther pointed out. "You two still just friends?"

Billy laughed. "If I'm lucky, we'll always be friends."

"Just like a cop to answer a question without really answering it."

Billy gave him a nod. "I learned from the best."

"Go see Beulah Alcott. She was about the only friend I ever saw Norah with and that was only once. I had to go see Beulah to question her about a missing fellow who was last seen at her place and Norah was there. Beulah said something about them being friends. 'Course, her definition of friendship might have meant whoever was paying her for a session at the time. You remember, she read palms and such. Sold herb remedies."

"I remember. Thanks for the tip. I'll pay her a visit. I didn't know she was still alive." Billy finished off his coffee. Like his moonshine, Luther's coffee was stout.

"Oh, yeah. She's still kicking. I saw her about a

month ago. Got some bad arthritis in my right shoulder. She fixed me up good."

"I always figured her remedies were nothing more than snake oil," Billy said.

"Always worked for me."

"You ever have her read your palm or tell your future?"

Luther chuckled. "Hell, no. Whatever's coming for me, I'd just as soon it be a surprise."

Billy stood. "If you think of anything else, Luther, give me a call. We're trying to figure out the connection between Norah and Addington."

"I'll poke around in some of my old notes, see if I forgot something."

Billy thanked him again and headed for Shake Rag. The community was a good ways out of town, much like where Luther lived, only on the other side of the county. Closer to Huntland. The drive took the better part of half an hour. Billy hadn't seen much more than trees and asphalt in the past fifteen minutes. Finally, he spotted the turnoff for Ms. Alcott's place. The narrow side road was badly grown over where it intersected the main road, making it almost impossible to see.

The shack Ms. Alcott called home was more than a mile off the main road. The yard, which had once been fairly large, had been invaded by the forest around it. The trees and undergrowth were overtaking it. He doubted the woman cared since she was older than dirt. A no-maintenance yard was a perk when you were closer to ninety than eighty.

He parked next to the narrow path leading to the house. Climbed out and followed the stones buried in the dirt, only the partially moss-covered tops showing.

The steps squeaked as he climbed up to the rickety porch. He removed his hat and crossed to the door, opened the screen and knocked on the wood slab behind it.

The voice that called out for him to come in was surprisingly loud and strong. He turned the knob and walked in. He blinked to adjust to the low lighting of a single kerosene lamp and the flames jumping in the fireplace.

"Ms. Alcott, I'm the chief of police—"

"Why I know who you are, boy. Take a load off, Billy Brannigan."

He'd only seen Beulah Alcott a couple of times. She was a tiny woman. Her dark skin looked even darker against her silvery hair. Her hair was fashioned into a coil on the back of her head. She wore a thick wool sweater that was gray like the boots peeking from beneath her long black skirt. Her gnarled hands were propped on the arms of the rocking chair that slowly moved back and forth in perpetual motion.

Billy sat down on the small sofa directly across from her. "I need some help with a case and I was hoping you might be able to assist me."

"You trying to help the undertaker's daughter, aren't you? I feel the trouble hovering over her like a black cloud."

Beulah Alcott was a self-professed fortune-teller. She read palms and tarot cards, and, he'd heard, she even had a crystal ball. But she was most known for her healing remedies. Folks way out here went to her more often than the doctor.

"I am and I'm hoping you can offer some insights."

"Her momma had the same trouble," Alcott said. "I read her palm once. Told her there was trouble coming." Her frail shoulders shook. "I could feel death all around her and I ain't talking about her living in that funeral home. She drew it like a magnet. It was one of the strongest impressions I've ever had come over me. She didn't act surprised. She knew what she was. You found all those bones, didn't you? They've been rattling in my dreams for decades."

"We sure did." Billy considered the best question to ask that might get a more direct answer. Not easy when the lady wanted to talk about spirits and impressions. He'd never been a believer when it came to fortunes and spirits.

"Carlos Sanchez was the one who buried all those bones. Do you know if Norah DuPont was involved with him or Julian Addington?"

He didn't expect the sort of answer he could use, but it might be interesting to see what she had to say. Unless someone told her, he had no idea if she had a clue who Addington was. She had no television. Maybe there was a radio around here somewhere, and there was always the possibility that she received the newspaper or heard gossip from some of her clients.

"You should believe, Billy." She stared directly at him. Her famous eyes, one blue and one green, were as vivid as if light poured out from them. "The only way you'll ever find the truth is if you believe."

"I'm trying, Ms. Alcott."

"Norah was a special person," Alcott explained. "They were drawn to her—those kind. The killing type, I mean. She made a mistake and she couldn't stop this thing she started. It destroyed her just as it will her daughter. She's special, too. She just don't know it yet."

"Special how?" Billy wanted to believe, and he wanted desperately to understand.

"They are drawn to her. She understands them and they need her."

"Who are *they*?" Billy needed her to be more specific.

"Why, the ones who spread death. Who else? They're coming for her, Billy. Be very careful. There is one who will do anything to have her. He has waited a long time and he don't like you one little bit."

Addington. Desperation swelled inside Billy. "What can I do to protect her?"

"Believe," she urged. "Believe in yourself, believe in her." She leaned forward ever so slightly. "Most of all, believe in what's coming. You can't stop it. You just have to face it when it arrives."

Billy thanked her and walked out of her tiny house. Heart thundering, he climbed into his truck and drove straight to the funeral home. He needed to see Rowan.

To convince her that she couldn't do this thing with Addington alone.

Twenty

Rowan walked through the viewing parlor for a final check. The chairs were lined up neatly. Boxes of tissue had been placed around the room, easily accessible for those whose emotions could not be contained. Flowers were already pouring in for Mr. Kramer from the local florists. She had dressed him in the handsome navy suit, pale blue shirt and striped tie his wife delivered. The elderly woman had smiled as she provided blue boxers and socks, as well as lace-up leather oxfords with a mirror shine. She said her husband liked matching accessories. Rowan promised she would see that all was exactly as Mr. Kramer preferred.

At five, he would be moved into the viewing room for the family to have some private time with him. Mrs. Kramer had requested that visitation begin at six. She wanted to be home by eight thirty. She and Mr. Kramer were always in bed by nine. At her expectant look, Rowan had made another promise, this one to ensure that Mr. Kramer was tucked in for the night no later than nine, as well.

In the corridor, Rowan read over the announcement

on the board. Surname was spelled correctly. Times stated for the visitation and tomorrow's funeral were correct. The funeral would begin at one tomorrow and the burial would follow at the family cemetery outside of town. The memorial pamphlets Charlotte had designed were lovely, as always. Neat stacks stood on the desk next to the guest registry.

All was ready.

A yawn had her putting her hand to her mouth. She hadn't slept well last night. Dreams of Raven had haunted her the first part of the night. She'd gotten up at two and paced the floor for a while. Ended up in her mother's room going through the pages of one of her journals. When she'd finally climbed back into bed again, Rowan had dreamed of her mother and, toward the end, of her father, too. The dreams had been confusing and disturbing. Her sister kept leading her through the woods. Each time Rowan would become lost and unable to find Raven again until she happened upon the water's edge and saw her body floating there.

The dreams of her mother had been calm, almost pleasant. They were picnicking in the backyard. The images seemed to be in black and white. The grass had looked brown rather than green. A white quilt was spread on the ground. She and Raven, as well as Norah, had been wearing white dresses. They had looked like the people in those old photos before color film was available. Pleasant enough but creepy somehow.

The dreams of her father were choppy and frustrating. She could see him and then he was gone. Each time she would start in one place, like the lobby of the funeral home, and then she was somewhere else. Like an old, flickering movie where parts of scenes had been lost to time and disintegrating film.

In the dreams, her father kept calling her name. *Rowan. Rowan. Rowan.*

She shivered, wrapped her arms around herself. The emotions from the dreams had lingered long after her second cup of coffee. When she'd had to go out into the cold morning to track down Freud she'd experienced that skin-crawling sensation that someone was watching her. Though she hadn't spotted anyone, the feeling just wouldn't go away and last night's dreams had whispered to her again. Of course, she'd wondered if Julian was out there somewhere watching her. But it could just as easily be someone else. Some of Dressler's people. The person or persons responsible for Stan Henegar's and Barney Thackerson's murders. She couldn't actually see any reason their murderer would be watching her. No one really had reason to connect her to the investigation in any capacity. Or maybe it was just someone from a neighboring business or home who wanted to watch the weird woman who lived in the funeral home.

Paranoia. It was spreading inside her like a disease she couldn't stop.

"Put your doctor's hat on, Rowan." She inhaled deeply, let out a breath slowly.

She was well aware how unhealthy long-term issues like the one involving Julian could affect one's mental health. This year had taken a toll. The past few months had been somewhat of a reprieve. She should have known better than to believe Julian might just disappear...or that he was dead.

No. He wasn't finished yet. And she had been a fool to allow her guard down, however slightly.

A knock on the front entrance made her jump. She pressed a hand to her chest and diverted from her destination, her office, to the front entry. She hated having to keep the door locked. This was a business. People needed to be able to walk in without the hassle of ringing a buzzer or knocking.

She checked the newly installed peephole and relaxed. *Billy.*

A quick twist of the deal bolt and she opened the door. "Why didn't you use your key?"

"I wasn't sure if you were here or if it was just Charlotte." He hitched his thumb toward her assistant's car, then removed his hat. "I didn't want to scare her by barging in unannounced."

A reasonable explanation. With all that had been going on around here, Rowan was immensely thankful Charlotte hadn't quit on her. She would be lost without Charlotte. This was not a one-woman operation.

"You have an update on the case?" She waited until he had clicked the dead bolt back into the locked position before heading toward her office once more.

"Afraid not. Well," he amended, "not really."

Rowan hesitated at the door and glanced at him. "Meaning?"

"Stan Henegar's sons came in for their interviews."

Rowan gestured to the chair in front of her desk as she walked around to her own. "Did you learn anything useful?"

It was at that moment that she realized her mistake. They were in her office. He'd kissed her right here in this room. She blinked. But then she was the one who'd kissed him after that. A rash decision at best. But one she could not regret, as foolish as the idea might be.

Deep breath. She braced her forearms on her desk and tried to appear relaxed. *You've known Billy your whole life, been friends most of that time. Be calm. Relax.* She trusted him…cared deeply for him.

She blinked, ordered her traitorous brain to focus.

"Steven, the older son, had a falling-out with Wanda when he was in high school. He swore he saw her fooling around with his coach. She denied it, of course, and Stan took her side. I can't confirm the story because the coach passed years ago. Asking around wouldn't accomplish anything other than to cause unnecessary harm."

Wanda was much younger than Stan. It was possible she'd felt the need for something more than he offered. It happened. It was a betrayal but certainly not the same thing as murder. Though it could be motive, yet an affair that long ago wasn't likely to be the reason Stan had been murdered just days ago. Rowan said as much and Billy agreed.

"The younger son, David, didn't like Wanda trying to play mother so they never really got along, but he didn't mention any instances of trouble the way his brother did. He was unaware of any sort of relationship with the coach."

Henegar's sons weren't happy about the insurance policy, Billy explained, but they weren't going to bother contesting the insurance since it wouldn't pay out until the murder investigation was resolved. If Wanda had nothing to do with their father's murder, they intended to let it go. If she had, the policy proceeds would go to them, anyway.

Rowan considered mentioning how she'd felt as if someone were watching her this morning, but she knew if she did Billy would only insist she needed a security detail. She didn't. She was prepared.

The lack of a security detail would facilitate the end result she was hoping for—Julian's return. She couldn't stop him unless he ventured close. She wanted him to come close again. Close enough to...

Rowan forced away the thoughts. It was at that moment that she considered that the former detective, Cash Barton, might be the one watching her. Anna Addington had hired him to find the truth about what happened to her daughter. It made sense that watching Rowan would be on his agenda.

Of course. She should have thought of that.

She decided something else as well, in that moment as Billy finished bringing her up to speed. "We should try talking to Sue Ellen."

"They both lawyered up." Billy shrugged. "I doubt either one is going to talk to us."

"She probably wouldn't give us the answers we want, anyway," Rowan agreed. "But for my purposes, she doesn't have to say a word. I only want to see her reaction to certain comments."

He leaned forward, hopeful that she'd come up with something that would help solve this case. "You onto something, Ro?"

Sadly, it was only a hunch. "If Sue Ellen and Wanda planned these murders, the idea came from somewhere. Julian has been all over the news, but the many, many ways in which he murdered his victims wouldn't be in a mere headline. To find the numerous MOs he used, one would have to sift through the articles. Read the details."

"Time-consuming," he noted, "but if a person felt compelled to find just the right method, he or she might go to the trouble."

"Or," Rowan countered, "he or she would do an internet search and have an entire list appear right before her eyes."

He nodded, not convinced enough to be excited just yet. "There were no computers, tablets or even smartphones at the Henegar residence. Wanda uses an old flip phone." His gaze narrowed. "I suppose she could have gone to the library or used a friend's computer or whatever."

Rowan watched the idea gaining momentum in his eyes. "Sue Ellen has a smartphone."

"And she has an online dating profile." He grinned. "Lincoln found it. Along with a Facebook page and an Instagram. Wanda doesn't have any of those, unless she's using an alias. Bottom line, Sue Ellen would be well versed in how to conduct an internet search."

"The idea—the seed of the plan—started with only one of them," Rowan suggested.

Now he had the itch, too. "My money's on Sue Ellen."

"Exactly. Let's pay the lady a visit." Rowan grabbed her bag and stood. "Then you can buy me lunch."

He pushed to his feet. "Did you just mention lunch?"

She looped the strap of her bag over her neck. "I did. Should we mark this day on the calendar?"

"I don't know about all that, but I would love to buy you lunch, Dr. DuPont."

Rowan smiled. This felt more like the way things

were supposed to be between them. Maybe the kiss was necessary to break the out-of-control tension. Now they could move on.

She dropped by Charlotte's office and let her know that she would be back in a couple of hours. Charlotte had already been out to lunch, since her list of duties included dropping by the post office and picking up supplies for the lounge. Rowan couldn't imagine trying to handle all that on her own. At the beginning of the year she intended to give Charlotte another raise. A really good one.

She did not want to lose Charlotte.

As they walked outside, Rowan asked, "Anything new on Utter?"

Billy shook his head as he settled behind the steering wheel of his truck. "Haven't located him. I have a feeling he's laying low."

"You think he knows more than he's shared?"

Billy started the truck. "Don't you?"

She nodded. "I do."

If Utter wasn't hiding out somewhere, he was likely dead. A smart killer didn't leave loose ends like an old man who could spill his guts. A smart killer cleaned up after himself as he went along.

Rowan couldn't say whether Carlos Sanchez had been smart or not, but Julian Addington was brilliant.

Sue Ellen Thackerson's vehicle was at her father's store. Technically it was her store now. The estate would need to go through probate, but, for all intents and purposes, it was hers. Unless it was discovered that she was involved in her father's death, at any rate. Then everything would change.

A new face was behind the counter in the store. Male. Thirtyish. Rowan didn't know him. Most likely Yancey Quinn had been fired for providing his two cents' worth about the relationship between Sue Ellen and her father.

"Sue Ellen in the back?" Billy asked.

"She is," the man said.

Billy gave him a nod and walked in that direction.

"I don't think she wants any company, though," the guy shouted.

Billy kept walking; Rowan did the same.

At the door that separated the back storeroom from the living quarters, Billy knocked.

Beyond the dingy door a female voice shouted, "Come on in. I didn't lock it."

Obviously, Sue Ellen thought the person at the door was the guy working behind the counter or some other friend she was expecting. Billy glanced at Rowan, then opened the door.

Sue Ellen looked up from the boxes she appeared to be packing. Her gaze swung from Billy to Rowan and back. "What do you want?"

"I have a couple of new questions for you, Sue Ellen."

The woman glared at Billy. "You can talk to my lawyer. You're not allowed to talk to me anymore."

She threw more items into a box and then reached for the next row on the bookshelf. Apparently, she was packing up her father's belongings. He wasn't even buried yet. *Why put off until tomorrow, what you can do today?* Rowan mused. The woman defined *heartlessness.*

"This is one of the most painful parts of losing a

father," Rowan said, thinking of her own father. She hadn't packed up any of his things. She'd left all of them right where they were. Just as he had Rowan's mother's things and Raven's things. Then again, what she and her father had done was called denial.

"It's no fun," Sue Ellen muttered, "that's for sure." More items went into the box. She seemed to pay little or no attention to what she tossed in. These were her father's personal possessions and she wanted none of them. No surprise there since she was, in all likelihood, the reason he was dead.

Silence throbbed in the air for five or six seconds.

"Chief Brannigan was telling me," Rowan began, "that the bodies may be released by the end of the week."

"Yeah, I heard that already." She looked Rowan up and down. "I'm still not answering any questions and I'm using a funeral home in Tullahoma."

"I understand." Billy gifted her with a patient smile. "It's just that we learned some disturbing information about Wanda Henegar that might impact the case."

Her eyebrows lifted the slightest bit. Rowan wanted to give Billy a high five. Very good move.

"What do you mean?" Sue Ellen dropped another item into the box and stared at Billy, waiting for an answer.

Oh, she was listening now and Rowan imagined she would be doing plenty of talking.

"Whoever killed your father and Mr. Henegar may have been trying to make the murders appear like the work of someone else."

"I'm not sure I understand." Caution weighted Sue Ellen's tone. "I thought that serial killer Addington was the top suspect. Are you saying he didn't do it? I'm positive the man I saw talking to my father was him."

"It's possible it was him," Billy said.

"But the work wasn't up to his usual standards," Rowan said for clarification.

For one single instant, fear gleamed in the woman's eyes. "There are standards for murder?"

"Murderers have MOs," Billy said. "Many of them are recognizable by those MOs. And we thought the MOs in your father's murder and in Mr. Henegar's were similar to one Addington once used. It was the execution of that MO that didn't live up to his standards. The work was sloppy, unfocused."

Sue Ellen shrugged. "Like on *CSI* or something like that."

Billy nodded. "Exactly like that."

"Except," Rowan said, infusing skepticism into her voice, "Addington killed more than a hundred people. I'm not sure all those murder methods, *MOs*—" she glanced at Sue Ellen "—were reported in the news. How did you say you thought this new suspect found what he needed to try framing Addington?" She directed the question to Billy.

Billy flared his hands. "That's the million-dollar question."

"What about on the internet?" Sue Ellen said. "You can find anything on the internet."

Rowan smiled. "My goodness, Sue Ellen. You sound like a detective yourself. You're absolutely right. We should have thought of that." She made a face at Billy.

The younger woman smirked, enjoying the compliment a little too much. "I've damn sure watched enough of those crime-scene shows to be one."

And there was the answer Rowan had come here looking for.

Her cell vibrated and she checked the screen. *Charlotte*. "Excuse me—" she looked from Sue Ellen to Billy "—I have to take this."

While Billy thanked the woman, Rowan moved into the storage area and answered Charlotte's call. "Hey. Everything okay?"

"I'm not sure."

The worry in her assistant's voice bumped Rowan's pulse into a faster rhythm. "What's wrong?"

"There's a woman here to see you."

Rowan's first thought was of Anna Addington. "Did she give you a name?"

"No. She said she would only talk to you."

Rowan licked her abruptly dry lips, ordered her nerves to stop their twitching. "Is there anything else I should know?"

"I can't pinpoint anything in particular. She doesn't appear to be dangerous."

That was good news, but Charlotte didn't sound as if it were good. Her voice was really low now. Rowan had to strain to hear.

"But she's odd."

Rowan relaxed a little. This was Winchester, there were a few odd folks. Maybe she wasn't the only one dealing with paranoia. "Is there anyone with her?"

"No, but she came in wheeling one of those big suitcases, as if she'd just gotten off a plane."

Renewed concern pulsed through Rowan. "I'll be right there. I want you to take Freud out. Tell her he needs to relieve himself and that I'm on my way. You go out the front door and keep walking."

"But what about—"

"Just do it, Charlotte. Now."

"Okay."

Rowan turned to find Billy coming up behind her. "Everything okay?" he asked.

"Not at all. We have to hurry."

As they rushed to his truck, she filled him in on the conversation with Charlotte.

"Damn." As he drove, he called Clarence Lincoln and told him to contact Sheriff Colt Tanner. Tanner had a deputy who was a former bomb expert in the military. Billy wanted him at the funeral home ASAP.

Rowan's throat tightened. She had no idea how far away the nearest bomb squad was. Her chest ached. As many times as she had hoped never to see the funeral home again, she did not want her father's legacy destroyed.

By the time they reached the funeral home, her heart was thumping against her sternum.

Billy parked on the street. "Stay put, Ro," he ordered as he climbed out.

"No way." She spotted Charlotte and Freud standing outside the shop across the street. She climbed out and waved to them. Freud barked.

Rowan started toward the funeral home and Billy blocked her path. "I mean it, Ro. You are not going in. You need to let me handle this."

"There's a very good chance we could be overreacting," she reminded him, though every nerve ending in her body was jumping.

"Could be," he agreed, his face impassive, "but you're staying right here while I check it out."

Before Rowan could launch a new protest, he turned

and strode across the lot, toward the funeral home and whatever waited inside.

Her brain told her to stop him but she felt frozen to the spot, as if the world were spinning out of control and she was helpless to stop it.

This could be Julian.

Billy could be walking into a trap.

Twenty-One

Billy Brannigan should have known better than to expect Rowan to follow orders. Especially when it came to all the damn trouble she seemed to draw like a magnet.

She entered the funeral home from the portico end. There was no way she was allowing him to face whatever was in there alone. Inside the door, she pulled her handgun from her bag, allowing the bag to slide down to the floor. She almost never stuck the damn thing into her bag. It usually took up all the room. But today, considering her dress slacks didn't have pockets and were a little snug in the waist, she'd left behind her wallet and sunglasses. The gun was more important, she had decided.

Moving silently along the carpeted corridor, she heard the front entrance as it opened. Heard Billy's low voice as he spoke to the woman waiting in the lobby to see Rowan.

"I can't talk to anyone but her," the woman insisted, her words a near screech.

"Why don't we step outside and you can speak to

her there?" Billy promised. "She's right outside waiting to see you."

Rowan somehow managed to shove the gun into her waistband at the small of her back and stepped into the lobby. The cold steel bit into her flesh. "Actually, I'm right here. How can I help you?"

Billy glared at Rowan but she ignored him. He would be the first to say that she'd become very good at ignoring him.

The woman stood from the bench where she'd been waiting. She was tall, thin and at least sixty, maybe older. "I need you to take care of this for me." She grabbed the handle of her suitcase and dragged it forward. "He said you could."

Rowan froze.

Billy had the suitcase wrenched away from the woman before she could take another step. She screamed at him. "Go," he shouted at Rowan.

Rowan held up her hands to show they were empty. "Why don't we go into my office?" she suggested to the woman shouting at Billy. Somehow the words came out calmly, though Rowan's heart was racing. "We can talk privately there."

This suggestion got the woman's attention. She stopped screaming and turned to Rowan. "Yes." She nodded adamantly. "We should talk privately."

Billy drew his weapon and pressed it into the woman's back. "Take one step and I will shoot." He arrowed another glare at Rowan. "Go. Now."

The woman turned to face Billy, his weapon now boring into her chest. "Go ahead, shoot me. I am not afraid to die. You, on the other hand, should be very afraid."

Oh, God. Rowan's heart sank all the way to the floor.

The entry doors burst open and uniformed officers poured in.

Rowan's knees gave out on her and she clutched at the wall for support.

The woman's screeching filled the air.

There was no bomb inside the thirty-two-inch wheeled bag.

Folded inside was the body of a young woman. Evidence techs and the coroner were called. Burt estimated the woman had been dead around twenty-four hours, maybe less. The car, in which the woman whose name they still did not know, was registered in Colorado, but it had been reported stolen yesterday.

Based on a photo from the databases Clarence had checked, the dead woman was twenty-nine-year-old Renae Cyrus from Denver, reported missing four days ago.

Dressler had arrived and was in the interview room with the presumed killer. Rowan, Billy and Clarence watched.

Billy was still a little irritated at Rowan for not following his orders. Tension radiated off him in tsunami-like waves, not easy to ignore in such tight quarters. The woman had been unarmed. There was cash in the glove box. Receipts from various gas stations along her journey. But no ID, no nothing, other than the wheeled bag with the body tucked inside.

Why the hell would some woman kill another woman and then drive from Colorado to Tennessee to speak with Rowan?

There was only one explanation.

Julian.

He must have sent her. There simply was no other explanation for this bizarre turn of events.

The woman continued to stare at Dressler without saying a word. As soon as she had been cuffed, she had stopped talking. She hadn't made a single sound since. As the officers had loaded her into a cruiser, she had stared at Rowan as long as possible. Rowan had asked Billy to allow her to interview the woman but Dressler had arrived and taken over. Rowan supposed she should be grateful that he had even agreed to allow them to watch the interview. But it was immensely difficult to be grateful to Dressler for allowing them to do what needed to be done.

After half an hour, Dressler stood and walked out of the room. Seconds later he squeezed into the observation booth. "She's not going to talk to me."

Rowan bit her tongue to prevent making a snarky retort.

"We can park her in a cell for a few hours and see if that changes her mind," Billy suggested.

Rowan wanted to shake both of them. The woman wanted to talk to her! The answer to getting her to cooperate was standing right here.

Dressler stared at the woman seated at the shabby table a dozen feet away, beyond the glass that allowed them to anonymously watch and discuss her. "I don't think time will change her mind."

Rowan refused to agree with him, though she did. To do so would be like taking his side over Billy's. Right now she wasn't on either man's side.

"Well, Agent Dressler, since your extensive charm

didn't work, what's your suggestion?" Billy turned to him and waited for his answer.

Rowan bit her lips together to prevent herself from smiling.

Dressler smiled that smug expression that made Rowan want to kick him. "I think it's time we allowed Dr. DuPont to interview the woman. After all, our Jane Doe came all this way to see her."

Billy shifted his gaze to Rowan. "What do you think, Ro? You interested in helping Agent Dressler get this done?"

"I don't know why I didn't think of that." She shrugged, knowing Billy would prefer she not go into the room, but that he now understood it was necessary. "She's secured. I'll be fine."

Dressler held up his hands in surrender. "Can we get on with it, please?"

Rowan crossed her arms over her chest. "Just waiting for you to move, Josh."

He smirked, then realized she was right and the sour expression that claimed his face made her want to smile. He exited the booth, Clarence did the same.

Billy hesitated. "I need you to be more careful, Ro."

She nodded. He was right. She had gone too far. Things could have turned out vastly differently. "I know. Sorry about earlier."

She owed him that apology on another level, as well. She had disrespected his position as chief and as her friend.

He gestured for her to exit first. When she reached for the door to the interview room, the men stepped back into the booth.

Rowan took a deep breath and opened the door.

She walked in and crossed to the table. Sitting down in the only vacant chair, she took a moment to get her bearings. Her chair was slightly offset from the other woman's rather than directly across from it. That way she wouldn't block the view of those in the observation booth.

"Well." Rowan placed her hands in her lap and met the woman's gaze. "This was certainly quite the commotion for the opportunity to speak to me. I apologize for all the hoopla."

The woman said nothing.

"You know who I am, but I don't know your name."

More of that silence. The way she stared at Rowan, with watery, pale blue eyes, was a tad unsettling. Her hair was light, mostly that white sort of gray that somehow looked good with her complexion. She was thin and tall but not frail. She looked strong. Her posture was very good. Straight spine, square shoulders. The only telltale indications that all was not right in her world were the dark circles under her eyes and the iron cuffs she wore. The pink sweater and khaki trousers and white lace-up tennis shoes were completely incongruent with her current situation and the body in the bag.

"I came a long way to see you."

The sound of her voice was like an ache in the air, filled with pain and defeat.

Rowan searched her face as she spoke. There was the vaguest accent. Something European or remotely Slavic. "You did. Should I be flattered?"

"You're supposed to fix this. No one else will— they're all afraid."

Rowan held her gaze. "I'm not afraid. Perhaps you can explain what you'd like me to fix."

"Her."

She said this as if Rowan should understand and, oddly, she did.

"Your friend."

She nodded. "It has to be you."

"You want me to prepare her?"

Another nod, this one a bit more frantic.

"I can do that, but first I need to know who she is. Who you are. Standard protocol," Rowan assured her.

"I love her." The woman blinked at the shine in her eyes. "You understand that, don't you?"

Rowan nodded. "I do."

"Please, it needs to be done quickly."

"I'm afraid the authorities won't release her to me without some information."

Fury ignited in her eyes, tightened her jawline. "You tell those bastards—" she glowered at the mirror above Rowan's head "—that I'll tell you everything. Who I am, where all the bodies are—as soon as you take care of her."

Rowan stood. "I'll speak to the man in charge and see what I can arrange."

The woman didn't respond.

Rowan walked out of the room and into the observation booth. "You heard what she wants."

Dressler shifted his gaze from the woman on the other side of the mirror to Rowan. He stared at her for a long moment, something like awe in his eyes. "Do it."

As if the woman had heard his agreement, she shouted at the mirror. "I want to watch. Unless I get to watch, no deal."

"No way," Billy said. "She is not going to be in the mortuary room with you, Ro. She's staying right here, in custody."

Detective Tara Stewart appeared at the open door. "Chief, we just received this in response to our latest round of inquiries."

Billy accepted the paper she held. He read over the typed words and then turned to Dressler. "We still don't have a name, but her prints have been associated with a dozen or so homicide cases over the past twenty years."

"Give her whatever she wants," Dressler said to Rowan.

Dressler won the battle but Billy won the war.

Rowan stood at the mortuary table, Renae Cyrus arranged before her. She had washed the body with disinfectant. Not exactly a pleasant job since the body had been stuffed into a suitcase for hours, but not the worst task she'd had to undertake by any means.

"She's beautiful," the woman who had, presumably, murdered her said.

The prisoner was shackled, wrists and ankles to a belly chain that made running or fighting impossible. She sat on a stool on the opposite side of the table, her secured hands braced on the edge of the cold steel.

This process was breaking numerous rules and no doubt a law or two. The deceased or a member of the deceased's family had not authorized this procedure. Rowan reminded herself that it would have to be done eventually unless her family was opposed for religious reasons.

Worst case, she would be sued, in which case she

would point to the Federal Bureau of Investigation and let them handle it.

"She is very beautiful." Rowan searched the older woman's obviously grieving eyes. "Are you certain you want to watch this? It's not pleasant."

If the report Billy had received was correct, this woman was most likely a killer. One who had perhaps been involved with many murders—maybe even this one. But every instinct Rowan possessed said that she loved the woman on the table.

The woman nodded. "She's my daughter." Her gaze locked with Rowan's. "I must watch."

Rowan nodded. There were similarities. The woman on the table had blond hair and blue eyes. Her complexion—under normal circumstances—would be similar. It was certainly possible.

"All right. Why don't you tell me what happened while I work?" Rowan began the steps of setting the deceased's face. She would seal the eyes shut, wire the jaw and seal the lips.

"She didn't smile much, so no big smile, okay?"

Rowan nodded at the woman on the other side of the table.

Silence hovered over them as Rowan did her work. Her heart rate and pulse slowed with the practiced rhythm. The lips, she decided, were identical to the older woman's. Their physical builds were similar, as well.

"I don't want to talk with him in here."

Rowan followed her gaze to where Billy leaned against the door.

"He's okay," Rowan assured her. "A good man."

The woman stared at her for a long moment. "She

was taken from me when she was two years old. Stolen." Tears brimmed on her lashes. "I was never going to have children because…" She swallowed hard, the movement tightening the column of her throat. "I knew it wasn't smart. But when it happened, I couldn't resist." She smiled, tried to wipe her cheek on her shoulder. "I wanted to know what it felt like to have someone love me unconditionally despite what I am." She released a big breath. "It almost killed me when I couldn't find her. I tried for years to forget her but I could not do it. After all this time, I finally found her."

Rowan paused in her work. "Where was she?"

"In Denver. A family there had adopted her. She was all grown-up and really smart. She's a teacher."

Was a teacher. Rowan looked at the dead woman on the table. "Was she married?"

The woman shook her head. "A boyfriend, though."

Rowan rested her gaze on hers. "It's time to do the next steps."

She nodded. "Okay."

Rowan readied the pump and prepared to make the necessary incisions. "How did she fall?"

She agreed with Burt's conclusion that the victim had fallen to her death. The visible external damage to the side of her head and the bruising of the neck on that same side suggested possible cervical injury along with the head injury. But, once her clothes were removed, it was the damage to her right shoulder that confirmed the scenario for Rowan.

"She wanted to spend some time with me. Getting to know me. School is out so we were going to disappear for a while. That way her family and friends couldn't interfere. She was going to call them. But she forgot her cell phone. She ran back inside to get it." She stared at her daughter for a long moment. "Her apartment building was an old one with no elevator, so there was only the stairs. I guess she got in too big of a hurry and tripped. When she didn't come back to the car, I went in to see about her. She was in the stairwell at the bottom of the stairs on the second floor." Tears slid down her cheeks and she rocked back and forth for a minute or more. "She was dead. I know when somebody is dead. I knew if I called 911 or whatever they would take her from me and I only just found her."

Rowan reached across the table and laid a hand on hers. "I'm so sorry for your loss."

When the woman had composed herself, Rowan turned on the pump and began the process of replacing the young woman's blood with preserving chemicals.

The woman stared across her daughter's body and said, "My name is Angel Petrov. I immigrated to this country with my family when I was five years old. I've killed many people, some who deserved it, some who did not. But I could never help myself. It is a curse." Her helpless gaze dropped to her daughter. "I have done only one good thing in this life." She looked at Rowan then. "I will tell you—" she lowered her voice to a near whisper "—their names and where the bodies can be found on one condition."

Rowan held her breath.

"The man—" she hitched her head toward Billy "—he must end my misery."

"I'm sure you're aware he can't do that," Rowan said just as quietly.

"Find a way," she said knowingly. "And I will tell you something very important that you need to know."

This woman was a self-professed killer, a serial killer. She had come to Rowan, which meant she was somehow connected to Julian or she had kept up with all the media buzz. Of those two possibilities, Julian was the far more likely scenario. Either way, Rowan had only one choice.

"You have my word," she promised. "I'll do what I can."

The older woman nodded. "You have paper and pen?"

Rowan removed the glove on her right hand, reached into her pocket and retrieved her cell phone. "Is it all right if I record you instead?"

She shrugged. "Why not?"

When Rowan had readied her phone, she gave the woman a nod.

"I started thirty-five years ago in Nevada."

By the time the embalming was complete, Angel had lapsed into silence. Rowan turned off her phone, slid it into her pocket and then shut off the machine. She removed the necessary hoses and closed the incisions.

"Would you like me to select her a nice dress?" Rowan asked.

Angel nodded. "Pink. She liked pink."

Rowan hesitated but only for a moment. "There's only one way you're going to get what you want, Angel."

She stared unblinkingly at Rowan.

"I think you know what I mean," Rowan said when she remained silent.

She nodded. "Very well. A deal is a deal. Watch

your friend closely or he will not be long for this world. He has a very large target on his back."

Her words confirmed Rowan's worst fears. "Thank you. Can you tell me who sent you to me?"

"You know the answer already."

Rowan dared to breathe. *Julian.*

"She wanted to protect you, but there was only so much she could do."

Rowan searched the woman's face. "Who do you mean?"

Petrov looked away. Clearly, she had said all she intended to say. Rowan had gotten more than she expected, so she let it go. "Let's pick out a dress."

While Angel looked through the dress options, Rowan was able to warn Billy to be prepared for a move out of the woman.

As much sympathy as she had for her loss, she would not help her escape justice, especially if it meant using Billy.

When the only right dress was selected and slipped onto Angel's daughter, she made her move. Billy stopped her and had her returned to a cell. Clarence called Denver and informed the detective on the Cyrus case that her body was here. The body had been placed in refrigeration.

Rowan had turned her cell over to Billy for access to the recording he would share with Dressler. Rowan had a visitation to oversee.

She and Billy could talk later. He was so worried about keeping her safe. But he was the one who needed to be careful. Julian wanted him out of the way and apparently he was telling people about it.

He had no doubt sent Angel here to distract everyone working on the case. To stir up emotions.

To prepare Rowan for what was coming.

Twenty-Two

Billy was ready to boot Dressler out of his office well before the son of a bitch was ready to go.

"We've listened to that recording half a dozen times. What else do you expect to get from what the woman said?" Billy was damn frustrated. Sitting huddled in his office with Dressler for the past two and a half hours was like trying to sleep on a bed of nails. The man had a way of getting under his skin and on his last damn nerve.

"Rowan isn't telling us everything." Dressler turned off the video he'd copied from Rowan's phone.

"What the hell, Dressler?" Billy pushed back his chair and stood. "I was right there in the room. What you hear is all that was said."

Dressler kicked back in his chair, propped his feet on Billy's desk. "So you watched them every second? Never looked away?"

"Of course I didn't look away." Billy gritted his teeth to prevent adding *asshole* to the end of that statement. "Do you think I would risk doing otherwise?"

Dressler dropped his feet back to the floor. "I need

to use your facilities and get myself some more of that coffee." He picked up his mug. "I'll be back in five."

Billy watched him go. Lincoln popped his head in. "I'd come in to give you this update but I'm afraid you'd rip my head off after spending that much time with Dressler."

For one second Billy started to motion for the detective to come in but then he changed his mind. To hell with Dressler.

"Walk with me," Billy said, skirting his desk. "You can tell me on the way to my truck."

"Okay." Lincoln looked surprised but he walked quickly down the back corridor along with Billy. "Petrov is still praying, or whatever she's doing. I think it's in Russian."

The woman had started to pray, or whatever it was, from the moment they stashed her back into her cell. They'd removed anything she could possibly hurt herself with. With the death of her daughter and her confession to all those murders, the woman was ready to leave this world, which was fine by Billy, but she wasn't doing it on his watch, by God.

"Keep a close eye on her. She might try to claw open her throat or something."

At the rear exit, Lincoln nodded. "What should I tell Dressler?"

What Billy wanted to tell him wouldn't be professional or polite. "Tell him I had a family emergency and that you will gladly take care of anything he needs."

"Thanks, Chief."

Billy settled his hat into place. "I owe you one."

"I think that might make it two or three."

Billy chuckled. "I'm good for it."

He hurried to this truck and climbed in. He drove the few blocks to the funeral home, parked on the street far enough away that Rowan couldn't look out a window and spot him. Then he called Culver.

About sixty seconds later, the man stood at the passenger-side door. Billy hit the unlock button and Culver got in.

"Any activity to report?"

Culver shook his head. "Not a damn thing. Since the visitation ended it's been deadsville around here." He laughed at his joke.

"Ha ha." Billy was not amused. "Is there any chance Rowan has spotted you?" Generally she was as sharp as a tack and spotted his surveillance details. Maybe Culver was better at this than he gave him credit.

"I guarantee you she hasn't spotted me. I'm good, Billy. Always have been."

Billy grunted, opting not to give him the satisfaction of a commitment one way or the other. "The woman who showed up at the funeral home today is a serial killer. She had a body with her."

"I heard about that, but I wasn't here. I was following Rowan and she was with you."

"I'm aware. My point in bringing this up is to remind you that you need to be on your toes. This is not a game and it's damn sure serious. You've got that, right?"

Culver nodded. "Look, Billy, I've got no desire to get myself dead. So, yeah, I'm paying attention. I get that this is a seriously screwed-up situation populated by some definite psycho types."

"Good. You keep me informed."

"I've got this, Billy." He reached for the door handle.
"Then you're going to owe me."

Billy nodded. "I already do."

Culver disappeared into the darkness. Billy stared
at the funeral home. He wanted to talk to Rowan. This
afternoon had been too intense and there had been no
time for a private discussion. He wasn't going to keep
waiting for this to be over to tell her all he needed to
say.

But first he had something he had to do and it
wouldn't wait until morning.

Beulah Alcott studied Billy for a long time after
she'd invited him to have a seat. She still sat in that
same chair. It was as if she hadn't moved since the last
time he was here.

"I knew you'd be back," she announced.

"Is that right?" She'd offered him tea or coffee but
he'd declined.

"You have more questions about her."

He did. "Norah was involved with bad people.
Somehow that association has trickled down to her
daughter and put her in danger."

"That's sure enough so," Alcott agreed.

"Did Norah ever speak to you about these associates
or what she had in common with them?"

"Death, of course." She stared at the flames in the
fireplace. "Like I told you, Norah was surrounded by
death. She drew it."

"Was she afraid of these people or were they her
friends?"

Another of those long assessments. "I can't answer

that question for you, Billy. That is the kind of question you must discover the answer to on your own."

He couldn't help wondering if that was code for "she had no idea."

"I want to protect Rowan. I can't do that without answers."

"Then you need to get out there and find them, boy. You won't find them here. What happens won't happen here."

"But everyone who was close to her mother is gone."

"Not everyone," she countered. "There is one who knew her better than all the others."

Well, damn. Julian Addington wasn't giving up his secrets.

"I'm not talking about him."

Something cold spread through Billy's chest. "Who do you mean, Ms. Alcott?"

"You'll see, Mr. Chief of Police. She won't be able to keep herself hidden from you long."

She?

"See yourself out, Billy Brannigan. I'm tired now."

Billy said good-night and did as the lady asked. As he walked through the darkness to his truck he wondered who in the hell *she* was?

He drove straight back to the funeral home and parked in the lot. It was late but the lights on the second floor were still on. Billy climbed out, hit the fob to lock his truck and headed for the front entrance. Rather than just unlock the door and go on in, he called Rowan's cell. After four rings it went to voice mail.

"Hey, maybe you're in the shower or something, but I'm coming up. I need to talk."

He hung up and tucked his phone into his pocket.

After unlocking the door, he deactivated the alarm. "Ro."

The silence was deafening. He closed and locked the door behind him. Even if Ro was in the shower, where was Freud?

"Freud! Come, boy!"

Billy palmed his weapon and moved toward the stairs. He took them two at a time. Living room, kitchen and dining rooms were clear. He moved on to the bathroom and the parents' bedroom.

Clear.

He paused at the bottom of the stairs leading to the third floor. "Ro?"

His throat constricted as he rushed up the stairs. He checked the bathroom first. No Ro. Bedrooms were empty, too.

"What the hell?"

He dug out his cell and called her again. After the first ring, he drew the phone away from his ear.

Her cell phone was somewhere in the house.

He hurried back down to the second floor. Called her phone again. It was on the sofa, half under a throw pillow.

He picked it up, watched as it went to voice mail.

He shoved it into his pocket and took off down to the first floor. He put through a call to Culver, as he raced from room to room downstairs. Kramer was in refrigeration, as was the body of Renae Cyrus.

Where the hell was Ro?

Culver's phone went to voice mail. "Call me back," Billy ordered.

He shoved his phone into his pocket, his heart thundering now. He moved down the corridor toward the rear entrance and the elevator that went down to the mortuary room.

The newly installed back door stood open.

Billy rushed out the door. He stumbled, almost fell flat on his face.

He righted himself and looked down to see what he'd tripped over.

Body. Blood, lots of blood.

"Son of a bitch." He crouched down and rolled the body over.

Culver.

His throat had been cut. Blood covered his shirt and jacket. Was all over the porch.

Hand shaking, Billy checked his carotid artery. He was dead. Skin was cold. Lips blue. He'd been dead half an hour or so.

"Goddamn it!" He laid the man back onto the porch and scanned the yard as he called for backup.

Once the call was made, he used the flashlight app on his phone and searched for tracks in the blood. He followed the small tracks—Rowan's tracks—down the steps until they disappeared in the grass.

"Where the hell are you?"

Barking drew his attention to the back gate. It was open. Billy ran in that direction. The lock had been pried away from the wooden gate post. Beyond the back alley, Freud was on the street at the corner of the block. When he saw Billy he started to bark again.

"You okay, boy?" Billy gave him a quick once-over. No visible injuries. "Where's Ro, boy?"

The dog stared at the street going away from the funeral home and started to bark again. Billy used the flashlight app again to check the sidewalk and the street. A smear of something dark on the sidewalk snagged his attention. He touched it, rubbed his fingers together.

Blood. Still damp.

He scanned the street in both directions. Whatever had happened, it ended right here, with Rowan being taken in a vehicle of some sort.

Billy thought of the way Culver's throat had been cut.

Addington.

Twenty-Three

The man was dead.

Rowan's body shook. He wasn't the first dying man she'd held in her arms by any means, but he'd died while telling her to *run*.

She blinked. Stared at the woman behind the wheel. Wanda Henegar had driven past on the side street that ran parallel to the funeral home at the exact moment Rowan had been running for help. Freud had been right behind her, but when Rowan got into Wanda's car, she had taken off before Rowan could help Freud inside. Her door had slammed shut with the momentum of the car's lunge forward.

Had Wanda seen something or someone? Had Freud frightened her? He had that effect sometimes.

Rowan felt her pockets. She needed her cell. Blood was the only thing she found. The man's blood. It was all over her from where she'd caught him as he'd fallen on her porch.

She'd left her cell phone upstairs—she'd only been going down to let Freud out one last time before going to bed. She hadn't planned to go outside. No need to take her phone or her weapon. It was a minute, only a minute.

Except she'd made a mistake.

"I need to use your cell phone." Rowan licked her lips. Her throat was so dry.

Wanda felt the pocket of her jeans. "Check the console or the floorboard. It's gotta be in here somewhere."

Rowan checked the cup holders, and between the console and the seats. She felt around the floorboard. Her heart thundered harder with each passing second.

"What happened back there? There's blood all over you."

"A man is dead." Rowan couldn't find the phone. Damn it! "He was murdered. I need to call Billy—the chief of police. I can't find your phone." Rowan looked out the windows to get her bearings. "Just take me to city hall. Someone will be there."

It was closer to city hall than it was to Billy's house. She could have the dispatcher call him. Send units to the funeral home.

Jesus. Mr. Kramer and Miss Cyrus were in refrigeration. She'd locked the unit. Something she'd started doing since that body was stolen. But the back door was open. She would have gone back into the funeral home and called for help except the dying man had told her to run and Freud had been standing in the doorway barking as if someone were inside that only he could see or hear. Rowan had instinctively run away from the threat, calling for Freud to follow.

Rowan blinked. Tried to gather her wits. She stared at the passing houses. Wanda was going the wrong way. Maybe she was upset. Confused. She'd run into

Rowan on the street with her covered in blood and shouting for help.

She turned to the driver. Only the console and about eighteen inches separated them. "City hall is the other way."

"Just stay calm, Ms. DuPont."

The words echoed in the car but Wanda's lips hadn't moved—the voice wasn't hers.

Rowan twisted around to see the woman to whom the voice belonged. Sue Ellen Thackerson sat in the back seat. The handgun she held was pointed at Rowan's head.

At least now she had confirmation that these two had been working together.

"You know—" Rowan looked from Sue Ellen to Wanda "—whoever talks first can probably cut a deal with the district attorney and get a lighter sentence."

"Sit down and put on your seat belt," Sue Ellen demanded.

Rowan sank back into the seat. Freud would be on the street barking his head off. Someone would hear him and call the police. Billy would come.

Unless whoever she was supposed to run from was still there. He might have cut Freud's throat, too. God. No.

Fear gnawed at Rowan.

"I have a question," she said, then drew in a deep breath.

"Shut up!" Sue Ellen kicked the back of Rowan's seat.

Rowan considered wrenching the door open and jumping out, but it was too late for that. Wanda was going too fast now. There was little chance she would survive the crash.

"This is important," Rowan insisted. "We could all be in danger."

Another kick to the seat back and a scream for her to shut up.

"Let her talk," Wanda snapped. "Maybe she knows something we need to hear."

Thank you, Wanda.

When Sue Ellen didn't argue, Rowan spoke again. "Did either of you kill that man back there? The one who was bleeding to death on my porch?"

Rowan had no idea who he was. She'd never seen him before. It wasn't a stretch to assume he was a cop Billy had ordered to watch her. Oh, hell, another dead cop. Agony welled inside her. She closed her eyes and fought back the overwhelming emotion. Now was not the time. She had to focus.

"What man?" Sue Ellen demanded. "We didn't even get out at the funeral home."

"What happened?" Wanda asked as she slowed for a turn.

Rowan had no idea where they were headed, but they'd left the city limits behind a mile or so ago.

"Someone cut his throat. He told me to run." Rowan tried to think if he'd said anything else. No. No, he hadn't said anything else.

"What man?" Sue Ellen demanded again.

"A cop. He was watching my house." That had to be the case. There was no other explanation.

"A cop?" Sue Ellen sat forward. She glared at Rowan. "There was a cop watching your place and someone killed him?"

Rowan turned to her, noted from the corner of her eye that Wanda was checking the rearview mirror repeatedly. "Yes. It was probably Julian. He's done this before. Remember that cop who was murdered in the funeral home parking lot back in May? That was Julian."

Silence.

Now they were scared. Rowan relaxed into her seat, facing forward once more.

Good.

She should screw the tension a little tighter.

With that in mind she suddenly twisted around to look at Sue Ellen again. "You should know he's capable of anything."

Sue Ellen looked taken aback. "How the hell would I know?"

Rowan had to bite the inside of her jaw to prevent herself from smiling. "You stated that you believe he murdered your father." She glanced at Wanda. "And your husband. If he's here, any one of us could be next."

Wanda slowed for a turn onto a road running through a field that went on as far as the moonlight would allow Rowan to see.

"No one followed us out of town," she said.

Sue Ellen turned around to stare out the back window. "I sure as hell hope not."

"It's me he wants," Rowan offered. "Let me go and I'll walk back to town. If he's out there, he'll follow me."

Silence lingered for half a minute.

"No," Sue Ellen said. "We can't do that."

"Why not?" Wanda argued. She parked in front of a dark house. "Nothing's happened yet. She doesn't know anything for sure."

Sue Ellen laughed. "Are you stupid? We just kidnapped her! That's, like, a federal offense. Can you say 'prison'?"

"Kidnapped?" Rowan said this as if she had no idea what Sue Ellen was talking about. "I thought you were helping me get away from a killer."

"We were," Wanda said.

Sue Ellen swore as she got out of the car. "You're pathetic," she mumbled as she opened Rowan's door. "Get out."

Rowan climbed out as ordered. She looked around. Beyond the small house was an old barn. It was too dark to determine the condition, but like the house, it leaned precariously. "What now?"

"Inside," Sue Ellen ordered.

Wanda was already at the door, unlocking it with the aid of a flashlight. Rowan climbed the two steps and moved carefully across the creaking wood porch. From what little she could see in the flashlight's beam, the house was fairly dilapidated. It was cold and dark. Obviously no electricity. Certainly no heat.

Rowan followed Wanda inside. Sue Ellen came in behind her and closed the door.

A flame flickered. Rowan blinked. Wanda lit what looked like an old-fashioned kerosene lamp. The lamp sat on a small rickety table. Other than the table, the only other furniture in the room was a wooden ladder-back chair.

"In the chair," Sue Ellen said.

Rowan exhaled a weary breath and crossed to the chair. She sat down. "Why are you doing this? I've done all I can to help you both."

The best way to stay alive was to pretend she had no idea what they were doing. Hopefully this ploy would also garner her the most information. People couldn't help themselves. They wanted others to know about their accomplishments even when they were illegal. It was human nature to want the admiration and/or respect of one's peers. Particularly one that wasn't expected to survive to tell.

When neither Wanda nor Sue Ellen answered, Rowan ramped up the stakes. "Did he pay you to bring me here?"

The two exchanged a look. Wanda was terrified; Sue Ellen not so much.

Sue Ellen asked, "How much do you think you're worth to him?"

This was priceless. Rowan could see the wheels turning in the woman's head. She was already calculating what she might do with even more money.

"He's a very wealthy man. I couldn't possibly estimate his worth but it's quite large. Millions, at least. He would do anything to have me."

Sue Ellen looked at Wanda, who remained uncertain and clearly terrified, and then back to Rowan. "Anything?"

Rowan nodded. "He's obsessed with me. Don't you watch the news?" She wouldn't have bothered asking her if she read the paper.

"We need to talk," Wanda said, anger radiating in her voice, making it shake.

"Give me a minute." Sue Ellen handed her the gun. "If she moves, shoot her."

Wanda stared at the gun as Sue Ellen went outside.

Rowan seized the chance. "Wanda, I don't know what's going on with Sue Ellen, but she's going to get you killed."

Wanda stared at her. "Just shut up and sit still."

Ah, a burst of bravado. "You don't understand," Rowan urged. "If the police find you—and they will—you'll go to prison for the rest of your life."

"They're not going to know it was us."

Rowan wanted to shake her. "They already suspect the two of you."

She shook her head. "We have alibis."

"Chief Brannigan knows you hired someone to do the killing."

Wanda's face paled. "No, we didn't. That's ridiculous. We had no money to do that. They controlled everything—including the money."

Keep talking, Rowan silently urged.

The door opened and Sue Ellen walked in carrying a backpack. Wanda clamped her mouth shut. Rowan refused to allow defeat to set in as she watched Sue Ellen pull a length of nylon rope, orange in color, from the backpack. Obviously, she should have watched a few more of those crime shows. She was hauling around the same kind of rope used to restrain her father when he was murdered. Oblivious, Sue Ellen set to work securing Rowan to the chair.

Rowan shifted her attention back to Wanda and held her gaze until she looked away. She was scared. This was good. As long as Wanda was scared, Rowan had a chance.

"Maybe—" Sue Ellen stood "—you're worth more to us alive than dead."

Wanda glared at her. "Shut up!"

Sue Ellen laughed. "You think she doesn't know why we brought her here? She worked for the police in Nashville. She's a damn shrink. She knows what we're doing. Don't you, Doc?" she sneered at Rowan.

Wanda shook her head. "I should never have listened to you."

Sue Ellen snatched the gun from her hand. "Then you'd still be stuck with that impotent old bastard for a husband and I'd still be kissing my daddy's ass hoping for a bread crumb."

"The person you hired is the one who will be charged with murder," Rowan lied. "The two of you could still get away with nothing more than a slap on the wrist. You could claim abuse. That's a surefire way to get away without any criminal charges and still get to keep the insurance proceeds and anything from the estates."

"Maybe you aren't as smart as we thought." Sue Ellen smirked.

Rowan held her gaze. "Perhaps not."

"We didn't hire anyone to do the killing," she explained.

"But you have alibis," Rowan protested with all the naivete she could muster.

Wanda looked as if she might throw up.

"I took care of her problem and she took care of mine. That way we each had an alibi for the time when the murder happened and we were equally committed to and invested in what had to be done."

Rowan wasn't completely surprised. This was where Billy's investigation was headed. They only needed a single piece of evidence to allow them to move on the theory.

"I didn't want to do it," Wanda admitted. "But Stan

was threatening to divorce me, leaving me with nothing. I would have nowhere to go."

"He was a piece of shit," Sue Ellen told her. "Just like my daddy. All they cared about was themselves and how good it made them feel to treat us like slaves."

The picture cleared for Rowan then. "You discovered your mutual problems and became friends?" She looked from Sue Ellen to Wanda.

"That's right," Sue Ellen snapped. She took Wanda's hand. "We found each other two years ago. Wanda was walking to town because Stan never allowed her to have the keys to her own car and I picked her up. I guess I was bored. We started to talk and one thing led to another." She glanced at the other woman. "A few months ago we realized what we had to do."

"But everything's a mess now," Wanda wailed. "None of it was as simple as you said it would be."

Sue Ellen shushed her. "Don't worry. We're going to get through this and we're taking all that money and disappearing. We'll lie on the beach somewhere and sip those pretty drinks and flirt with the kind of men who will appreciate us."

"Screw the insurance," Wanda urged. "We have enough without it. Let's just leave now."

"In a minute," Sue Ellen promised. She glowered at Rowan. "Just so you know, that other hundred-and-something thousand that was missing? Quince took it. The bastard. I fired him, but he threatened to tell Chief Brannigan that he knew me and Wanda were friends, so I let him keep the money." She turned to Wanda. "All the men here are such assholes."

"No one would blame the two of you for wanting

better lives," Rowan said. "But the police are onto you. You should leave now, like Wanda said."

Sue Ellen shook her head. "Tell me how to get in touch with *him*."

Just as Rowan suspected, the woman was greedy. No amount of money would ever be enough. "You want to call Julian and offer me to him for whatever he's willing to pay?"

Sue Ellen nodded. "Why not? Then we don't have to worry about the insurance or anything else. We can just go."

"He won't recognize your number, so he isn't likely to answer your call," Rowan warned, "but you can leave him a voice mail. He monitors his calls closely, hoping that he'll hear from me."

"How do we know he'll call us back?" Wanda asked, still visibly nervous.

"Trust me," Rowan said, "he wouldn't miss an opportunity to get to me. There are only two or three people who know his cell number. He won't ignore the voice mail."

"Give me the number."

Rowan called off Julian's number. She hated that she knew it by heart.

Sue Ellen started to enter the digits and Wanda stopped her. She glanced at Rowan. "This could be a trick."

Sue Ellen sent a menacing stare at Rowan. "If this is a trick, I will kill you."

"The number I gave you is Julian's," Rowan confirmed. "He'll identify himself when the call goes to his voice mail."

She left out the part about how the FBI was one

of the two or three who had his number. They were monitoring Julian's number for any communications.

"You'll have to tell him where to come and how much you want." She shrugged as best she could with her arms secured so tightly behind her and to the chair. "You have to trust me. I don't want you to kill me."

"Won't he kill you?" Wanda asked, a glimmer of concern in her voice.

"No. He wants me alive." Rowan wasn't really sure about that part, but it didn't matter. Billy would get here before Julian. Hopefully. It was a risk she was willing to take.

Sue Ellen made the call. "We have something you want, Addington. You bring us a million dollars—no, two million—and she's all yours. We're…" She stared at Rowan for a second. "You call me back when you have the money and I'll tell you where we'll make the exchange."

The woman wasn't as stupid as Rowan had suspected. There was nothing to do now but wait…and hope Dressler's people came up with a way to make these two believe Julian Addington was on the way with a couple of million dollars.

Unless he was already here…watching and waiting.

Twenty-Four

Billy's officers were crawling all over the funeral home.

Burt and Ledbetter had bagged Culver and were ready to take away the body. The idea that he'd gotten Culver killed made Billy sick to his stomach.

"Son of a bitch."

Freud stared up at Billy as if he expected him to do more. God Almighty, how he wanted to do more.

They had questioned every single person for a full city block all the way around the funeral home. Sheriff Colt Tanner had his deputies checking gas stations. Every road going in and out of town now had a roadblock. The trouble was, Rowan could be anywhere, and he had no conclusive timeline to go by.

The one thing that gave him hope that she was close, and that she hadn't been gone long, was the fact that Culver's blood had still been wet. Burt was confident he had been dead less than an hour when he arrived.

"Chief, we may have just gotten lucky." Lincoln hurried along the sidewalk to where Billy stood.

Hope welled in his chest. "Did you find a witness?"

"The lady who lives in the house on the corner." Lincoln pointed in that direction. "We thought no one was home but she was asleep. Her son heard on his police scanner what was going on and called her to see if she was okay."

"Did she see someone?"

Lincoln smiled and nodded. "She did. She said the dog was raising a real ruckus so she looked out her front window to see what was going on. She saw Rowan get into a car. She said the driver drove away like a bat out of hell."

"Tell me about the car." Billy's chest felt ready to explode.

"Blue. Old. Four-door with a big dent in the rear quarter panel, or as the lady said, near the back tire on the driver's side. Best of all, she says she is certain the driver was a woman." Lincoln grinned. "Wanda Henegar has a car just like that."

"Let Colt know. I want an APB out on that car, as well as ones on Wanda and Sue Ellen. Those two are working together as sure as hell."

Billy started toward his truck. Freud followed.

"Where you going, Chief?" Lincoln called after him.

"To find Ro."

Lincoln caught up with him. "In that case, I'm going with you."

Billy shot him a glare.

"Hey, I can make those calls while you drive."

True enough, Billy supposed.

Billy put Detective Tara Stewart in charge. He opened the rear driver's-side door. "Let's go, boy." Freud scrambled into the seat.

Lincoln settled into the passenger seat as he made the calls and passed along Billy's directions. Billy slid behind the wheel and started the engine. It was hard as hell to see two women he'd known for years as the kind of criminals who would kidnap a person, much less murder anyone. What the hell?

The two things that gave him reason to be hopeful about Rowan's safety was that she was incredibly smart and she was experienced in homicide investigations. She would know how to handle herself in a situation like this.

"Hang in there, Ro," he murmured. "We're coming."

The cell in his pocket vibrated. He dug it out and checked the screen. Dressler. Another knot joined the thousands of others in his gut. He accepted the call. "Brannigan."

"What the hell is going on, Chief?"

"What do you want, Dressler?" Billy had already talked to Dressler. They had nothing. He swore he had no one watching Rowan so he didn't have a clue what had happened to her and he damn sure didn't have any idea where Addington was. In fact, he'd been no damn help at all.

"Apparently someone in your shithole little town thinks she can make a deal with Addington."

"What?" Billy slowed for the turn to the Henegar farm.

"The cell that called Addington's number belongs to one Sue Ellen Thackerson."

If Sue Ellen called Addington, Rowan had to have given her the number. He grinned. *Smart girl.*

"How fast can you figure out where that call came from?"

Next to Billy, Lincoln had asked Colt, the Franklin County sheriff, to stand by.

"She's definitely in Winchester," Dressler said. "My people are triangulating the area now. You'll get the location when I do. See you there."

The call ended. As much as Billy hated that guy, he was damn thankful for him just now.

Twenty-Five

"How long do you think it will take to hear back from him?" Wanda asked.

Rowan kept an eye on Sue Ellen, who was pacing the floor like a caged animal. Since that call, a half hour maybe, Rowan had been working to loosen her bindings. Her wrists burned from the scrapes and tears in her skin, but she kept at it, careful not to allow her movements to draw the attention of her captors.

"I'm sure he won't be long. No matter where he is, he has resources everywhere."

Sue Ellen zeroed in on one aspect of Rowan's answer. "Are you saying he might be somewhere else? Mexico? Canada? Someplace far away?"

Before Rowan could answer, Wanda shook her head. "We should just leave before the police find us." When Sue Ellen ignored her, she grabbed her by the shoulders and forced her to meet her gaze. "We don't need any more money. We have enough."

Sue Ellen stared at her for a long while. Rowan hoped she would see reason and leave. After that phone call, Rowan wasn't concerned about not being found. It was cold in this old house, but not cold enough to cause her any real physical difficulties. She wasn't going to freeze to death.

"What I meant," Rowan offered, "is that no matter where Julian is, he has resources. Even if he isn't nearby, he'll send someone for me."

Sue Ellen wagged her head side to side. "I don't believe her." She turned to her partner in crime. "She knows too much. We can't just leave her."

The words sent an icy chill through Rowan's chest. Not exactly how she was hoping to see this play out.

"What difference does it make?" Wanda protested. "We'll be long gone."

Sue Ellen drew in a big breath, as if she were struggling for patience. "Right now they can't prove anything. They have suspicions but no evidence. She knows! She can tell them what we did. If they ever find us we could get the death penalty."

Apparently, this hit the right chord with Wanda. "Okay. I get it. We don't want that. We'll do whatever you think is best."

Rowan tugged a little harder at her bindings. This was the perfect time for a distraction. "Did you hear something?"

Both women turned to the door. "Watch her," Sue Ellen said. "I'll check it out."

Sue Ellen went to the door. Wanda hugged her arms around herself. "Be careful," she urged.

Rowan felt the skin ripping on her hands. Didn't care. She had to get free of this rope. Sue Ellen had made her decision and she'd swayed Wanda to her side. Rowan was out of time.

Sue Ellen closed the door behind her as she exited.

Wanda watched the door as if she feared her friend wouldn't be back.

"If you help me," Rowan said, "I can help you get immunity." A lie, but it could work and she was pretty desperate at the moment.

Wanda stared at Rowan as if she had slapped her. "I can't betray her. I would never have escaped that bastard if not for Sue Ellen."

"Then you're going to prison," Rowan said, "and one or both of you will likely get the death penalty." Probably not, but the woman didn't know that.

"Stop talking." Wanda returned to her vigil of watching the door.

Now if she could just get her right thumb through that loop. Rowan bit her lips together against the pain.

The door opened and Sue Ellen came in. She slammed it behind her. "There is no one out there." She arrowed a nasty look at Rowan. "Let's do this and get out of here."

Damn. Rowan ripped her thumb from the bindings. Almost free.

The door suddenly burst inward. Rowan swung her gaze from the gun in Sue Ellen's hand to the man at the door. Tall, broad-shouldered, bald.

A flash of light blazed from the gun in his hand and the sound of the bullet exiting exploded in the room. Once. Twice.

Wanda screamed.

Sue Ellen dropped to the floor, her weapon spinning away on the dusty hardwood.

Wanda stared at the widening circle of red on her blouse and then she joined the other woman on the floor.

Rowan's attention shifted back to the man. He stared at her. The long beard on his chin seemed odd considering his shiny, bald head.

He walked toward her. Rowan braced herself. Tried to calm her galloping heart.

"Did Julian send you?" The acrid smell of gunpowder in the air filled her lungs as she spoke.

He pulled out a knife. Was it the one he'd used to kill that officer who had been watching her?

Rather than rake the blade across her throat, as she expected, he stepped behind her and sliced through the nylon rope.

Her hands fell free, both numb from being tied so tightly.

She bolted from the chair. Almost tripped over Wanda's body.

The man stared at her as he sheathed the knife.

He stood between her and the door. There was no way she could get around him. There was at least one other room in this shack. She thought of darting through the opening behind her but he still held the gun. If she managed not to get shot, what if there wasn't a door? Or a window?

"Julian didn't send me."

His voice was deep, guttural. Menacing.

Could this man be another of Billy's officers? She doubted the biker beard fell within the police department uniform guidelines.

If not, then who was he? Some passing stranger who heard about the trouble on a police scanner and wanted to play Good Samaritan? Or maybe he wanted to cash in on a potential asset.

"Who sent you?" She hated that her voice trembled.

He turned his back on her and walked toward the door.

Rowan's body started to shake. The receding adrenaline, she realized, but she could do nothing to stop it. She should be grateful he was leaving, but somehow she wasn't.

"Who?" she demanded.

He paused, his hand on the doorknob.

"Who sent you?" she repeated.

He glanced back at her for only a moment. Just long enough to say the words that would change everything... that would turn her world upside down all over again.

And then he was gone.

Rather than debate the feasibility of what he had said, she walked out of the shack. She crossed the creaky porch and descended the rickety steps.

She couldn't see it, but she heard the roar of an engine fading in the distant darkness. Motorcycle engine.

Then she started to walk toward the highway with nothing but the moonlight to guide her.

Before she reached the end of the long drive, she saw the blue lights. Heard the sirens.

Relief washed through her, warming her against the cold.

Billy was coming.

Twenty-Six

Rowan dropped a fistful of treats into each bag. "There you go. Happy Halloween."

Thank-yous and squeals echoed in the air as the band of little ghosts and ghouls rushed away from the funeral home.

Rowan sank back onto the bench next to Billy. Freud sat like a statue next to her, uncertain what the festivities were all about. In their Nashville neighborhood, populated by mostly career-oriented singles and couples, they'd never experienced a Halloween like this one. Crowds of children had been popping by for over an hour. It was dark, and the air was just cold enough to make her shiver. She hugged the black cape more tightly around her.

"You cold?"

Billy smiled at her and she lost her breath. A moment was required to gather her composure once more. "I'm okay."

He reached for the thermos his mother had sent. "You need more hot chocolate."

She managed a smile. "It was so sweet of your mother to send homemade hot chocolate."

"Don't kid yourself—she lives for this stuff." He passed a mug to Rowan before filling his own. "She starts planning the holidays months in advance."

"That's what mothers are supposed to do," she said, her voice almost wistful. She wished she could remember her mother doing something like this.

Your mother sent me.

That was what the bearded man with the bald head had said to her.

But that was impossible because Rowan's mother was dead. The memory that stood out in Rowan's mind more than any other was the day Norah died. Rowan had watched her father pull her mother's body over that railing. Stared as he cut her free of the rope and then held her in his arms, crying like a small child.

Her father—the man who was fearless and as steady as a rock. He had cried until the police and the ambulance arrived. Finally, he had realized Rowan was standing there, in shock by then. He'd fallen to his knees and hugged her fiercely to him. They had cried together.

Norah was dead.

No question.

Whatever reason that man had for telling her Norah had sent him, he had lied.

More games. Julian loved his games. She hadn't recognized just how much until two nights ago. Obsessed with Rowan, he might be, but he did not care about her. A man who cared about her would never have done the things he had. Using her mother to hurt her. Using her sister.

Julian knew all Rowan's secrets. He understood every facet of her. He recognized what would hurt her most.

All of this, she had decided in the hours before daylight this morning, was a game. He had created this entire facade to hurt her. The note she found in her dead father's pocket. His own daughter's bones so near to where Raven had died. And all those lies about her mother, as well as her father.

She couldn't trust any of it.

At this moment, she had no idea what a single thing she had uncovered meant—if anything. The man and all his tattoos. The drawings on the cave walls and all those bones. The photos she had found in Herman's house. His bizarre message before blowing his brains out. The stranger on the motorcycle who had saved her from certain death. None of it fit together.

None of it made the slightest bit of sense.

"Here comes the next crowd." Billy stood, set aside his mug. "It's my turn."

He met the kids a few steps away and distributed the Halloween candy. Rowan smiled, watching him. He wore his cowboy hat and a long duster with a big tin star pinned on it. He looked like a sheriff from the old West. Rowan wore a black wool cape she'd found in her mother's closet, along with black boots and a black velvet hat with a mesh veil that partially covered her face.

What else would a female undertaker wear?

Billy waved to the kids as they hurried off to their next stop. He strode back to where Rowan sat, and her breath caught. She looked away. She had to get this new fierce, needy streak under control.

He sat next to her for a moment without saying anything, but she understood that he had something on his mind. He'd been avoiding saying whatever it was for a couple of hours now.

"It was a long day," she said, as much to herself as to him.

"Sure was." He leaned back, propped his arm across the back of the bench.

In the darkness outside that shack where she was supposed to have died, Rowan had stopped in the middle of that dirt road and waited for Billy and the others to reach her. He'd parked, his headlights pinning her in place. He jumped out of his truck and rushed to her. The fear on his face and the worry in his voice as he'd asked her a dozen questions had ripped at her heart.

Evidence techs had come. Burt and his assistant had arrived. Dressler had appeared in the middle of her recounting of events. He'd added his questions. She'd thought for sure he and Billy were going to tear into each other. She'd watched Wanda's and Sue Ellen's bodies being bagged and taken away.

Rowan couldn't hope to analyze the two, on what little she knew. What she understood with complete certainty was that they had been desperate to be free. Free of the men who controlled their lives. Free and away from here.

"I thought I lost you."

Billy's voice pulled her back to the here and now. She closed her eyes and searched for the strength to meet his gaze. When she did, she could hardly bear the hurt she saw there.

"But you didn't. You found me."

He stared into his mug for a second or two. "I think I told you this already but having Sue Ellen call Addington was ingenious. Dressler was able to track your location and get us there way faster than we could have on our own."

"Nothing ingenious about it. Having her make that call was the only strategy available to me," Rowan admitted. "It was an act of desperation."

"Even Dressler was impressed."

The memory of how Billy had checked every place where he saw blood on her squeezed her heart all over again. "I'm sorry about your friend Culver."

"You believe the guy on the motorcycle killed him?"

Rowan wished she knew. "He was certainly carrying the right knife for the job. A big hunting knife."

"Did you say he had a hunting knife?"

Rowan nodded. "Yes. Didn't I say that when I gave my statement?" She'd told them everything back at that shack. Hadn't she?

"Yeah, yeah, you did. But I didn't think to ask whether or not the knife had a serrated edge. Did you see it? I'm sure it happened so fast you might not have noticed."

Rowan thought back to the moment when he drew the knife. She closed her eyes and replayed his hand wrapping around the handle, the knife slipping from its sheath. The glint of the lantern light on the blade. The rough, uneven edge…

"Yes. It was definitely serrated."

"Hang on." Billy pulled out his cell and made a call.

"Hey, Burt, I know it's Halloween and all, but can you check something for me?"

As the two men talked, Rowan thought back to the victims whose throats had been slashed by Julian. None had been done with a serrated blade. Of course, if the bearded bald man was the one who had killed Culver, Burt should be able to determine that a serrated blade was used.

Clearing up one more homicide would be useful, though it still wouldn't tell them who had sent the bearded bald man. It certainly wasn't her mother.

The idea was ludicrous.

"Thanks, Burt."

Billy ended the call, tucked his phone back into the pocket of his duster. "The blade used to cut Culver's throat was not serrated."

Rowan rubbed her forehead. "So the man who cut me loose didn't kill him."

"Guess not. It's possible his knife had both a serrated and a smooth side."

"He cut me loose. Let me go. Why would he have killed Culver, anyway?" The scenario wasn't logical, but killers were often irrational.

"Dressler and I had the same discussion. If he came to save you—which would beg the question, how did he know where you were unless he followed you from the funeral home?"

"And if he did," Rowan added, "what took him so long to act?"

"If he didn't follow you, how did he get his information before I did?"

His eyes said the same thing she was thinking. A leak in the FBI.

"Damn."

Rowan agreed wholeheartedly with that summation. "I guess we should talk to Dressler about this."

"We should," she confirmed.

Another minute of quiet passed between them. The distant laughter and squeals of children whispered in the darkness. Freud cocked his head in first one direction and then the other, trying to determine the source of the sounds. Rowan rubbed his head to reassure him.

"I can't lose you, Ro." Billy turned to her. "We can't avoid having this conversation forever. We have to talk about *us* soon."

She set her mug on the ground and turned to him, her knees pressing into his. "Billy, you are an amazing man. You are incredible at your work, a great son and everyone loves you." She dared to reach up and touch his jaw, allowing her hand to linger there. "I cannot imagine my life without you."

"But…" he prompted.

She dropped her hand away. Clasped it in her other one. "You deserve so much better than I can hope to be."

He took her hand in his. "What the hell does that mean, Ro?"

She shook her head. "I don't know exactly. There's something wrong with me. I don't know how to be in that kind of relationship. It's never worked for me and I don't want anything to ruin what we have." She took a breath and said the rest, "And I can't risk Julian trying to use you to get to me. If he hurt you—"

"Addington doesn't worry me." His long fingers curled around hers. "I'm willing to take my chances on both counts."

Rowan was well aware of how he felt and it scared her to death. "Let's agree to take this slow and see what happens."

He nodded. "I can live with that."

He frowned, then reached into his jacket pocket and snagged his phone. He checked the screen and his frown deepened. "Dressler. It's kind of creepy that he would call when we were just talking about him."

Rowan made a face. "Definitely creepy."

He shrugged then answered.

Another huddle of kids skipped across the lot toward them. Rowan took the bucket and met them a few feet away. The children ranged in age from toddlers to preteens. The mothers held toddlers' hands and urged them to recite the expected greeting of "trick or treat." The older kids shouted the words, then giggled and whispered among themselves.

"You're so cute," Rowan said as she dropped candy into a little pumpkin's treat bag.

Not for the first time, she wondered if she would ever have children of her own. Her biological clock was quickly winding down. She glanced back at Billy and her heart squeezed. He would be a good father. He should have kids. She wasn't so sure if she was mother material. She'd had no role model growing up.

Thank-yous and squeals twittered through the kids as she finished dropping goodies into the treat bags. She watched them hurry away before turning back to Billy.

He was right behind her. She jumped. "I didn't hear you walk up."

The worry on his face told her the news from Dressler was not good. "What did he say?"

"The forensic lab that's working on all those bones and the faces inside the skin binders sent him a preliminary report."

Which meant they had discovered some matches to victims in their databases. "That's good news, right?"

Billy's troubled expression and tone didn't correspond with the concept of good news.

"They've found some matches in databases but so far none are people who've been listed as missing."

"How is that possible? That would mean the matches aren't to victims. Why would they be in a database if they're not victims?"

"So far the bones and skin masks appear to belong to inactive serial killers."

Rowan absorbed the ramifications of the words. They shook her to the very core of her being, but disbelief refused to allow the meaning to fully penetrate. "You're saying that the victims of Sanchez—or Santos, whatever his real name is—are documented serial killers?"

Billy nodded. "That's what I'm saying."

This news changed everything. Rowan just wasn't certain if the change was for the good or what it meant about her mother...or her father.

How would she ever sort through all this and find some semblance of the truth? Each step forward was immediately followed by two steps back. Every new answer was twisted into one or more new questions. No sooner had she solved the puzzle of who one character in this bizarre story was than another one, or three, appeared.

All of it, every single twisted move, led back to Julian.

Rowan pushed away the disturbing realizations and questions. What she did know was that she couldn't keep pretending her own life didn't matter just because she couldn't figure out the past.

She refused to allow Julian Addington to control her any longer.

This was her life and she intended to live it from this moment forward.

She reached out, took Billy's hand in hers. She searched his eyes, saw the promise and the reassurance there. She trusted him. She needed him. She wanted him.

"Stay with me tonight."

He reached up, cupped her cheek in his hand. "You sure about that?"

"I've never been more sure of anything."

And she was. She was absolutely certain for the first time in her life.

* * * * *

*When Allison James got married, she didn't know
the charismatic man was the son of an illegal drug
and weapons kingpin. After her husband's murder,
she escapes and is placed in witness protection.
Now US Marshal Jaxson Stevens, a man from her
past, is the only person standing between her and
certain death…*

Read on for a sneak preview of
Witness Protection Widow
by USA TODAY *bestselling author Debra Webb.*

One

Sunday, February 2
Winchester, Tennessee

It was colder now.

The meteorologist had warned that it might snow tomorrow. The temperature was already dropping. She didn't mind. She had no appointments, no deadlines and no place to be—except *here*.

Four days.

Four more days until *the* day.

If she lived that long.

She stopped and surveyed the thick woods around her, making a full three-sixty turn. Nothing but trees and this one trail for as far as the eye could see. The fading sun trickled through the bare limbs. This place had taken her through the last of summer and then fall, and now winter was nearing an end. In all that time she had seen only one other living human. It was best, they said. For her protection, they insisted.

It was true. But she had never felt more alone in her life.

Bob nudged her. She pushed aside the troubling thoughts and looked down at her black Labrador. "I know, boy. I should get moving. It's cold out here."

Allowing herself to get caught out in the woods in the dark—no matter that she knew the way back to the cabin by heart—was a bad idea. She started forward once more. Her hiking boots crunched the rocks and the few frozen leaves scattered across the trail. Bob trotted beside her, his tail wagging happily. She'd never had a dog before coming to this place. Her mother's allergies had never allowed for pets. Later, when she was out on her own, the apartment building hadn't permitted pets.

Even after she married and moved into one of Atlanta's megamansions, she couldn't have a dog. Her husband had hated dogs, cats, any sort of pet. How had she not recognized the evil in him then? Anyone who hated animals so much couldn't be good.

She hugged herself, rubbed her arms. Thinking of him, even in such simple terms, unsettled her. Soon she hoped she would be able to put that part of her life behind her and never look back again.

Never, ever.

"Not soon enough," she muttered.

Most widows grieved the loss of their spouses. She did not. No matter the circumstances, she had never wished him dead, though she had wished many, many times that she had never met him.

But she had met him, and there was no taking back the past five years. At first, she had believed the illusion he presented to her. Harrison had been older, very handsome and extremely charming. She had been born in small-town Georgia on a farm to parents who taught her that fairy tales and dreams weren't real. There was only reality and the painful lessons that came from hard work and bad luck. Suddenly, at nearly twenty-six, she was convinced her parents had been wrong. Harrison swooped into her life like Prince Charming poised to rescue a damsel in distress.

Except she hadn't been in distress really. But she had been hopeful. Desperately hopeful that good things would one day come. Perhaps that was why she didn't see through him for so long. He'd filled her life with trips to places she'd only dreamed of visiting, like Paris and London. He'd lavished her with gifts. Exquisite clothing, endless jewels. Even when she tried to tell him it was too much, more came.

He gave her anything she wanted…except children. He had been married once before and had two college-aged children. He had no desire to go down that path again. She had been devastated at first. But she had been in love, so she learned to live within those disappointing parameters. Soon after this revelation she discovered a way to satisfy her mothering needs. She volunteered at Atlanta's rescue mission for at-risk kids. Several months after she began helping out part-time, she was faced with her first unpleasant truth about her husband. To her dismay, there were those who believed he and his family were very bad people.

The shock and horror on the other woman's face when she'd asked, "You're married to Harrison Armone?"

Alice—of course, that wasn't her name then—had smiled, a bit confused, and said, "I am."

The woman had never spoken to her again. In fact,

she had done all within her power to avoid her. At least twice she had seen her whisper something to another volunteer, who subsequently avoided her, as well. Arriving at the center on her scheduled volunteer days soon became something she dreaded rather than to which she looked forward. From that moment she understood there was something wrong with who she was—the wife of Harrison Armone.

If only she had realized then the level of evil the Armone family represented. Perhaps she would have escaped before the real nightmare that came later. Too bad she hadn't been smart enough to escape before it was too late.

She stared up at the sky, visible only by virtue of the fact that the trees remained bare for the winter. She closed her eyes and tried to force away the images that always followed on the heels of memories even remotely related to him. That first year and a half had been so blissful. So perfect. For the most part she had been kept away from the rest of the family. Their estate had been well away from his father's. Her husband went to work each day at a beautiful, upscale building on the most distinguished street in the city. Her life was protected from all things bad and painful.

Until her co-volunteer had asked her that question.

The worry had grown and swelled inside her like a tidal wave rushing to shore to destroy all in its path. But the trouble didn't begin until a few weeks later. Until she could no longer bear the building pressure inside her.

Her first true mistake was when she had asked him—point-blank—if there was anything he had failed to disclose before they married.

The question had obviously startled him. He wanted to know where she had gotten such a ridiculous idea. His voice had been calm and kind, as always, tinged with only the tiniest bit of concern. But something about the look in his eyes when he asked the question terrified her. She hadn't wanted to tell him. He had been far too strangely calm and yet wild-eyed. Fear that he would track down her fellow volunteers and give them a hard time had horrified her. After much prodding and far too much pretending how devastated he was, he had let it go. But she had known that deep down something had changed.

Whether it was the idea that the bond of trust had been broken, or that she had finally just woken up, she could not look at him the same way again.

The worst part was that he noticed immediately. He realized that thin veil of make-believe had been torn. Every word she uttered, every move she made was suddenly under intense scrutiny. He became suspicious to the point of paranoia. Every day was another in-depth examination of what she had done that day, to whom she had spoken. Then he allowed his true character to show. One by one those ugly family secrets were revealed by his actions. Late-night business meetings that were once handled at his father's house were suddenly held in their home.

One night after a particularly long meeting with lots of drinking involved, he confessed that he had wanted to keep the fantasy of their "normal" life and she had taken it from him.

From that moment forward, she became his prisoner. He punished her in unspeakable ways for taking away his fairy tale.

Even with him dead, he still haunted her.

She shook off the memories and focused on the moment. The crisp, clean air. The nature all around her. She'd had her reservations at first, but this place was cleansing for her soul. She had seen so much cruelty and ugliness. This was the perfect sanctuary for healing.

And, of course, hiding.

Only a few more days until the trial of the century. She was the star witness—the first and only witness who had survived to testify against Harrison Armone Senior. The man had built an empire in the southeast, and Atlanta was his headquarters. The Armone family had run organized crime for three generations, four if you counted her husband, since he would have been next in line to head the family.

But he no longer counted because he was dead.

Murdered by his own father.

She had witnessed Mr. Armone putting the gun to the back of Harrison's head and pulling the trigger. Then he'd turned to her and announced that she now belonged to him, as did all else his son had hoarded to himself. He would give her adequate grieving time, and then he would expect *things* from her.

Within twenty-four hours the family's private physician had provided a death certificate and another family friend with a funeral home had taken care of the rest. No cops were involved, no investigation and certainly no autopsy. Cause of death was listed as a heart attack. The obituary was pompous and filled half a page.

It wasn't until three days after the funeral that Alice had her first opportunity to attempt an escape.

She had prepared well. For months before Harrison's

death she had been readying for an opportunity to flee. She had hidden away a considerable amount of cash and numerous prepaid cards that could not be traced back to her. She'd even purchased a phone—one for which minutes could be purchased at the supermarket. When the day came, she left the house with nothing more than the clothes on her back. The money and cards were tucked into her jacket. The entire jacket was basically padded with cash and plastic beneath the layer of fabric that served as the lining. She'd worn her favorite running shoes and workout clothes.

Days before, at the gym, she had stashed jeans, a sweatshirt, a ball cap, big sunglasses and a clasp for pinning her long blond hair out of sight beneath the cap.

That day, she'd left the gym through a rear exit and jogged the nearly three miles to the Four Seasons, where she'd taken a taxi to the bus station. She'd loaded onto the bus headed to Birmingham, Alabama. In Birmingham, she had boarded another bus to Nashville, Tennessee, and finally from Nashville to Louisville, Kentucky. Each time she changed something about her appearance. She picked up another jacket or traded with another traveler. Changed the hat and the way she wore her hair. Eventually she reached her destination. Scared to death but with no other recourse, she walked into the FBI office and told whoever would listen her story.

Now she was here.

The small clearing where her temporary home—a rustic cabin—stood came into view. The setting sun spilled the last of its glow across the mountain.

In the middle of nowhere on a mountain, she was awaiting the moment when she would tell the world what kind of monster Harrison Armone Senior was.

His son had been equally evil, but no one deserved to be murdered, particularly by his own father.

Those last three and a half years of their marriage when he'd recognized that she knew what he was, his decision to permit her to see and hear things had somehow been calculated. She supposed he had hoped to keep her scared into submission. She had been scared. Scared to death. But she had planned her escape when no one was looking.

The FBI had been thrilled with what she had to offer. But they had also recognized that keeping her alive until and through the trial wouldn't be easy. She had been moved once already. The security of the first location where she'd been hidden away had been breached after only three months. She'd had no idea anything was going on when two marshals had shown up to take her away.

So far things had gone smoothly in Winchester. She kept to herself. Ordered her food online and the marshal assigned to her picked up the goods and delivered the load to her. Though she had a small SUV for emergencies, she did not leave the property and put herself in a position where someone might see and remember her.

Anything she needed, the marshal took care of.

The SUV parked next to the house was equipped with all-wheel drive, since she lived out in the woods on a curvy mountain road. US Marshal Branch Holloway checked on her regularly. She had a special phone for emergencies and for contacting him. He'd made her feel at ease from the beginning. He was patient and kind. Far more understanding than the first one.

For this she was immensely grateful.

Yes. She had married an evil man. Yes. She had been a fool. But she hadn't set out to do so. She had been taught to believe the best in everyone until she had reason to see otherwise.

Well over a year. Yes. It had taken a long time to see past the seemingly perfect facade he had built for her, but she was only human. She had loved him. She had waited a very long time to feel that way again after her first heartbreak.

"Get over it," she muttered to herself. Beating herself up for being naive wasn't going to change history.

This, she surveyed the bare trees and little cabin, was her life now.

Witness protection was made to look like a glamorous adventure in the movies, but that could not be further from the truth. It was terrifying. Justice depended on her survival to testify in court. The FBI had shown her how much bigger this case was than just the murder of her husband and the small amount of knowledge she had absorbed. The Armones had murdered countless people. Drugs, guns and all sorts of other criminal activities were a part of their network. She alone held the power to end the Armone reign.

No matter that the family was so obviously evil, she still couldn't understand how a father could murder his son—his only child. Of course, it was Harrison's own fault. He had been secretly working to overthrow his father. The old man was nearing seventy and had no plans to retire. Harrison had wanted to be king.

Instead, he'd gotten dead.

Alice shuddered at the idea that his father—after murdering him—had intended to take his widow as his own plaything.

Sick. The man was absolutely disgusting. Like his son, he was a charming, quite handsome man for his age. But beneath the skin lived a monster.

Once the trial was over, she hoped she never had to see him again.

Staying alert to her surroundings, she unlocked the back door and sent Bob inside ahead of her. He was trained to spot trouble. She wasn't overly concerned at the point. If anything had been amiss, he would have warned her as they approached the cabin.

Dogs were a new addition to the witness protection family. She hadn't had a dog at the first location. It wasn't until she'd arrived here and had Bob living with her that she'd realized how very lonely she had been for a very long time. Well before her husband was murdered.

She locked the door behind her. Taking care to check all the locks. Then she followed Bob through the three rooms. There was a small living-dining-kitchen combination, a bedroom with attached bath and the mudroom-laundry-room at the back door. Furnishings were sparse, but she had what she needed.

Since cell service was sketchy at best, she had a state-of-the-art signal booster. She had a generator in case the power went out and a bug-out bag if it became necessary to cut and run.

She shivered. The fire had gone out. She kept on her jacket while she added logs to the fireplace and kindling to get it started. Within a couple of minutes, the fire was going. She'd had a fireplace as a kid, so relearning her way around this one hadn't been so bad. She went back to the kitchen and turned on the kettle for tea.

Bob growled low in his throat and stared toward the front door.

She froze. Her phone was in her hip pocket. Her gun was still in her waistband at the small of her back. This was something else Marshal Holloway had insisted upon. He'd taught her how to use a handgun. They held many target practices right behind this cabin.

A creak beyond the front door warned that some-one was on the porch. She eased across the room and went to the special peephole that had been installed. There was one on each side of the cabin, allowing for views all the way around. A man stood on the porch. He was the typical local cowboy. Jeans and boots. Hat in his hands. Big truck in the drive. Just like Marshal Holloway.

But she did not know this man.

"Alice Stewart, if you're in there, it's okay for you to open the door. I'm Sheriff Colt Tanner. Branch sent me."

Her heart thudding, she held perfectly still. Branch would never send someone to her without letting her know first. If for some reason he couldn't tell her in advance, they had a protocol for the situation.

She reached back, fingers curled about the butt of her weapon. Bob moved stealthily toward the door.

"I know you're concerned about opening the door to a stranger, but you need to trust me. Branch has been in an accident and he's in the hospital undergoing surgery right now. No matter that his injuries were serious, he refused to go into surgery until he spoke to me and I assured him I would see after you, ma'am."

Worry joined the mixture of fear and dread churning

inside her. She hoped Branch wasn't hurt too badly. He had a wife and a daughter.

She opened her mouth to ask about his condition, but then she snapped it shut. The man at her door had not said the code word.

"Wait," he said. "I know what the problem is. I forgot to say *superhero*. He told me that's your code word."

Relief rushed through her. She moved to the door and unlocked the four dead bolts, then opened it. When she faced the man—Sheriff Tanner—she asked, "Is he going to be okay?"

The sheriff ducked his head. "I sure hope so. Branch is a good friend of mine. May I come in?"

"Quiet, Bob," she ordered the dog at her side as she backed up and allowed the sheriff to come inside before closing the door. She resisted the impulse to lock it and leaned against it instead. Holloway wouldn't have trusted this man if he wasn't one of the good guys.

Still, standing here with a stranger after all these months, she couldn't help feeling a little uneasy. Bob sat at her feet, his gaze tracking every move the stranger made.

"Is there anything you need, ma'am? Anything at all. I'll be happy to bring you any supplies or just…" He shrugged. "Whatever you need."

The kettle screamed out, making her jump. She'd completely forgotten about it. "I'll be right back."

She hurried to the kitchen and turned off the flame beneath the whistling kettle. She took a breath, pushed her hair behind her ears and walked back to where he waited.

"Thank you for coming, Sheriff, but I have everything I need."

"All right." He pulled a card from his shirt pocket and offered it to her. "Call me if you need anything. I'll check on you again later this evening and give you an update on Branch's condition."

She studied the card. "Thank you." She looked up at him then. "I appreciate your concern. Please let the marshal know I'm hoping for his speedy recovery."

"Will do." He gave her another of those quick nods. "I'll be on my way, then."

Before she opened the door for him to go, she had to ask, "Are his injuries life-threatening?"

"He was real lucky, ma'am. Things could have been far worse. Thankfully, he's stable and we have every reason to believe he'll be fine."

"What about his wife?"

"She wasn't with him, so she's fine. She's at the hospital waiting for him to come out of surgery. If you're certain you don't need me for anything, I'm going back there now."

"Really, I'm fine. Thank you."

When the sheriff had said his goodbye and strode out to his truck, she locked the door—all four dead bolts. She watched as the truck turned around and rolled away. She told herself that Marshal Holloway's accident most likely didn't have anything to do with her or the trial. Still, she couldn't help but worry just a little.

What if they had found her? What if hurting the marshal was just the first step in getting to her. Old Man Armone was pure evil. He would want her to know in advance that he was coming, just to be sure she felt as much fear as possible. Instilling fear gave him great pleasure.

Harrison Armone Senior had a small army at his beck and call. All were trained mercenaries. Ruthless, like him. Proficient in killing. Relentless in attaining their target. They would be hunting her. If being careful would get her through this, she had nothing to worry about. But that alone would never be enough. She needed help and luck on her side.

With this unexpected development, she would need to be extra vigilant.

"Bob."

He looked up at her eagerly.

"We have to be especially alert, my friend."

The devil might be coming.

And he wouldn't be alone.

Two

Jaxson Stevens left Nashville as soon as he heard the news of the accident. He and Branch Holloway had been assigned together briefly before Holloway transferred back to his hometown of Winchester. Holloway was a good guy and a damned fine marshal. Jax was more than happy to back him up until he was on his feet again.

He parked his SUV in the lot and headed for the hospital entrance. He hadn't been in the Winchester area in ages. He hailed from the Pacific Northwest and he'd taken an assignment in Seattle when he completed training with the marshals service. He had ended up spending the first decade of his career on that side of the country. Then he'd needed a change. He'd landed in Nashville last year.

Truth was, he hadn't exactly wanted to spend any time in the southeast, but it was a necessary step in his career ladder. There was a woman he'd met when he was in training at Glynco. The two of them had had a few very intense months together and he'd wondered about her. He'd kept an eye on her for years. Certain that they would end up together again at some point. They'd both been so young when they first met. He'd checked in how she was doing in college. Had anonymously helped out when her father passed away.

Then his notions of a reunion came to a grinding halt in Atlanta.

She'd gotten married. He shook his head. All those years she had haunted his dreams so many times. He'd thought he had known her, thought they had something. He'd definitely never felt that connection with anyone else.

But he had been wrong. Dead wrong.

A woman who would marry a man like that was not someone he knew at all. He imagined she well knew what the world thought of her choice about now.

Irrelevant, he reminded himself. The past was the past. Nothing he could do about the years he wasted wondering about her. He was happy in Nashville for now. He had just turned thirty-two and he had big career plans. There was plenty of time to get serious about a personal relationship. God knew his parents and his sister constantly nagged him about his single status.

Maybe after this case was buttoned up. The witness had to be at trial on Thursday. After that, he was taking a vacation and making some personal decisions. Maybe it was time he took inventory of his life rather than just pouring everything into the job.

The hospital had that disinfectant smell that lingered in every single one he'd ever stepped into. The odor triggered unpleasant memories he'd just as soon not revisit in this lifetime. Losing his younger brother had been hard as a ten-year-old. He couldn't imagine what his parents had suffered.

His mom warned him often that he shouldn't allow that loss to get in the way of having a family. He had never really considered that he chose not to get too serious about a relationship because of what happened when he was a kid, but maybe it had. His parents had spent two decades telling him that what happened wasn't his fault. Didn't matter. He would always believe it was. He should have been watching more closely. He should never have allowed his little brother so close to the water's edge.

He should have been better prepared to help him if something went wrong.

Damn. Why the hell had he gone down that road?

Jax shook his head and strode across the lobby, kicking the past back to where it belonged—behind him. A quick check with the information desk and he was on his way to the third floor. He followed the signs to Holloway's room.

His gaze came to rest on his old friend and he grimaced. The left side of the man's face was bruised and swollen as if he'd slugged it out and lost big-time. What he could see of Holloway's left shoulder was bruised, as well. "You look like hell, buddy."

Branch Holloway opened his eyes. "Pretty much feel like it, too. Glad you could make it, Stevens."

Jax moved to the side of his bed. "What happened? You tick off the wrong cowboy?"

Tennessee was full of cowboys. Jax had tried a pair of boots. Not for him. And the hat, well, that just wasn't his style. He was more of a city kind of guy. Jeans, pullovers and a good pair of hiking shoes and he was good to go. He was, however, rather fond of leather. He'd had the leather jacket he wore for over a decade.

"I wish I could tell you a heroic story of chasing bad guys and surviving a shoot-out, but it was nothing like that. A deer decided my truck was in his way. I didn't hit him, but I did hit the ditch and then a couple of trees. One tree in particular tried real hard to do me in."

Jax made a face. "Sounds like you're damned lucky."

"That's what they say, but I gotta tell you right now I'm not feeling too lucky. My wife says I will when I see my truck. It's totaled."

"Can I get you anything?" Jax glanced at the water pitcher on the bedside table.

"No, thanks. My wife was here until just a few minutes ago. She's hovered over me since I got here. Between her and the nurses, I'm good. Trust me."

Jax nodded. "You didn't want to discuss the case by phone. I take it this is a dark one." Some cases were listed as dark. These were generally the ones where the person or persons who wanted to hurt the witness had an abundance of resources, making the witness far more vulnerable. Sometimes a case was dark simply because of the priority tag associated with the investigation. The fewest people possible were involved with dark cases.

There were bad guys in this world and then there were *really* bad guys.

"Need-to-know basis only," Holloway said. "We're only days out from trial. Keeping this witness safe is essential. At this point, we pretty much need to keep her under surveillance twenty-four hours a day until trial. This couldn't have happened at a worse time."

"Understandable," Jax agreed.

"I'm sure you're familiar with the Armone case. It's been all over the news."

Jax's eyebrows went up with a jolt of surprise. "That's not a name I expected to hear. I knew the patriarch of the family was awaiting trial, but I haven't kept up with the details."

"They've kept the details quiet on this one to the extent possible. Even with all those precautions and a media blackout, her first location was jeopardized."

Her? A bad, bad feeling began a slow creep through Jax.

"Hell of a time for you to be out of commission," he said instead of demanding who the hell the witness was. This could not happen. Maybe it was someone else.

"Tell me about it," Holloway grumbled.

"Why don't you bring me up to speed?" Jax suggested. "We'll go from there."

"The file's under my pillow."

Jax chuckled as he reached beneath the thin hospital pillow. "I have to say, this is going the distance for the job."

"We do what we have to, right?"

"Yeah. Right." Jax opened the file, his gaze landing on an eight-by-ten photo. He blinked. Looked again. She looked exactly as she had ten years ago.

"You okay there?" Holloway asked. "You look like you just saw a ghost."

"Full disclosure, Holloway, I know this woman." Jax frowned. No. That was wrong. He didn't just know this woman; he knew her intimately. Had been disappointed in and angry with her for years now.

"Well, hell. If this is a problem, we should call someone else in as quickly as possible. I've got the local sheriff, a friend of mine, taking care of things now. But I can't keep him tied up this way. No one wants this bastard to get away this time. We've got him. As long as she lives to testify, he's not walking."

Holloway was right. The Armone family had escaped justice far too long. "I've got this." Jax cleared his head. If Holloway thought he was not up to par, he would insist on calling in someone else. Jax was startled, no denying it. But he wanted to do this. He had to do this. For reasons that went beyond the job. Purely selfish reasons. "You can count on me. I just needed to be up front. We knew each other a long time ago."

"If you're sure," Holloway countered. "I'm confident I can count on you. I just don't want to put you in an unnecessarily awkward situation. Sometimes the past can adversely affect the present."

Jax felt his gut tighten. Maybe he wasn't as ready for this as he'd thought.

No choice.

If he didn't do this, he would never fully extract her from his head.

The what-ifs would haunt him forever.

"I can handle it. Like I said, we haven't seen each other in years," he assured the other man. "No one wants this family to go down more than me."

That part was more true than he cared to admit.

"If we're lucky, that family will be history when this trial is done," Holloway said. "The son is dead. Now all we need is for the father to be put away for the rest of his sorry life." Holloway searched his face as if looking for any uncertainty. "I can ask Sheriff Tanner to show you the way to her location, if you're sure we're good to go."

"That works."

"Thanks, Stevens. I owe you one."

The cabin was well out of town. Sheriff Colt Tanner had met Jax at the courthouse and led the way. Tanner had last checked on the witness an hour ago. At this stage, Jax wasn't to simply check on her, he was to stick with her until she walked into that courtroom to testify. Protect, transport…whatever was necessary.

On the drive to her location, he had decided he really didn't have a problem with doing the job. He couldn't deny that he had spent a great deal of time trying to find Allison James, aka Alice Stewart, the widow of Harrison Armone Junior, illegal drugs and weapons kingpin of the southeast. In fact, he wanted to do this. He wanted to learn what had happened to the sweet young woman he had known during his training. How had the shy, soft-spoken girl become the wife of one of the most wanted bastards on the minds of FBI, ATF and DEA agents alike? Maybe it was sheer curiosity, but he needed to understand how the hell that happened.

The actual problem, in his opinion, was how she would feel about him being the one charged with her safety. She no doubt would understand that he was well aware of who she had gotten involved with and would be disgusted by it. Members of law enforcement from Atlanta to DC had wished for a way to eradicate this problem.

He guessed he would find out soon enough.

Jax parked his SUV next to hers and got out. She was

likely watching out the window. Tanner had updated her on Holloway's condition and told her that a new marshal would be arriving shortly. Jax had no idea whether the sheriff had given her his name. If he had, she might be waiting behind that door with her weapon drawn. Not that she had any reason to be holding a grudge. He'd asked her to go with him to Seattle, but she had turned him down. No matter that he shouldn't—didn't want to—he wondered if she had attempted to track him down at any time during those early years after he left and before she made the mistake of her life.

Had she even thought of him?

He hadn't asked her to marry him, but they had talked about marriage. They had talked about the future and what they each wanted. She'd had expectations. He had recognized this. But that hadn't stopped him from leaving when an opportunity he couldn't turn down came his way. She wouldn't go. Her father was still alive and alone. She didn't want to move so far away from him. What was he supposed to do? Ignore the offer he had hoped for from the day he decided to join the marshals service?

That little voice that warned when he had crossed the line shouted at him now. He had been selfish. No question. But he'd had family, too, and they had been on the West Coast. An unwinnable situation.

He walked up to the porch. Climbed the steps and crossed to the door. Aware she was certainly watching, he raised his fist and knocked.

She didn't say a word or make a sound, but he felt her on the other side of the door. Only inches from him. He closed his eyes and recalled her scent. Soft, subtle.

She always smelled like lemons. Never wore makeup. She had the most beautiful blue eyes he had ever seen.

The door opened and she stood there, looking exactly the way she had ten years ago—no makeup, no fussy hairdo, just Ali. The big black Lab the sheriff had told him about stood next to her.

For one long moment, she stared at him and he stared at her.

He inhaled a breath, acknowledged the scent of her—the scent he would have recognized anywhere.

"Say it."

For a moment he felt confused at her statement.

"Say it," she repeated. "I'm not letting you inside until you do."

He understood then. "Superhero."

She stepped back and he walked in. The door closed behind him, locks tumbled into place. The dog sniffed him, eyeing him suspiciously.

She scratched the Lab's head and the dog settled down. "No one told me you were the one coming."

She stood close to the wall on his left, beyond arm's reach. She looked thinner than before. Fear glittered in her eyes. Beyond the fear was something else. A weariness. Sadness, too, he concluded.

"I didn't know it was you until I arrived in Winchester." He held her gaze, refused to let her off the hook. He didn't want this to be easy. Appreciating her discomfort was low. He knew this, and still, he couldn't help it. "I'm glad I'm the one Holloway called. I want to help. If that's okay with you."

"I'm certain Marshal Holloway wouldn't have called you if you weren't up to the task." She shrugged. "As for the past, it was a long time ago. It's hardly relevant now."

She was right. It had been a long time. Still, the idea that she played it off so nonchalantly didn't sit so well. No need for her to know the resentment or whatever the hell it was he harbored related to her decisions or the whirlwind of emotions she had reeling inside him now. This was work. Business. The job. It wasn't personal.

He hitched a thumb toward the door. "I picked up a pizza. It's a little early for lunch, but I was on the road at the crack of dawn this morning."

"Make yourself at home. You don't need my permission to eat."

No, he did not. "I'll grab my bag and the pizza."

He walked out to his SUV. He took a breath. Struggled to slow his heart rate. He had an assignment to complete and it was essential he pulled his head out of the past and focused on the present. What happened ten years ago or five years ago was irrelevant. What mattered was now. Keeping her safe. Getting her in that courtroom to put a scumbag away.

He grabbed his bag and the pizza and headed back to the cabin. She opened the door for him and then locked the four dead bolts. He placed the pizza on the table and dropped his bag by the sofa. He imagined that would be his bed for the foreseeable future. The place didn't look large enough to have two bedrooms.

"This is Bob, by the way," she said of the dog, who stayed at her side.

He nodded. "Nice to meet you, Bob."

Bob stared at him with a healthy dose of either skepticism or continued suspicion.

"Would you like water or a cola?"

Since beer was out of the question, he went for a cola. She walked to the fridge and grabbed two. On the way to the table she snagged the roll of paper towels from the counter and brought that along, as well. She sat down directly across the table. Apparently she had decided to join him. He passed her a slice, grabbed one of his own and then dug in. Eating would prevent the need for conversation. If he chewed slowly enough, he could drag this out for a while.

She sipped her drink. "You married?"

He was surprised she asked. Left her open for his questions. And he really wanted a number of answers from her. At the moment dealing with all the emotions and sensations related to just being in the room with her was all he could handle.

"No. Never engaged. Never married."

Silence dragged on for another minute or so while they ate. Keeping his attention away from her lips as she ate proved more difficult than he'd expected. Frankly, he was grateful when she polished off the last bit.

"Technically," she pointed out as she reached for a second slice, "*we* were engaged—informally."

He went still, startled that his heart didn't do the same. He hadn't expected her to bring that up under the circumstances. *"Technically,"* he repeated. "I suppose you're right."

"How long were you in Seattle?"

"Until last year." He wiped his hands on a napkin. "I'm sorry about your father."

"It was a tough time."

"Yeah, I'm sure it was." He had come so close to

attending the funeral, but he wasn't sure he would have been welcome.

He bit into his pizza to prevent asking if that was why she'd run into the arms of a criminal. Had she wanted someone to take care of her? A sugar daddy or whatever? Fury lit inside him. He forced the thoughts away. It didn't matter that they had spent months passionately focused on each other, practically inseparable. That had been a long time ago. Whatever they had back then was long gone by the time she married Armone. All this emotion was unnecessary. Pointless. Frustrating as hell, actually.

"What about your parents?" She dabbed at her lips with a napkin. "Your sister?"

"The parents are doing great. Retired to Florida. Is that cliché or what?" He managed a smile. Hoped to lighten the situation.

She looked completely at ease. Calm. Maybe he was the only one having trouble.

Her lips lifted into a small smile. "A little."

"My sister is married with three kids." He shook his head. "I don't know how she does it."

"She's lucky."

"You have kids?" He knew the answer, but he didn't know the reason.

"No. *He* didn't want children. He had two with his first wife." She stared at the pizza box for a moment. "Looking back, I was very fortunate he didn't."

For now, he guided the conversation away from the bastard she'd married. So he asked another question to which he also had the answer. "You were determined to finish school. Did you manage?"

"I did. With taking care of my father, it took forever, but I finally got it done."

"That's great."

More of that suffocating silence. He stared at the pizza, and suddenly had no appetite.

"Your career is going well?" she asked.

"It is. The work is challenging and fulfilling."

She stood. "Thank you for the pizza."

He watched as she carried her napkin and cola can to the trash. She stood at the sink and stared out the window.

The urge to demand how she could have married a man like Harrison Armone burned on his tongue, but he swallowed it back.

"I think maybe they should send someone else."

Her words surprised him. He stood, the legs of his chair scraping across the wood floor. "Why? I see no reason we can't put the past behind us."

She turned to face him but stayed right where she was, her fingers gripping the edge of the countertop as if she feared gravity would fail her. "If *he* finds me, he will kill me. If you're in the way, he'll kill you, too."

Don't miss
Witness Protection Widow *by Debra Webb,*
available February 2020 wherever
Harlequin® books and ebooks are sold.

www.Harlequin.com

Get 4 FREE REWARDS!

We'll send you 2 FREE Books plus 2 FREE Mystery Gifts.

FREE
Value Over
$20

Both the **Romance** and **Suspense** collections feature compelling novels
written by many of today's bestselling authors.

YES! Please send me 2 FREE novels from the Essential Romance or
Essential Suspense Collection and my 2 FREE gifts (gifts are worth about
$10 retail). After receiving them, if I don't wish to receive any more books,
I can return the shipping statement marked "cancel." If I don't cancel, I will
receive 4 brand-new novels every month and be billed just $6.99 each in the
U.S. or $7.24 each in Canada. That's a savings of at least 13% off the cover
price. It's quite a bargain! Shipping and handling is just 50¢ per book in the
U.S. and $1.25 per book in Canada.* I understand that accepting the 2 free
books and gifts places me under no obligation to buy anything. I can always
return a shipment and cancel at any time. The free books and gifts are mine
to keep no matter what I decide.

Choose one: ☐ **Essential Romance**   ☐ **Essential Suspense**
　　　　　　　(194/394 MDN GNNP)　　　　　　(191/391 MDN GNNP)

Name (please print)

Address   Apt. #

City   State/Province   Zip/Postal Code

> Mail to the **Reader Service:**
> **IN U.S.A.:** P.O. Box 1341, Buffalo, NY 14240-8531
> **IN CANADA:** P.O. Box 603, Fort Erie, Ontario L2A 5X3

Want to try 2 free books from another series! Call 1-800-873-8635 or visit www.ReaderService.com.

---

*Terms and prices subject to change without notice. Prices do not include sales taxes, which will be charged (if applicable) based
on your state or country of residence. Canadian residents will be charged applicable taxes. Offer not valid in Quebec. This offer is
limited to one order per household. Books received may not be as shown. Not valid for current subscribers to the Essential Romance
or Essential Suspense Collection. All orders subject to approval. Credit or debit balances in a customer's account(s) may be offset by
any other outstanding balance owed by or to the customer. Please allow 4 to 6 weeks for delivery. Offer available while quantities last.

Your Privacy—The Reader Service is committed to protecting your privacy. Our Privacy Policy is available online at
www.ReaderService.com or upon request from the Reader Service. We make a portion of our mailing list available to reputable
third parties that offer products we believe may interest you. If you prefer that we not exchange your name with third parties, or if
you wish to clarify or modify your communication preferences, please visit us at www.ReaderService.com/consumerchoice or write
to us at Reader Service Preference Service, P.O. Box 9062, Buffalo, NY 14240-9062. Include your complete name and address.

STRS20